Island Girls

To Joanne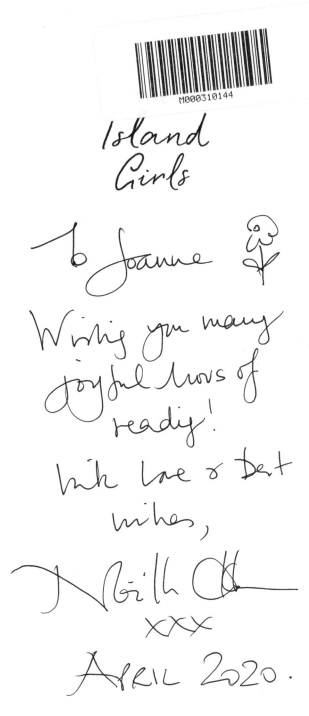

Wishing you many joyful hours of reading!

With love & best wishes,

Nicola Clifton

xxx

APRIL 2020.

BOOKS BY NOELLE HARRISON

The Island Girls

The Gravity of Love
The Adulteress
The Secret Loves of Julia Caesar
I Remember
A Small Part Of Me
Beatrice

THE

Island

Girls

Noelle Harrison

Bookouture

Published by Bookouture in 2020

An imprint of Storyfire Ltd.
Carmelite House
50 Victoria Embankment
London EC4Y 0DZ

www.bookouture.com

Written by Noelle Harrison

ISBN: 978-1-83888-177-1
eBook ISBN: 978-1-83888-176-4

For Lydia, for gifting me a story.
And for Becky, for coming to the island with me.

Chapter 1

Emer

10th October 2011

Emer was far away now, the last year trailing behind in the jet stream of the small ferry as it ploughed through the sea. It was a perfect day, after all. Lifting her face to the sky, Emer felt the warmth of the sun on her damp cheeks, as her whole body rocked to the rhythm of the boat. She should have been lulled by the gentle motion of the ocean, but she was far from calm.

The boat chugged through island waters glittering azure, her sister's favourite colour. Orla loved the sea, a natural sailor. That was how she'd met her husband, Ethan, both of them on the ocean every single weekend. But Emer had never developed sea legs, despite her sister's enthusiasm. She'd gone out with Orla and Ethan several times, and even when the sea had been smooth as glass she'd feel panic building up inside her. Like now. It felt like the longest journey ever, although it was only an hour and fifteen minutes. Her heart beating furiously inside her chest, and her mouth dry with fear. She'd been steadily drifting further and further away from her life before. She would never get it back. She knew that. But maybe her destination was a place where she could forget, and be forgotten? That was all she wanted right now.

Emer sat on the tiny deck, fighting back the urge to be sick, staring into the cold Atlantic Ocean. The water was so clear she could see all the way to the lobster pots settled on its bed.

The Vinalhaven ferry wove between the brightly coloured lobster pot buoys bobbing up and down among the fishermen's boats. How Orla would have loved the pretty little harbour of this Maine island with its wooden houses all different colours and the wharf sitting high atop wooden stilts. Sunlight was dancing on the dappled water, the scent of the sea everywhere, its salty tang on Emer's lips. How many times had her sister declared her dream of island life? Well, here Emer was, living her sister's dream, running away from her own nightmare.

As she walked off the boat, it hit Emer how quiet the island was. All she could hear were the gulls crying, and the water lapping against all the fishermen's boats. A lone vehicle driving down the road. It was almost unnerving not to hear the sounds of busy traffic. Not only that, she hadn't considered how isolated this island really was. As she walked down Main Street, it felt as if she were walking back in time. Most of the shops were closed, some with signs saying they wouldn't be open again until next season. It felt a world away from Boston: the packed subways, the bustle of the crowded streets and the noise and urgency of the hospital. Emer had left behind her previous life as a nurse in Massachusetts General Hospital to become the companion and palliative care nurse for one patient, Susannah Olsen, on the island of Vinalhaven off the mid-Maine coast. Her new employer, Susannah's niece Lynsey, had told her Vinalhaven was packed in the summer months, but now in October it was clear tourist season was over. There was that same faintly sad feeling Emer got whenever she went to a seaside town in the winter. The fun was over for another year. Time to hibernate.

She checked the address Lynsey had given her, and carried on. Emer's route took her all the way down Main Street. Past a food

und table and white wicker chairs with
he garden was a glory of fall abundance
of hydrangeas and a large horse-chestnut
mer spied more gleaming conkers. In the
an ancient apple tree laden with red apples.
eps of the porch, opened the porch door
inside door but there was no answer. She
ce, so she tried the door and it opened.
and brightness of the garden, the interior
a thorough airing. Emer itched to pull back
n the windows. The place was a mess. Piles
s were stacked on old mahogany furniture.
esk at the one window where the drapes were
an old typewriter and a stack of papers.
called out, but there was no reply. She kept
into the back of the house and the kitchen. A
as piled with old crockery, but the kitchen was
ntidy.
alled out again. No reply. She unlatched a door
d climbed up to a narrow landing. Two doors.
aybe Susannah Olsen had already taken to her
urgent need of pain relief. Emer knocked before
room was a bathroom, and the second clearly
room. There was another flight of stairs at the end
presumably up to another bedroom in the eaves
Emer stepped into Susannah's bedroom. There was
ed covered with the most beautiful quilt Emer had
colours in contrast to the deep shades of fall. This
l of spring pink, sunny yellow, light green, grassy
s orange and baby blue as little sprigs, petals, flower
iny polka dots created an overall pattern bursting
. Orla would have loved it. Emer admired the quilt

store, which was open, and a bar. She heard music inside and
the low hum of conversation – so at least some people came out.
She took a right down a leafy street with large wooden houses –
white, green, grey – all the way down on either side. The gardens
were festooned with hydrangeas, the ground littered with horse
chestnut shells. She found a perfect conker and slipped it into her
pocket, its smooth contours soothing in the palm of her hand.

It was warm for October, and Emer shifted her rucksack on her
sticky back. A lone grey cat sauntered past her, and she spied an old
lady raking up leaves on her lawn. A truck cruised by, its driver an
old man with a shaggy beard, giving her a friendly wave just like
back home in Ireland. She remembered Lynsey telling her there
weren't too many permanent residents on the island any more.

'A lot of the houses are for summer visitors, empty all winter,'
Lynsey had explained. 'Those staying all year are either boat
builders or lobster fishermen. They can make good money from
the lobsters, so a lot of young men don't bother with college.'

'It costs a lot to go to college in the States, doesn't it?'

'You're telling me,' Lynsey moaned. 'My aunt never lets me
forget how much it cost her to educate *a circus attraction*, as she
calls me. In any case, Vinalhaven has an interesting history. It
used to have a big granite industry, but that all died out. And you
know, I'm not sure how much longer it's going to work out with
the lobsters either. What with climate change, they're moving
north to colder waters.'

Emer had never eaten lobster. She didn't eat meat or fish, not
since she and Orla had made their pact as teenagers. But she
didn't want to put Lynsey off her so she didn't ask her how a vegan
might fare on Vinalhaven, food-wise. A jar of peanut butter and
a loaf of bread could be found anywhere, surely?

'Anyways,' Lynsey said to her. 'It's very, very quiet there. I
felt like I slept most of my teenage years because there was like,

nothing to do, ever. My sister Rebecca loved it. She and Aunt Susannah hiked together, but my aunt's not able enough for that now. You'll be okay being so alone?'

'The quiet life is just fine for me,' Emer said firmly.

'Are your parents gonna visit?' Lynsey asked her. 'There's a few places for rental if they'd like to come?'

'Maybe,' Emer had said, not elaborating. Lynsey had waited for her to say more, but what could Emer tell her? Her father had no idea she had even applied for the job on Vinalhaven.

She followed the road now as it curved out of town to a small bridge crossing an estuary of the sea. Water rushed beneath it and she paused to listen to the clinking of the fishing boats, and the sounds of seabirds she couldn't name. There was a pier off the road, with several pick-ups parked and mountains of lobster traps stacked in the yard. She guessed this was one of the places the fishermen set out to get the lobster. The houses thinned out as she kept going, passing a sign to *Lane's Island Preserve*. She was walking beside marshland, thick with golden reeds and giant bulrushes. Crows were cawing loudly from the treetops, and she could hear crickets chirruping.

Turning the corner, Emer heard the sound of children, their high-pitched voices flung upon the wind. Two little girls were swinging on a hammock slung up in the front porch of a blue wooden house, a row of orange pumpkins lined up on its steps. The older girl had blonde hair, the younger red. Just like her and Orla. They didn't even notice her as she walked by, and she was trying not to stare at the children, but it felt like a sign. An image connecting her to the bond with her own sister. The reason why she had committed to this job.

As if on cue, her cell phone vibrated in her pocket. All the text messages coming through which she'd been unable to receive while on the boat. Five missed calls from Lars. Without even

listenii
one tex

Hello
to gree
Aunt S
on her c

Another t
then a third n

Just to war
need looking
her great. Tha

Her heart sank.
patient on this remo
was too late now. Ce
ever. She was here, so
There were fewer h
either side of the road,
in the breeze as if whisp
the glint of blue, ever n
remained as a never-endi
crows above. The stillness
all sound, even the beating
hands and focused on findi
Susannah Olsen's house
expected. It was constructed c
houses, and painted white. T
exterior and it looked like it n
The roof sagged a little in the mi

a large swing-seat, a ro
patchwork cushions. T
with blooming bushes
tree, beneath which E
middle of the lawn was
She climbed the s
and knocked on the
knocked again. Silen
After the beauty
was dark. It needed
the drapes and ope
of books and pape
There was a small d
rumpled. Upon it
'Hello?' Emer
going, wandering
big blue dresser w
clean, if a little u
'Hello!' she c
to a stairwell an
Both closed. M
bed and was in
opening. One
Susannah's bec
of the landing
of the house.
a big double l
ever seen, its
quilt was fu
green, joyou
heads and
with energ

for another moment before walking over to the window and looking out. The view was of the boughs of the apple tree. She felt as if she could almost lean out of the window and pick an apple.

'What are you doing in my room?'

Emer swung round, her face colouring as she got the first glimpse of her new patient. A small, slender woman with a bob of silver hair, Susannah Olsen didn't look sick. In fact, she was carrying a big basket brimming with groceries. It must have weighed quite a bit.

Emer found herself feeling strangely shy. She had no idea why she should be. She'd been employed to help Susannah Olsen.

'I'm Emer Feeney, the nurse,' she said. 'Did your niece Lynsey not tell you I was coming?'

'I know who you are all right, young lady, but I just wondered what you were doing snooping in my room?'

'I thought you might be in bed,' Emer explained. 'I was looking for you.'

'Well as you'll see, I'm quite all right,' Susannah said tartly. 'Don't know why those girls are fussing over me so.'

'They want to make sure you're cared for.'

'Been managing just fine on my own for years,' Susannah said.

They looked at each other. Emer smiled awkwardly, feeling fake, but Susannah didn't return the smile.

'Well, seeing as you're here now you may as well make yourself useful,' she said, passing Emer the basket of vegetables. 'Come on downstairs and we'll have some tea.'

Emer was taken aback by the older woman's gruffness, but then what had she been expecting? Susannah was hardly going to be over the moon at the arrival of a nurse who by her very presence was going to remind her every day that she was dying. Lynsey had told Emer that Susannah had been diagnosed with pancreatic cancer, which would be terminal regardless of whether Susannah chose to have chemotherapy. Emer had felt sorry for Susannah being so alone at the end of her life. No family nearby. Her closest living relatives were Lynsey, who lived a good five-hour trip away in Salem, and the other niece, Rebecca, who lived in England.

But clearly Susannah did not view herself as a victim. She turned around and walked out of her bedroom. Emer followed her down the stairs. Nothing about Susannah seemed to give the sense she was weak and frail. It was only when the older woman got to the bottom of the stairs and straightened up that Emer noticed her flinch in pain. Slightly. She was thin, too.

'Don't think you can stuff me with drugs now,' Susannah snapped at her, as if she knew Emer was appraising her. 'This is my home and I'm going to carry on exactly as I want. Got it?'

'Well, my job is to make you comfortable,' Emer said carefully.

'I will tell you when I need help. Right? Don't you be doping me up so I can't think right. If I can't read my books I may as well be gone anyway.'

It wasn't too late. Emer could call up Lynsey. Tell her she'd changed her mind. Apologise. Explain she'd not been herself when she'd signed up as a private palliative care assistant. They always said you should never make big life changes when you're grieving. How could she possible stay on this remote island in this woman's dark, depressing house and witness her end? Watch her in *pain*? And know that was what it had been like for her own flesh and blood?

Because you owe me.

Orla's voice inside her head. She heard her all the time now she was gone.

Emer took off her rucksack and put it down on the ground with shaky hands.

'Of course, whatever you wish.' She was surprised by how steady her voice was, and how calm she sounded. 'My role is to help you, Susannah. You call the shots.'

Susannah crossed her arms and narrowed her eyes at her.

'We'll see,' she said, scowling. 'I know how you nurses like to take over!'

She picked up the kettle to fill it with water and Emer saw her grimacing in pain again. She reached forward to take the kettle from her, but Susannah pushed her away.

'See, you're already at it.'

Emer felt a flash of irritation, bit back a retort. But then, she'd seen behaviour like this before in cancer patients. Emer knew it came from fear, and denial. She of all people should understand those emotions. If she could help Susannah, if she could do this right, at least, maybe the weight on her heart might press less heavy. Would the guilt ever go away?

Chapter 2

Susannah

July 1951

She was going to make Mother angry again. Her job had been to bake the bread this morning. Simple enough. But she'd burnt it. Kate did the baking most days no problem, while Susannah collected the eggs from their neighbours. But this morning her sister had to help their mother finish up the fine lacing for the cuffs and hems of Sarah Wilkinson's wedding dress. Even at ten years of age, Kate was the 'best little lacer' on the whole island. It filled Susannah with awe to watch her sister's nimble fingers at the lacing stand, sitting on the other side to their mother, as they wove the shuttles through the threads to create perfect miniature lattices or bigger looping nets. It took Susannah an age just to thread a needle, and then she always managed to prick herself. She hated lacing, along with sewing, cooking, cleaning and all the domestic tasks she should be good at because she was a girl.

She hadn't even smelt the bread burning because she'd been lost deep inside Daddy's boyhood copy of *Treasure Island*. It was Kate who came tearing into the kitchen and flung the oven open.

'Susie! The bread!'

Susannah jumped up from the table. 'Oh no, oh shoot, Katie!'

'Quick! Hide the book. She could be back any moment,' Kate said, opening the door and flapping the tea towel to clear the kitchen of the black billows of smoke.

'Are they ruined?' Susannah asked, stuffing the book under a cushion.

Kate took out the trays of blackened loaves. Slipped the oven gloves off.

'I'd say so,' she said, smothering a giggle.

'Why are you laughing? I'll get the brush handle for this,' Susannah said despairingly, but her sister's giggles were infectious. A laugh bubbled up inside her. Kate looked so funny with threads of lace hanging off her skirt, hair all wild, and well – here Susannah was again, being the dreamer as Mother always complained.

'I'll make some pancakes, they're quick enough,' Kate said. 'Tell her it's my fault the others burnt. I was watching the bread while you were out getting the washing down.' Kate waved at the window to the sheets flapping on the line outside. 'She won't hit *me*!'

It was true. Their mom clearly favoured Kate. Well, any mother would. Kate was so good at everything their mother viewed as important – lace-making, sewing, cooking and gardening. Susannah tried to do things right, but she got caught up in her books. She'd decide to read to the end of a chapter, put the book down and help Kate out, but then the story would kidnap her and hours might pass before she realised Kate had done all their domestic tasks on her own. Her sister never told on her, but often their mother would catch Susannah out. Curled up on her bed, buried in a book. A loud slap on the leg was her resounding wake-up call to join the 'real world' as their mother called it.

'Vinalhaven isn't the real world, Mom,' she'd talk back, her leg and dignity smarting from the slap. 'The real world is what's happening out there.' She waved her arm towards the window and the view of the blustery Atlantic Ocean, as the daily craving to know what was really going on beyond the borders of the tiny island dug into her heart.

'That's where you're wrong, my girl,' her mother told her. 'The real world is right inside these four walls, where you, your sister and I have to make our living, and provide for ourselves all on our own.'

Susannah immediately felt guilty. She always did when her mother reminded her how much she had to sacrifice to look after her two daughters with no husband to help. What good were books when you had to make a living on the island of Vinalhaven, miles from the mainland, let alone an actual city?

Susannah picked up the laundry basket.

'She won't believe you burnt them.' Susannah was glum now as she spoke to Kate. Her backside was still sore from yesterday's smack for dropping one of their precious eggs.

But Kate wasn't listening. She was all a bustle, cleaning out the burnt tins and getting together everything she needed to fix Susannah's mess.

Susannah headed out into the garden, glad to be outside the house. It was a blustery day and the sheets flapped around her in the wind. She walked through them, imagining she was wandering the streets of a bazaar and these were brightly coloured banners. She closed her eyes, went to a place her daddy had been during the war. Morocco. She could smell the street vendors' exotic foods, hear the strange language they were speaking, see the beautiful women with dark eyes, beauty concealed behind veils. She had never forgotten the stories her daddy told her on his one visit home. If she squeezed her eyes shut, really tight, he was right before her. *Come on, my little Susie.* One hand for her, one hand for Kate. Daddy had his girls again and he was going to show them the world. Yes, she could hear the cries of the vendors now, smell the spices and the heat of Casablanca as Daddy took them on an adventure. Weaving through tiny streets and alleys. Searching for ancient wisdom in a land far older than their own.

A sheet slapped her in the face, and she opened her eyes, her dream disappearing fast into the blue western sky. She gazed out to sea. This was where they lived. Perched on a rise of land, the back garden opening out onto a rocky slope all the way down to the Atlantic, and in the other direction blueberry bushes, and pine woods.

Susannah pulled down one of the sheets and wrapped it around her. She was the daughter of a gypsy. She drew the sheet across her nose and mouth, and made her eyes big and round. What would it be like to live in a tent in the desert? To ride a camel? Would she dance with her sister around the desert fires? What would they eat? She didn't think it would be pancakes. Maybe fruit? Sweet and juicy, something like plums.

'Susannah! What are you doing, girl? You're dragging the sheet in all the dirt.'

Her mother loomed over her, arms crossed, frowning. Always frowning at Susannah. She was tall too, the only physical feature Susannah had inherited from her mother. It was Kate who shared the same fair hair and blue eyes as their mother. Although her sister never looked as severe as their mother did now: the rosebud contours of her lips drawn into a thin line of disapproval.

'Sorry, Mom, I was hanging the laundry,' Susannah said, not daring to look her mother in the eye.

'Well, it sure looks a funny way to be doing it.' Her mother grabbed the now dirty sheet from her hands. 'It'll have to be washed all over again. Not that I don't have enough to be doing.'

This was the anthem of their childhood. All the chores her mother had to be doing. But for who? That's what Susannah wanted to shout out. She and Kate didn't care if the house was less than perfect.

'Mom likes to keep standards up,' Kate had tried to explain to Susannah when she'd complained about all their back-breaking chores all summer long.

'None of the other kids on the island have to work so hard,' Susannah said. 'They get to have fun, swimming and all.'

'But they've all got daddies,' Kate said to her. 'Mom has to work extra hard at looking after us so we don't starve. That's why we've got to do the house for her, so she can lace.'

'Well, I still don't know why we're doing so much work for just us three,' Susannah continued to moan.

'Because of the Olsens, silly!' Kate had declared. 'Daddy's family could come over any time. She don't want them to see her down.'

That was one thing all right. Their mom was proud, and Susannah admired her for that.

After their regular dinner of fish and potatoes, their mother relented on grounding Susannah for dirtying the sheets and let them out for the last few hours in the summer's day. The two sisters ran like crazy down the stony track to Lane's Island's Bridge Cove. Susannah suggested they swim in the old quarry on Amherst, but Kate had said the woods were too scary when it started to get dark. She preferred to be out in the open, on the edge of their island and looking out at the ocean. All Susannah cared about was getting into the blessed cool water after the long hot day. She didn't mind all the midges swarming around them as she hopped from foot to foot to get her shorts off. They never bit her anyway, only Kate.

The two girls ran into the water, squealing with delight. Susannah submerged herself immediately and began swimming out further from shore.

'Don't go too far,' Kate called as she splashed about in the shallows.

Susannah was the stronger swimmer. Kate never ventured too far from land, even if it was calm like today. It was their daddy who'd taught Susannah how to swim, the summer he'd been back on leave. She'd been four, old enough, but Kate had been too little and their mother had refused to let her baby in the sea. Their mother never swam.

Susannah had never forgotten her daddy carrying her into the ocean with him until the sea was up to his shoulders and she felt it swaying all around her. She'd been scared and excited all at the same time. Safe in the knowledge her daddy would never let her sink to the bottom, but also wanting to show him she was a brave girl. He had held her hands and her legs had swung out behind her, lifted by the buoyancy of the salty water.

'Kick your legs, Susie!' he had encouraged her. 'Make waves!' he'd laughed.

The first time he'd let her go, he hadn't warned her and she had almost screamed with fright, but then he kept saying:

'I'm here, Susie, right here; you can do it, my girl.'

The water was home right from the beginning. It carried her and she had trusted it. Began to swim all on her own, much to her daddy's delight. She was a mermaid, flipping her tail, and diving beneath the surface. Following her father under the water, their red hair waving like sea flora, both their eyes open, bubbles all around them.

The last three summers, Susannah had been trying to teach Kate to swim. Susannah had wanted to pass on what she'd learnt from their daddy, but Kate never took to it like she had. Started screeching when Susannah pulled her too far out from the shore, declaring she didn't like it when she couldn't put her feet down on anything.

'But that's exactly what I love,' Susannah had said in astonishment. 'I feel so light!'

*

Susannah kept swimming. It hurt her heart to think of her daddy. She tried not to, but sometimes she just couldn't help thinking about what had happened to him. Their mother had never spoken about details during the war. Just told the girls their daddy was never coming back, and Susannah couldn't even remember exactly when that had been.

It was only at the beginning of this summer that Mrs Matlock, the librarian, had told her a little about what had happened to her daddy. Apart from the ocean, Vinalhaven's small town library was Susannah's favourite place to be. Often, she'd hide away for hours reading all the history books. There was plenty on the Civil War, and the history of English kings and queens but Susannah was looking to read about what had just happened in the world. When she'd drummed up enough confidence to ask Mrs Matlock, she'd been told the war was not history yet.

'I've some old newspapers catalogued,' she told Susannah, looking in surprise at her over the rim of her glasses. 'But why would you want to be reading about something as terrible as the war? Wouldn't you prefer a nice story book? Have you read *Little Women*? It's a favourite of mine.'

Susannah had shook her head. 'I want to know what happened,' she'd said to Mrs Matlock.

It was as if the older woman knew without being asked. 'Is it about your father?' she said, her eyes gentle.

'Did you know him?'

'I sure did.' Mrs Matlock smiled fondly. 'Spent nearly as much time as you in this library when he was a boy.'

It pleased Susannah to hear this about her father. He had liked books too.

'Has your mother never told you what happened to him?'

'All I know is he was posted to North Africa,' Susannah said. 'He came back once on leave. But when he went back he got killed.'

Mrs Matlock nodded sadly. 'Yes that's right, your father was posted to North Africa after the Anglo-American occupation of Casablanca. But he didn't die there. Your mother told me he was killed in action during the allied invasion from North Africa to southern Italy in 1944.'

Susannah sat quite still. North Africa. She remembered him telling her about the dry heat, the desert nights packed with stars. But Italy? She'd no idea her father's life had ended there.

'Has your mother never spoken to you on it?'

'No,' Susannah whispered.

'Oh, Lord,' Mrs Matlock said. 'I do hope I haven't spoken out of turn. How old are you now, Susannah?'

'Eleven. Nearly twelve.'

'Well, I guess you're old enough.'

'Where's Casablanca?' Susannah asked Mrs Matlock. She'd heard of the movie. Everyone had, but she had no idea where it was in northern Africa.

The librarian took down one of the big atlases and spread it open on one of the library tables. Susannah pored over the map until the library closed. By the time Mrs Matlock had locked the door and waved her goodbye, Susannah knew that Casablanca was situated facing the Atlantic Ocean on the north-western coast of Morocco. It was founded by Berbers in the seventh century BC and called Anfa. In the fifteenth century it was ruled by the Portuguese, and then the Spanish, from where it got its name – *Casablanca* – 'white house'. Colonised again this time by the French, during the Second World War the city was part of French territory. Susannah traced her finger all the way from Casablanca across northern Africa to Tunisia, and the short blue leap of ocean over to the heel of Italy. She read that it was less than 1000 kilometres between Tunisia and Sicily. Susannah knew all this, but she still didn't know how her father had died. Where in Italy? Had it been during the invasion of Rome? Or a skirmish with Germans in a small hillside village in southern Italy? Had her father's end been a hero's death?

Susannah stopped swimming now, and trod water. If she had a boat, she could sail across the Atlantic Ocean. Right over on the other side was Casablanca. One day, she'd go there. See through the eyes of her father. She turned back towards shore. Kate had got out of the water already and was beachcombing. It was one of her sister's compulsions. Collecting shells and small pebbles off the beach, leaves, tree bark, berries and stones from the woods. Their bedroom was filled with all Kate's treasures from nature in baskets and bowls, even in some of the clothes drawers.

'Oh, looky at my ring!' Kate declared, holding up a stone with a hole all the way through it, as Susannah waded out of the sea. Kate slipped the stone on her finger. 'I do, I do!' She twirled on the sand. 'I'm going to marry Johnny Carver! He said so to me.'

Shivering from the cold, Susannah looked at her sister in disbelief. 'Oh no, Katie, his nose is always dirty. You don't want to marry a boy with a runny nose!'

'But his daddy has the biggest boat, and he's going to be the *best* fisherman on the whole island. Just like Daddy was.'

Kate was always saying what a great fisherman their father was, like their mother did too. That he had been an island man through and through, and his family belonged here and nowhere else. That this was where they had to stay forever. Ever and ever.

But Susannah knew it wasn't true. Their daddy had been an adventurer. He had gone right the other side of the huge Atlantic Ocean to a whole new continent to do his duty for his country. To be part of history. Her daddy was a man of significance, not only a fisherman. She wanted to tell Kate this, but there was no point. Kate didn't understand.

As the sun set, the two sisters walked back to the house. Susannah was still damp from the sea, the scent of the ocean on her skin, and her eyes red from being in the water so long, but she felt better now she'd been in it. Kate was still chattering away about her future wedding to the runny-nosed Johnny Carver. Susannah didn't hear the woods rustling until two boys jumped out on to the road in front of them. Kate gave out a scream in fright, but Susannah scowled. She wasn't afraid. It was only Silas Young and his younger brother, Matthew. The boys came from one of the oldest fishing families on the island. Youngs and Olsens went way back. Their fathers had both fought in the war, but the boys' father had come back. Most of the girls at school were as afraid as Kate of Silas. He would chase them around the yard, trying to get kisses from them.

'Where you two girls been?' Silas asked. He was only one year old than Susannah, but because he was so tall and lanky he looked almost like a grown man.

'None of your business,' Susannah said, as Kate put her hand in hers.

'Bet they been skinny dipping in the sea,' Matthew teased them. 'Wait until I tell my mom and she'll go and tell yours. Boy will you be in trouble for going naked in the ocean.'

'We weren't skinny dipping,' Kate blurted. 'We had our bathers on, see!' She pulled up her top to show Matthew her wet swimsuit, falling right into his trap.

'Nice boobies!' Silas howled as Kate went red with mortification.

'Leave us alone,' Susannah said, furious, as the boys walked in step with them.

'Or what?' Silas said, as Matthew pulled on Kate's damp ponytail.

'Ow!' she protested.

'I sure do like your hair, Katie Olsen; it's the colour of butter,' Matthew said, giving it a tug again.

'Hey, leave her alone,' Susannah said, giving him a kick on the shin.

The boy hopped back in surprise.

'Well, ain't she the wild one,' Silas said, all sly-like.

'Leave us be, alrighty?' Susannah said, grabbing her sister's hand and tugging her on. They broke out into a run towards home.

'Run on home, girly girls!' Silas called after them.

By the time they got home, Kate was in tears. Susannah wiped her face with her sleeve outside the door. 'Don't mind those stupid boys, Katie,' Susannah said. She was anxious their mother would notice Kate's distress and ban them from going out so late again. If she couldn't get into the ocean on a summer's evening, she'd just die with boredom.

'But why don't they like us?' Kate asked. 'Why are they so mean to us?'

'I don't know! Why do you care? They're idiots!' Susannah said, exasperated. Sometimes Kate was so wet.

Susannah needn't have worried. Their mother was hard at work at the lacing stand, and barely looked up when they came in. Susannah shooed Kate up to bed.

Her sister, as always, fell asleep as soon as Susannah turned off their lamp. But despite having been up so early, and having to get up so early tomorrow, Susannah couldn't sleep. She could hear Mother down below, working the shuttle. All summer long, ever since the day in the library when Mrs Matlock had shown her the map, Susannah had been dying to ask her mother the details of what had happened to her father. But instinct warned her not to. A part of her understood. Her mother kept them so busy because she couldn't let herself sink into the grief. The shuttle going back and forth, lacing yarn, twine, threads, whatever she could, to mesh nets and more nets. Susannah hated those nets. Because they trapped her mother, and they trapped her and Kate on Vinalhaven, in a house which always felt empty because of their father's absence.

Chapter 3

Emer

29th September 2011

The train had been nearly empty, apart from those obviously going to Salem. A goth couple in black leathers, piercings and tattoos, and three girls dressed in witches' hats and beautiful corseted dresses. Each hat was decorated differently – one with garlands of dark purple flowers, the second with tiny black spiders and glittering webs, and the third with tiny orange pumpkins. Emer had slid into her own row of red leatherette seats, and stared out of the window as they pulled out of North Station. It had been a wet and windy fall day, the edges of Boston grey and dreary as they travelled north. As the ticket inspector approached her, Emer couldn't help noticing she had a green shamrock attached to her ticket machine.

'Irish?' Emer asked her. 'Me too.'

'Yeah,' the girl said, though her accent was strong Bostonian. She had inky-black hair, which fell out of a lopsided ponytail upon which her inspector's cap was perched at an angle. Emer longed to neaten it up, braid the shiny black tail of it, or tuck it into her cap. She had braided Orla's hair the day before she'd died. Just how she'd done it when they were little girls. The way their mam had taught her. Orla's red hair had always had a will of its own. Emer remembered how frustrated she would get trying to tame her sister's wild curls. Orla would laugh at her, not really caring how she looked. The braids never lasted the day in school, and by the time they were both home for their dinner, Orla's unruly locks would have broken free. But after the chemo, when all Orla's hair grew back, it was different. No longer curly, but straight and thick. It was darker, too. And though she had tried to escape Emer's hairbrush when they were little, after her hair had returned, Orla had asked Emer to constantly brush it. Once braided, Orla's hair had gleamed the same shade as glossy chestnuts.

Emer's phone vibrated in her pocket as the train pulled into Salem. She pulled it out, knowing instinctively it was Lars. It was usually at this time of day they'd eat lunch together if they could. She was tempted to take the phone out of her pocket, tell him she was in Salem. A place he'd said he'd take her one day. But the phone remained buzzing on the palm of her hand, because she didn't know how to speak to Lars now it had been so many weeks. Finally, the phone stopped. She slipped it back into her coat pocket, feeling even more confused. Why couldn't she be clear and tell him it was over for good? The phone buzzed in her pocket to indicate he'd left a message, but she didn't trust herself to listen to it yet.

It began to rain as she left the train station at Salem. She followed the three witches, walking downtown until she stood outside a shop selling an assortment of books, witches' hats, wands, sage, incense, crystal balls, tarot cards and all sorts of other New Age paraphernalia.

Her interview was conducted in the store, in the curtained-off tarot reader's corner by Susannah's niece, Lynsey de Luna. Lynsey was beautiful, tall and willowy with dyed red hair, pale skin and black kohled eyes. She was wearing a long purple velvet dress and black lace fingerless gloves, with a white quartz pendant hung on a chain around her neck.

'Thank you for coming all the way from Boston,' Lynsey said. 'I know you'll be fine. You're Cancer, right? With Virgo ascending?'

Emer had no idea what Virgo ascending meant, but she confirmed yes, she was a Cancerian. Orla had been into all the star signs, but Emer had never believed in any of it, no matter how much her sister tried to convince her otherwise.

'Cancer and Virgo: the perfect combination for a caregiver.' Lynsey nodded sagely. 'But my sister insisted I check you out in person,' she said. 'Rebecca's in the UK. She can't make the trip right now. She really wanted to come over and be with our aunt since she got the prognosis, but Rebecca's a lecturer. It's the beginning of a new semester, so difficult for her to get away. And I've got a business to run.' Lynsey spread her arms to take in the whole circumference of the reader's tent.

'When Aunt Susannah told us she had cancer, I tried to persuade her to come to Salem so I could mind her, but she hates it here.' Lynsey gave a short mirthless laugh. 'My aunt calls Salem a tasteless theme park. She says it's making money on the back of an historic tragedy.' Lynsey sighed. 'But you know, I think it's neat Salem isn't just a museum, but a place for people like me to feel normal.'

Lynsey picked up her deck of tarot cards and began to shuffle them.

'Rebecca did all the right things. Went to college. Studied hard. She's a professor now. My aunt's pride and joy! Now, when it comes to me – well, I did it all wrong. Dropped out. Travelled. A free spirit and mystic.' Lynsey pulled out one tarot card and placed it on the table. The image was of a dancing fool skipping off the edge of a cliff, a merry smile on his face. 'See, that's me.' She smiled. 'The eternal Fool!'

There was an awkward pause. Lynsey picked up the card and put it back in the deck, before placing the cards face down in front of her. 'So back to you, Emer, and what you'll need to do for my aunt Susannah. She's made the decision not to have radiation or chemo. Your role is to strictly manage her care.'

'Did she not want treatment?' Emer had asked.

'She was diagnosed with pancreatic cancer, which as you know is a terminal prognosis. Susannah was of course offered chemo to prolong her life…' Lynsey's voice cracked as she gazed down at the deck of cards, her expression concealed. 'But she said she wanted to live her life to the full as long as she could. No matter how much we tried to persuade her otherwise, she refused to have chemo.'

Lynsey looked up. Behind the bravado, Emer detected sadness. She'd seen it many times before in the hospital.

'And now it's too late anyways,' Lynsey said. 'So you'll be helping with pain management.'

'That's no problem,' Emer had said. 'I used to work on an oncology ward.'

Lynsey looked her in the eye again. 'That must have been tough.'

'You get used to it,' Emer said, looking away as her stomach cramped from the lie.

After the interview, Emer wandered around Salem on her own. Anything other than return to the desolation of Orla and Ethan's house in Quincy. She had said she'd help her brother-in-law pack up, but she wasn't ready to put her sister's life into boxes yet.

Without meaning to, she found herself sitting down at the table of another tarot card reader. She'd never had her cards read before. Always thought it rubbish, and yet here she was, clutching at anything to help her make sense of the mess she'd made of things.

It was dark by the time she came out of her reading. The rain had got heavier, and she had to run across the street, diving into a bar. Her head was swimming with the imagery of the tarot cards and what the reader had said to her. She needed a drink.

Taking a big gulp of her cider mimosa, she savoured the cinnamon rim around the top of the glass. She adored the taste of cinnamon. The first time she'd gone for coffee with Lars, they'd shared a cinnamon roll and he'd told her about the ones his mother made back in Norway. The taste of the cinnamon drink brought him back to her. The name he had called the buns was beautiful – *skillingsboner*. It sounded soft and full, like the buns themselves. She remembered his phone message from earlier. She'd still not listened to it. She took out her phone and dialled voicemail.

'Hey, Emer, it's Lars.' She could hear his nervousness in the pause. 'Please call back. Let me know you're okay. I'm worried.'

Emer hovered her fingers over the phone. If she called him back now, he'd persuade her to go see him when she got back to Boston. She'd be swept up again in her emotions. Ever since Orla had died, she couldn't think straight. All she wanted was to get away from her old life, and the guilt. Lars was part of the guilt, no matter how much she wished he wasn't.

Emer cradled her drink as she sat at the bar and people-watched. She had expected Salem to be a tacky tourist trap, and it was to a certain extent, but she also liked the fact it seemed to be a place which welcomed the different. In Salem, you could let your inner goth go wild, and no one would bat an eye. It felt like the most liberated place she'd been to so far in the three years she'd been living in the States.

She tried to remember what cards she'd got in her reading. There was the Death card. Well, obviously there would be death in her reading – but this was in the future, not the past. The reader had explained it meant change and new beginnings rather than an end. There was also the Queen of Cups, which was supposed to be her, and two Kings. A conflict of some sort. She didn't like that. And last of all, the Devil came up, too. It was all a bit of a hazy mess. Now, what did the Devil mean again? Orla had had a deck of tarot cards. Used to bring them out at dinner parties to read for friends.

'It's a bit of fun,' Orla had reassured Emer. 'Not to be taken too seriously.'

Emer's tarot reader had been a girl about the same age as herself. Why hadn't Emer asked Lynsey de Luna to read her cards? She'd probably have done it for free. But then she didn't want her new employer to know too much about her. She needed this job, not just because she was flat broke, but because she needed to go somewhere she had never been before. Not Ireland, not Boston. Somewhere new, where Orla's imprint didn't exist.

Emer's reader had looked her in the eyes, and given her a warning. 'Be careful,' she'd said to her.

Had the girl been a charlatan or the real thing? Was Emer's journey to the island going to change her forever?

Chapter 4

Susannah

November 1953

There had been Olsens on Vinalhaven since they first came from Sweden to work in the granite quarries in the 1800s. Susannah loved looking through the boxes of all the pictures her mother kept under her bed. Black and white photographs of her great-great-grandparents' wedding back in Sweden. Her father's great-grandfather, Karl, had arrived on the island from Jonköping in the mid-1800s with his wife, Greta. He had been a master sculptor and was immediately employed by one of the granite quarries to carve huge sculptures, commissioned and sent all over America. Greta had worked in the netting factory, making horse nets with big tassels to keep the flies away from the horses. Work in the quarries had dried up at the turn of the century, forcing Karl's son – Susannah's grandfather – to take to the sea and become a lobsterman like most of the men on Vinalhaven. However, the Olsen women had continued to work in the netting factory until it closed down in the 1920s.

Susannah's grandmother, her mother's mother, had also worked in the netting factory, side by side with her father's mother. The two women had been firm friends, and it was through this connection Susannah's parents had met.

Susannah pulled the box out all the way and opened up the lid. She took out the stack of old photographs. She knew them all by heart, but even so she laid them out on the wooden floor.

There was the old wedding picture in Sweden, and one of her grandparents' wedding in Vinalhaven, on the steps of the old church. One of her favourites was the picture of all the women who worked in the netting factory. Three rows of serious faces all dressed in black. She loved to think about the stories of all those women. Had they all grown up in Vinalhaven? Did they have dreams and desires beyond the island? Had any of those women managed to escape to the world outside of Maine?

She sifted through the photos and found what she was really looking for. The picture of her dad in his American army uniform. He looked so pleased with himself. A big smile plastered on his face, with his officer's cap on top of his slicked-back hair. Had he really been so happy to go off to war? Or was it to escape the island? She imagined all the places he'd got to see before he met his end in Italy. She had been five, Kate four, when their father had died. Her memories of him from before the war were hazy, but she remembered those hallowed times when he had read to them at night. He had given her a love of books. Susannah stared at her father's face. She sought in this photograph an understanding of who she was.

It had been snowing, the day their mother had received the telegram. The day before Thanksgiving, and their mother had been cooking in preparation for her husband's family's annual visit. Every time Susannah smelt or tasted pecan pie, its sweetness brought back the sound of their mother's cry. A long, low wail, like a wounded animal. Terrifying in its depth. A sound neither she nor Kate had ever heard their mother make before.

Their mother had run out of the house, snow falling as she plunged through white drifts towards the sea. Kate had been terrified.

'What's wrong with Mom?' she'd asked Susannah, her small face white with shock, tears welling in her eyes.

'It's something to do with Daddy,' Susannah said to her sister, picking up the telegram. She had not been reading for long and grasped at the words. 'I think he's dead,' she whispered, her heart feeling big and huge in her chest. It had never occurred to her that her father might never come back from the war. 'He was killed.'

But Kate wasn't listening. She had followed their mother out into the garden, slipping along the trail her mother had made through the snow in her house shoes. Susannah watched Kate go to their mother, and pull on her arm. Bring her back from the brink of her despair. Their mother turned to Kate, bent down and scooped her up. Held her tight to her chest. Susannah watched her mother and sister together in loss, their mother clinging onto her child to stop herself from walking into the icy sea. The two of them shaking with cold and grief, yet still not turning back into the house and their new reality. Susannah didn't know why she hadn't joined them. But she held back, with her forehead pressed to the chill windowpane, feeling outside of her family, tears trailing down her cheeks. Why had God taken her father from her?

It had been almost nine years since that terrible day. The very worst day in her life by far. She had woken this Saturday morning to a white world, the first snows of the winter. Always, it reminded her of her father's death. The whole morning, she'd been aching to dig out the box of photographs and find his picture. She was afraid that one day she would forget what he looked like. Already, he had become a shadowy memory.

Susannah heard her mother calling up to her from down below. She'd gone upstairs to sweep the floors and get her mother's new glasses. Her mother hated wearing them, but she needed them when she laced.

Susannah put the photograph back in the box and shoved it under her mother's bed. She picked the glasses up from her mother's dressing table.

Downstairs, her mother and Kate were both sitting either side of the lacing stand, working on net bags for pool tables. The table was in the window for the best light. Outside it had stopped snowing and the sun had come out, sparkling on the snow and illuminating the room. Her mother had a big order to fulfil and she and Kate had been working away since the early morning, while Susannah had cleaned the whole house.

'How come it takes you twice as long as your sister to sweep upstairs, young lady?'

'I was looking so long for your glasses,' Susannah lied.

'You know right well I always leave them on my dressing table,' her mother said, not believing a word. 'Were you daydreaming again in one of your books?'

'I read,' Susannah snapped. 'That's not daydreaming.'

Kate gave her a warning look, but Susannah was annoyed. Why did her mother always try to stop her from reading? 'I've homework to do for school on Monday,' Susannah said. 'I don't have any more time to do chores!'

Their mother stopped lacing and gave Susannah an icy stare. 'Well, it will have to wait,' she said. 'We have to finish this, as well as attaching the taffy lacing to Mary Carver's dress.' She stood up from the lacing stand and put down her shuttle. 'In fact, you can take over for now, and help your sister finish these bags off while I finish off the dress,' she said. 'Luckily it doesn't take any great skill.'

'I can't, I've homework to do, I told you,' Susannah said defiantly.

'You are trying my patience, young lady,' their mother said. 'If we don't get these jobs done, we don't eat – or do you think reading your books will feed us?'

'Come on, Susie.' Kate tried to diffuse the tension between their mother and Susannah. 'It won't take us long.'

Susannah reluctantly sat down at the lacing stand.

'Why can't you knuckle down like your sister?' her mother said as she pinned the taffy lace to the cuffs of the wedding dress. 'Learn useful skills, so you'll find a good husband who could provide for you and a family.'

'The idea of having a baby makes me feel sick,' Susannah declared, slamming the shuttle through the yarn.

'Oh, you don't mean that, Susie,' Kate said, looking shocked. 'I can't wait to be a mother. I want at least one of each. A boy and a girl.'

'Your father and I planned to fill this house with children,' their mother said, her voice sad. 'Ronald always wanted a son to follow in his footsteps.'

Her mother's words hurt Susannah's feelings. Had she not been enough for her father because she was a girl? Why were daughters of less value than sons?

'That's why you girls need to be good in the house, because we've no man to take care of us now,' their mother said.

'But what if I went to college?' Susannah ventured. 'Get a good job after I graduate. I could take care of us!'

'College!' Their mother stopped sewing, looking at Susannah as if she'd suggested she wanted to fly to the moon.

'Mr Samuels says my grades are the best he's ever had,' Susannah said proudly. 'He thinks I've potential. I could become a teacher, or work in a library like Mrs Matlock.'

'Mom, Susannah really is the best at school, everyone knows it!' Kate said, and Susannah felt a flood of gratitude towards her sister.

'Wake up, girl!' their mother snapped. 'We've discussed this before. I don't have money to send you to college.'

Their mother put Mary Carver's dress down and walked over to the lacing stand. Stood over Kate, so she was facing Susannah.

She seemed even taller than ever, standing against the white frame of snow outside, her fair hair gleaming in the light from the window, her blue eyes glacial.

'Even if we could afford it, why would you want to leave your sister and I?' she said, sounding injured. 'College isn't for the likes of us. We belong here, on Vinalhaven.'

'No, I don't, I don't!' Susannah stopped lacing and yelled at her mother in frustration. 'I hate this island and I hate our life. Everything is slow and old-fashioned.'

Their mother picked up one of the shuttles and slammed it onto the top of the stand, so that both girls jumped in fright. 'Don't you dare raise your voice to me,' she bellowed at Susannah, as tears started in Kate's eyes. 'You're a disgrace. Why can't you be more like your sister?'

Susannah jumped up from the lacing stand, faced her mother. 'I'm getting out of here one day. I will, you know,' she spat.

'Go to your room this instant!' their mother shouted, her voice shaking with anger. 'I can't abide to look at you!'

Susannah ran out of the room and up the stairs, her heart thumping with the drama of the argument. She would not cry. She was sorry for making Kate cry. Her sister always wept when she argued with her mother. But she refused to submit.

It was only hours later that their mom came up the stairs. She sat on the end of the bed and put her hand on Susannah's shoulders as she turned away from her.

'I only want what's best for you, Susannah,' her mother said. 'I don't want you to be disappointed.'

Susannah said nothing, buried her face further into the pillow.

'You'll understand one day,' her mother said to her. 'When you have children of your own.' She stood up, sighing.

Susannah wanted to shout at her in frustration. She didn't want children, so she never would understand! But she knew there was no point. From now on, she'd keep her dream secret – but she would never give up on it.

Chapter 5

Emer

11th October 2011

When Emer had woken up this morning, Susannah had already been at her desk, typing away on an ancient typewriter. Emer loved the sound of her fingers tapping the keys, and the zip of the return.

'Can I get you anything?' she'd asked Susannah. 'Have you had any breakfast?'

But Susannah had waved her away.

'Not hungry,' she had said gruffly.

'Tea, then?' Emer pushed. She knew Susannah must be in pain if she didn't want to eat, but she should have something.

'I suppose.' Susannah sniffed. 'Black, no milk. It doesn't agree with me.'

When she'd brought back the tea, Emer had been careful to place it on a little side table by Susannah's desk. 'What would you like me to do?' she asked Susannah. 'I can do some cleaning or laundry for you?'

Susannah stopped typing, looking up at Emer in surprise. 'Oh, is that what Lynsey said you should do?'

'I'm here to help,' Emer said, feeling useless. She was used to the urgency of the hospital, but here in Susannah's house she felt like she was moving in slow motion.

'Well now,' Susannah said, her tone a little kinder. 'It's a beautiful fall day. You should take yourself for a walk around town.'

'Where would you recommend?'

'Amherst Hill is just down the road. You can take the short trail past the stone quarries where we used to swim as kids in summer, and go up onto the granite slabs. There's a great view from the top.' Susannah took a sip of her black tea and curled her nose in distaste, clearly missing the milk. She put the cup down again. 'On your way back, pick up some groceries. How's that sound?'

'What should I buy? Do you want to give me a list?'

'I really don't care,' Susannah said, a distracted tone to her voice as she opened the drawer in her desk, and took out a bank card. Waved it at Emer. 'Use this.'

Emer took the card, trying to take a peek over Susannah's shoulder at the sheet in the typewriter, but the words were obscured by a big pile of books.

'What are you writing?' she asked her.

Susannah looked up at her, pushing her glasses down the end of her nose. 'Private correspondence,' she said, emphasising the word *private*.

Emer felt chastised. She had to remember her place was as a nurse, nothing more.

'Can I get you anything before I leave? Are you in pain?'

'Of course I'm in pain,' Susannah snapped, 'but the morphine messes with my head. I can't think straight, so I'll take the pain and clarity.'

'Okay.' Emer paused, remembering how hard Orla had resisted taking painkillers too. Though sometimes, Emer could see the defeat in her sister's eyes as she'd ask for relief. It had broken Emer's heart.

'You take what you need, darling,' she'd said to Orla.

'It makes my dreams so crazy,' Orla had whispered to her. 'I don't like it.'

But when she'd taken the morphine, the tension in Orla's face would soften, and at least she would be able to sleep.

'I'm here to help you in any way I can,' Emer said, returning to the present, and the pained hunch of Susannah at her typewriter. 'You need to take it easy.'

'Seeing as I've been in this body for the past seventy-two years, I think I know what it needs better than anyone, don't you?'

Emer backed away, out of the room. Lynsey had warned her Susannah might be difficult, but she hadn't expected such open hostility. Susannah didn't want her there, clearly. Her resentment was palpable. It occurred to Emer that she didn't belong anywhere any more. Not back home in Ireland, nor in Boston now Ethan was gone to his family in New York. As for Lars, anything that might have happened there was ruined for good. This island and Susannah Olsen were all she had right now.

It was a dull morning on Vinalhaven, but against the backdrop of the grey skies, the fall foliage appeared even more intense. Emer was sure there were colours in those trees she'd never seen. Every possible nuance of red, orange, brown and green. She couldn't stop herself from picking up fallen leaves, holding them in her palms, and studying each one for the secrets of their colours.

Emer remembered the night she'd arrived in Boston for the first time. She'd still been raw from her father getting together with one of their neighbours, Sharon Madigan. It had seemed outrageous to Emer at the time that her father would want another woman to move into the house. Especially since Emer had been convinced Sharon had had designs on their father even before their mother had passed away. A widow herself, she had called over nearly daily with a cooked dinner for their dad.

'How can he be so naïve?' Emer had given out to Orla. 'He and Mam used to take the mickey out of Sharon Madigan looking like mutton dressed as lamb, and now he's only moving in with her!'

Orla had talked her down. 'He doesn't do well on his own, you know it's so, Emer.'

What her sister had said next made Emer shiver with the memory of it.

'If anything ever happened to me, I'd want Ethan to find someone else.'

'Stop,' Emer had said. 'You'd only be devastated, wouldn't you, Ethan?'

'No one could compete with you, babe,' Ethan said to Orla. 'Well, maybe Mila Kunis.' He'd winked at Emer.

Orla had laughed as Ethan put his arm around her waist and kissed the top of her head. 'I guess not even Mila can match you, honey.'

Ethan. The ghost brother-in-law. All joy had now been washed out of him by the loss of his young wife. Emer couldn't face talking to him just yet, after the emotion of helping him pack up. She should have been on the phone every day. Checking he was doing okay. She justified her silence by the fact he was back home in New York, surrounded by his family. But still, she and Ethan had loved Orla the best. This united them.

As for her father, he and Sharon had flown back to Ireland the day after the funeral. To be fair to him, he'd tried to persuade Emer to come home with them, but the idea of returning to the place she and Orla had shared so many childhood memories horrified her.

'We can set up your old room, nice and cosy for you,' Sharon had tried.

'Don't bother,' Emer had told her. 'It's not my home any more.'

She had seen the hurt in Sharon's eyes, but what did she expect? How could she come close to replacing her mother and sister?

'Ah, Emer, now, don't be like that,' her dad had said, giving her big hug. 'There's always a place for you at our table.'

She choked back the tears. She knew they meant well, but she felt as if she'd lost her dad too.

'I need to stay in Boston for a while,' she'd lied. 'My job.'

Emer kept walking until she crossed a tiny bridge. Behind her lay the curve of the harbour, pleasure boats and lobster boats bobbing side by side in the afternoon calm. On her left, the land had become marshy, reminding her of the bogs back in Ireland. Everything in America was on a bigger scale – the sky, the sea, the woods. A pick-up passed her, a white husky pushing its face out of the open window, and the driver, a guy with black hair and a baseball cap, waved to her. Everyone appeared so friendly here, in contrast to Susannah. Although the other side to this attentiveness was feeling watched the whole time. Emer had always been shy. Hated to be the centre of attention. Her place had been in the shadow of her sister. And she had liked that position. It had felt safe and protected. But Orla was gone now, and Emer was exposed. Blinded by grief. Struggling to make sense of it.

Tears stung her eyes. She turned around, head down, terrified someone would see her distress. There was an opening to the woods on her right and she crossed the road and followed a path between the trees. Huge boulders of granite emerged from the undergrowth, and as she came into an opening, she realised she was at one of the old granite quarries on the island, where Susannah had told her locals went swimming in the summer. The pool was small but the water still and dark with deepness, slabs of granite around its circumference. She kept going, into the trees on the other side of the quarry pool, following the trail uphill, and reaching out to touch the golden leaves. Although it was past midday, cobwebs were still strung with dew where they laced patches of blueberry bushes. The only berries left were white with age. She saw plenty of other berries – black, pink and bright red – but wasn't sure if they were edible so steered clear.

On top of the hill was a plateau of granite and a view across the island all the way to the distant sea. Emer read a plaque about it having been a lookout point for U-boats during the Second World War. Spreading her coat on the granite plateau, Emer sat down, and drew her knees to her chest, trying to contain the sorrow. The tears came all the same. She had never got to say goodbye to Orla. She would give up every moment of happiness in her future if she could share one more hour with her sister. But Orla was gone, just like their mam. Daddy now had Sharon. Emer was sisterless, motherless, all alone. And despite the fact Lars kept trying to contact her, she couldn't have him, could she? It was because of Lars she'd let Orla down, when her sister had needed her the most. How could it ever work out with him now?

Emer dawdled as she continued on her way to the grocery store. She took a look at the old netting factory, now a garage, before continuing up to the old church and the library. She didn't think she'd been in a library since she was at nursing college in Dublin, five years ago now. As she walked up the steps, she noticed the pick-up which had passed her earlier with the white husky still sitting in the front, gazing at her as she pushed the door open and walked inside.

The hush of the library felt sacred. She wandered through the stacks, not really knowing what she was looking for. Orla had read a lot. Said words inspired her art. But Emer wasn't like her sister. All she wanted from books, and films too, was to escape. A few hours away from work and all the drama she saw every day in the hospital. The only title she recognised on the shelves was *Twilight* by Stephenie Meyer. A girl in love with a vampire.

That would do. A story to take her away from her own reality. She took the book off the shelf and made her way to the counter. 'I'd like to join the library,' she said.

'Sure,' the librarian said. She was quite young, not much older than Emer, with John Lennon glasses and long brown hair. 'Are you living on the island?' The librarian took her glasses off, had a good look at her. Emer felt herself blushing. 'Oh, I bet you're the nurse who's minding Susannah Olsen, aren't you?'

Emer nodded.

'How's she getting on? I've been meaning to call over but she's not the most social of ladies. Still, Susannah's an important part of our community.'

'She's doing fine,' Emer said. What could she say? *She's dying, slowly?*

As the librarian introduced herself – 'Peggy Steel, pleased to meet you' – Emer recognised the owner of the pick-up with the white husky as he came up to the counter with a big stack of books. She sensed him listening to Peggy's continued interrogation – where was Emer from? How long had she been in the States? Where had she lived before she came to Vinalhaven? Emer tried to keep it short, but Peggy the librarian clearly craved a chat.

'Hey, Henry, you met Susannah's Olsen's nurse? Your name is Emma, right?

'No, Emer.'

'So Emma here is from Ireland, Henry.'

'That so? Beautiful, Ireland,' said Henry, giving her an appreciative look. 'Well, good for you; Susannah Olsen is something else.'

'Susannah used to be Vinalhaven's librarian,' Peggy said. 'Going on thirty-odd years. She trained me in!'

'I remember going to her reading circle for kids,' Henry told them. 'She got me reading all the greats, but I was only interested in the cooking books.'

'Henry here runs one of the restaurants on Vinalhaven,' Peggy enthused. 'It's called The Haven. You might have seen it on the way through town.'

'It's closed for the season now,' Henry said. 'Got good intentions to read all these books over the winter.'

'You still doing your sculptures, Henry?' Peggy asked him. The librarian was all fluttering eyelashes.

'Sure am,' Henry replied, flashing a big smile at Peggy.

'Henry is one of Vinalhaven's artists,' she told Emer. 'We've a few living here, as well as writers.'

'We love the seclusion,' Henry told her. 'Very peaceful for creating.'

'But of course Henry is also a born islander, unlike me,' Peggy tittered. 'Though I feel like this is where I belong, for sure.'

'Vinalhaven worked its magic on you, right, Peggy?' Henry winked at Emer. She felt a little awkward with this familiarity.

'Well, isn't it just so beautiful here?' Peggy turned to Emer.

'Yes, it is, really the prettiest place I've been,' Emer said honestly. 'All the wooden houses, with pumpkins lined up outside, and the leaves on the trees are just stunning.'

'Yeah, we take Halloween very seriously here on Vinalhaven.' Henry grinned at her. 'Fall has to be the time of year when the island looks its best.'

'All the fall foliage,' Peggy agreed. 'Isn't it gorgeous? Is this time of year as pretty in Ireland?'

'It can be,' Emer said, wishing she could get away without being rude. She craved to be walking on her own again. 'But mostly it rains a lot in Ireland. We get very grey days.'

'Oh, I don't like the rain,' Peggy prattled on. 'Prefer the snow to the rain.'

'Have to agree, nothing beats the purity of first snow,' Henry said.

'So you here on your own?' Peggy grilled Emer. 'Got a husband with you? Kids?'

'Oh no, no,' Emer said, edging away.

'My husband's an island man,' Peggy chatted on, oblivious to Emer's discomfort. 'Three kids. Bobby is five, Ellie seven, and Tammy nine.'

'Hard to believe,' Henry said. 'You look so young, Peggy.'

Peggy giggled like a schoolgirl. 'Must be island life,' she said. 'And we all go to bed not long after Teddy because he has to be up so early for the fishing. You know, all those early nights must count for something.'

'I'm a bit of a night owl,' Henry said. 'How about you, Emer?'

'Oh well, it depends,' she said. 'I used to have to work night shifts.'

'That so?' Peggy asked. 'What hospital did you work in? Was it here or in Ireland?'

'Boston,' Emer said quickly, and then made a pretence at looking at the time on her phone. 'Oh, I'd best be going. Sorry, Susannah's expecting me.'

Henry gave her a knowing look as Peggy waved goodbye.

'Do come back soon!' she said. 'I love a good chat.'

Emer slipped out of the library and down the steps. She hadn't considered what it might be like to live in an island community. All she'd been thinking about when she took the job was getting out of Boston, and going somewhere new. A place Orla had never been. A place with no memories. But she should have known. Growing up in rural Ireland meant everyone knew everybody's business. There were no secrets in their townland in Meath. This could be supportive, but also unbearably claustrophobic. It had been the reason why Orla had gone off travelling when she was barely eighteen, not even bothering to go to college. Once Mammy was gone, Orla couldn't bear to stay in Ireland. Emer had been more of a homebody: still training as a nurse in Dublin and coming home every weekend to see Daddy. It wasn't fair. Why had she had to witness both her mother and her sister struck down with cancer? And now here she was, putting herself through it all over again for a stranger. It wasn't the same as being a nurse in a hospital. Caring for Susannah Olsen would be more personal, no matter how much professional distance she tried to maintain.

'Emer, wait up!'

She jumped to hear her name, and spun on her heel. It was Henry.

'You forgot your book,' he said, holding out the library copy of *Twilight*.

'Oh, thanks,' she mumbled, not looking at his face, embarrassed for him to see her choice of reading matter.

'Let me know if it's any good.' She could hear the tease in his voice, and looked up. He had eyes the colour of autumn, brown flecked with amber and green. He looked taller, too, outside the library. Although his dark head was streaked with a few grey hairs, and he was clearly a bit older than her, there was a boyishness to his open smile.

'I was just looking for something light,' she said.

'I wouldn't say vampires are very light,' Henry said, grinning. 'But I've seen this book everywhere. Peggy was just saying the teenage girls are obsessed with it on the island.'

Emer winced to think of Peggy comparing her reading taste with Henry to that of a teenage girl. 'Oh well, that sounds a bit rubbish,' she said, stuffing the book into her bag.

They stood for a moment in awkward silence. She waited for him to get into his pick-up, feeling it was rude just to walk away.

'Hey, would you like to go for a coffee sometime?' Henry suggested.

'Oh, I don't know,' she faltered, surprised by his forwardness.

'We could go for one now,' he pushed, giving her a warm smile.

Emer felt panic rise in her chest. This man Henry was very nice, and a coffee was just a coffee, but it felt a little like a date and she wasn't ready for a date right now with anyone.

'Oh, thank you, but I can't,' she said hastily. 'Like I said in the library, I have to get back to Susannah.'

'I thought you were just making that up to get away from Peggy,' he said. 'Another time then.' He made for the pick-up and his white husky dog, who was almost clambering out of the open window, so keen was he to see his master returning. 'Good luck with Susannah,' Henry said as he got in the pick-up.

After buying some groceries in the market shop, Emer walked fast back to Susannah's house, feeling guilty she'd been so long. By the time she got back she felt warmed up and better for the first time in ages. Despite still feeling so bad about Lars, Henry's invitation had lifted her spirits. She had no intention of going for a coffee with him, but the fact he'd invited her was flattering. Both he and Peggy had been interested in who she was, and that she was helping Susannah. They didn't view her as a nuisance. She was going to make things up to Orla by taking the greatest care of Susannah Olsen. Her sister, and her mam, would be proud of her. It was one small way to stay connected to those she had loved the most.

Chapter 6

Susannah

April 1954

Susannah marched up the hill ahead of Kate, who was, as usual, dawdling on her way to school.

'Come on, we're going to be late,' Susannah called back. But Kate seemed to be going even slower.

They had a big math test today, and Susannah was anxious to get to school early so she had time to go over the book again. Math was her weakest subject, but she knew it was crucial she did well if she was to have any chance of getting off this island and going to college. It was a big dream, but Susannah was determined to aim high. She believed it was what her father would have wanted.

She stood at the top of the hill by the church, her hands on her hips.

'Hurry *up*!' she scolded.

Kate broke out into a reluctant run to join her. 'Aw, Susie, we're going to be there before everyone else.'

'That's the point,' Susannah said crossly.

'Why are you always so serious?' Kate complained. 'You never come out in the yard at recess. You don't know about anything that's going on with anyone else in school.'

'I don't care to know what's going on,' Susannah said.

'Sometimes I have to stop the boys calling you names,' Kate said, looking at her slyly.

'Like what?' Susannah asked, surprised. She hadn't even thought any of the boys noticed her in school. They were all so loud and stupid.

'Matthew Young said you're like a schoolteacher already; an old woman, he called you,' Kate told her. 'I said you were three times as clever as him and he's only jealous of you.'

Susannah linked Kate's arm, touched by her sister's defence. 'Thanks, Katie.'

'You're welcome,' Kate said. 'But you should come out and talk with me and the girls, because you know you do act like an old woman sometimes.'

'But you know I want to go to college, Kate,' Susannah said. 'I have to stay in and study as much as I can.'

Her sister was quiet for a moment. They could hear the patter of rain on the leaves above them as the sky clouded over.

'Come on, it's starting to rain, let's run the rest of the way,' Susannah said, tugging on Kate's arm, but her sister held back.

'Why are you so fixed on getting off the island, Susie?' Kate said. 'Don't you love me and Mom enough to stay?'

'You know that's not why, Katie,' Susannah said, exasperated. She had given up trying to get her mother to understand, but she had hoped Kate would. The rain began to fall in earnest. 'Come on,' she said, tugging her again. 'We're going to get wet.'

The two girls broke out into a run for the last stretch to the school gates.

The math test went better than Susannah had hoped. Rather than stay in the classroom and read as she usually did at recess, Susannah decided to go out and look for Kate. Try to be a bit more social. They were in different years, but even in the dinner hour they didn't hang out together. Susannah wasn't fond of Kate's two best friends in school – Annie Young, the sister of Matthew and Silas, who was as dim as her two brothers, and Rachel Weaver, the daughter of the owner of the island hotel, a spoilt Daddy's girl who was always boasting about how rich her father was.

As she walked out of the building, she noticed all the kids were standing in a circle on the other side of the yard, and some of the girls were crying. She saw Kate's blonde hair among the throng.

'Hey what's going on?' she asked Kate as she pushed in next to her.

'Oh, look at the poor thing,' Kate said, pointing to a seagull which was thrashing around in the yard. 'It just dropped out of the sky right in front of us.'

'Its wing is broke,' Annie said, stating the obvious.

'Oh, I can't stand to look,' Rachel said, burying her head in her hands.

'But how did it happen?' Susannah asked. For a seagull to drop out of the sky with a broken wing was completely illogical.

None of the girls answered her. Instead, Annie's two brothers came busting into the crowd.

'Don't worry, girls,' Silas said to them. 'We'll put the poor thing out of its misery.'

Matthew knelt down by the bird, while Silas handed him a stone. Matthew raised his arm, and with one swift movement slammed the stone down onto the poor bird's head. All the girls screamed in unison; even some of the other boys looked white. Matthew kept repeating the action until the bird was clearly long dead. Susannah felt her stomach lurch. That was just too quick. Couldn't they have tried to fix the bird first?

'What's going on here?' Mr Samuels said, marching towards the gang of teenagers.

'It had a broken wing, Sir,' Silas said.

'We did the kindest thing,' Matthew joined him.

'I see, well, good. Thank you, boys,' Mr Samuels said. 'Go on back inside, everyone. We'll get Mr Jenkins to clear it up.'

They all moved away towards the school buildings. Susannah couldn't bear to look at the dead bird again. It made her stomach churn.

'Oh, the poor bird,' Kate said to her. 'But they did the right thing, didn't they?'

'I guess,' Susannah said as they walked behind Matthew and Silas Young. But as they were going through the doors back into school, she got a glimpse of the top of a slingshot sticking out of Silas Young's trouser pocket. They had shot the bird down! Her immediate instinct was to run back to Mr Samuels and tell him. But what good would that do? Just make everyone else hate her for telling on the two most popular boys in school.

Had Matthew known his brother had shot the bird out of the sky, or did he genuinely want to end its suffering? Susannah had never forgotten the way Matthew and Silas had taunted her and Kate when they'd gone swimming down at the cove. But no matter how many times she reminded her sister how mean they were, Kate never minded it any more, saying they were just boys being boys. Susannah knew that was just one big fat lie. She didn't understand any of the boys in their school. She really hoped one day she'd meet a boy she liked. All she had to do was get off the island.

Chapter 7

Emer

15th October 2011

Emer woke as the sun rose. She hadn't drawn the curtains in her room. From her bed, she could see rosy light seeping into the sky. She got out of bed and watched the sun rising above the pine trees on an islet in the bay. The view from her bedroom looked out over Vinalhaven harbour and all the moored boats used over the summer months. The water was deep blue, with smooth, slow ripples rocking against the sides of the pleasure vessels. The fishing boats had already taken off in the morning dark. Susannah had told her last night the fishermen went out at four in the morning, returning at one every afternoon.

'From the lobster pots straight to The Sand Bar every darn day,' Susannah had said, her tone critical. 'But always going home to bed at four in the afternoon.'

Emer took in the fragile beauty of the day. She was used to being up this early from working in the hospital. It was a time she'd always loved. The untouched quality of early morning, like new snow. But ever since that dreadful day she'd woken up next to Lars, rolled over and turned on her phone, dawn's magic had been ruined. It had become the time when she'd found out her sister had died. And she hadn't been there, all because of Lars. No – she couldn't blame him. It had been she who had run away from the hospital – Ethan, her dad and Sharon all sat around Orla in the bed. She'd banged on Lars' door in the middle of the night. Orla had held on for so many weeks. Why had she chosen those exact hours, when her sister was absent, to let go?

Emer wiped the tears off her face with the back of her hand. She had to get it together. Her job was to be a support to Susannah. She couldn't be wallowing in her own grief. She had to stay upbeat for her new patient. She put on her best comfort sweater – an old one of her mam's, deep green and soft – over her pyjamas and pulled on a pair of thick woolly socks. She was going to see if she could put together a breakfast Susannah might feel like trying, despite her dwindling appetite.

A short while later, balancing coffee and scrambled eggs with toast on a tray she'd found in the back of the big blue dresser in the kitchen, Emer climbed the stairs to Susannah's bedroom. She tentatively knocked on the door. No answer, but she could hear Susannah coughing. She knocked again and walked in.

Susannah hadn't closed her curtains either. Her bedroom was bathed in gold, illuminating dust and cobwebs but also displaying the beautiful quilt on her bed. Every time Emer looked at it, she saw another detail she hadn't noticed before. This morning it was a series of tiny apple-green hearts with white sprigs in the print at the four corners of the quilt.

'Good morning,' Emer said, in her most cheerful nurse's voice. 'That really is such a lovely quilt. Did you make it?'

No answer from Susannah's bed, although the old lady was awake, giving her a look half-way between surprise and outrage.

'I made you some breakfast.' Emer placed the tray down on the table by the bed and turned to help Susannah sit up, but she was already getting out of bed. 'Oh, don't you want the food I made?'

'Sure, sure,' said Susannah, looking cross. 'But I ain't bed-bound yet.'

'I know, but I thought it might be nice for you to be treated to breakfast in bed.'

'Well, we eat downstairs in this house.'

Emer picked up the tray again. 'Okay, sorry,' she said, trying not to sound as wounded as she felt.

'I don't need help dressing, either,' Susannah snapped, making sure Emer got the hint.

Half an hour later, by the time both the coffee and toast were stone cold, Susannah came downstairs, dressed in a sky blue sweater and denims. Her silver hair was brushed and she was even wearing a little make-up. Emer was mortified to still be in her pyjamas. She could feel Susannah's disapproval as they sat at the kitchen table in silence. But Susannah said nothing, perusing the very thin local paper, and picking at her breakfast while Emer forced down toast and fried tomatoes.

'You not eating eggs?' Susannah said, surveying Emer's breakfast plate.

'No. I'm vegan.'

'So, you don't eat meat? No fish, dairy?'

'Not since I was fifteen.'

Susannah grunted. 'Shame you won't eat the lobster. It sure is good here.' She pushed away her plate of eggs.

'Are they no good?' Emer ventured.

'They're fine.' Susannah's tone softened. 'It's just hard to eat.'

'I'll do some experimenting,' Emer offered. 'We'll find something you can eat.'

'What's the point?' Susannah said, pushing her chair back and standing up. Emer was about to go back into cheerful nurse mode and dish out some positive platitudes when Susannah's phone began to ring.

Susannah began hunting for her phone. 'That'll be my niece, Rebecca,' she said, looking much happier all of a sudden. 'She rings nearly every morning, between lectures. Did I tell you she's a history professor at King's College in London?'

'No, Lynsey did.'

'Now where is the darn thing?' Susannah declared.

Emer found the phone on top of a pile of books on the dresser, and handed it to Susannah, who gave her the first – if tight – smile she'd offered her since Emer had arrived.

'Hello, honey.' Susannah's tone immediately softened as she answered the phone.

Emer got up from the table.

'It was Rebecca's mom, my sister Kate, who made the quilt,' Susannah said to Emer, putting a hand over the mouthpiece.

So Susannah's sister had been a seamstress. Had she made all the furnishings in the house? Cushion covers, quilts on all the beds, and quilted throws on the couches? Emer left the kitchen, wandering into the main downstairs room, coffee mug in hand. The view overlooked the front porch with a swing seat, round table, wicker chairs and a white trellis covered in red leaves. Beyond the porch was the garden. Many years ago it might have been looked after lovingly, but now things clearly needed some management. She'd never been much of a gardener, but the way Susannah was reacting to her help inside the house, she guessed she'd have plenty of time on her own to give it a try.

Surveying the front room, which also appeared to be Susannah's study, Emer determined it could do with a big clean and tidy up. Her eyes were drawn to two photographs in frames on Susannah's desk. In the first one she recognised Lynsey, though a child, the red hair blazing around her pale face, and next to her was a younger girl, with blonde hair and blue eyes. Clearly her sister, the adored Rebecca. Emer put the photograph down and picked up the second frame. It was an old black and white photograph of a young woman sitting on the same veranda she had just looked at and smiling shyly. Emer guessed this must be the sister, Kate. She was very pretty. Emer peered at the photograph but it was hard to make out her features in the dim light. Balancing her coffee mug on top of a stack of papers on the table at the window, Emer leant across to pull back the curtains properly. Dust flew up from the heavy drapes, making her sneeze. She put down the framed picture as she sneezed again, lifting her hand to cover her nose, and knocking over her coffee cup. Dark brown liquid streaked across the stack of papers. Emer picked up the top papers in a panic, making the mess even worse in the process.

'What the hell are you doing?' Susannah came storming into the room and snatched the papers from her hand.

'I'm so sorry. I was opening the curtains and I knocked my cup over.'

Susannah looked furious as she dabbed the top of her papers with her handkerchief.

'You have copies, don't you?' Emer asked in a panic.

'Of course I don't have copies!' Susannah indicated the old typewriter. 'Can you not just mind your own damn business?'

'I really am so sorry. Please, what can I do?' Emer felt stress and panic building up in her body.

Susannah shook her head. 'This isn't working out. You being here, I mean. It's not personal. I just can't have anyone else in my house.'

'It was an accident,' Emer defended herself.

'That may be, but this house is too small to have a stranger living in it with me,' Susannah countered. 'You can see I am quite able to look after myself.'

Susannah stood tall, but Emer could see the pain outlined in the face. Her mouth was pulled into a severe line, her forehead creased with focus, and her eyes glared with pain.

Emer took a breath, determined not to get annoyed with Susannah. 'You might think you don't need me, but things can change all of a sudden with pancreatic cancer,' she said. 'Besides, Lynsey is paying me to help you. I can't just walk away.'

'Don't know why she doesn't come and mind me herself,' Susannah moaned. 'But oh no, I forgot, she's too busy being a charlatan fortune teller, making money on the back of the real history of persecution and suffering in Salem.' Susannah shook her head, looking fierce. 'My niece is an embarrassment.'

Emer felt sorry for Lynsey, responsible for an aunt who clearly thought her career as a tarot reader was shameful.

Susannah shrugged. 'Well, I guess you'd better stay if Lynsey is paying you,' she said, trying to sound indifferent. 'Rebecca's coming back soon. You won't need to stay on then, she'll help me.'

Emer plastered a smile on her face. Its rigidity made her chin tremble. 'That's good,' she said. *The sooner the better.* Emer wanted to have a go at Susannah. Tell her how lucky she was to have a nurse all to herself. How it had been a constant stress to give all of her patients on the oncology ward the attention they needed, and yet Susannah, one woman, seemed to take up so much more space in her life after only a few days.

Chapter 8

Susannah

July 1957

What was taking Kate so long? Susannah had been sitting outside the library for nearly a quarter of an hour waiting for her sister. Like every other day this week, she'd gone straight from school to the library. Sat at the table right at the back and by the window, away from the island gossipers up front, waiting for Mrs Matlock to come down to her. The foliage on the trees was thick, casting a green light on her hands as she turned the pages of the book. Everything was bursting with life outside. But Susannah had a lot of study to do if she was going to have any chance of her scholarship. It was less than a year ago that Mr Samuels, the principal of their small island high school, had called her in for a meeting. He had told Susannah her grades were the highest of any of their pupils in years, and encouraged her to apply for college.

'But we can't afford it,' Susannah had said.

'There are scholarships,' Mr Samuels had told her. 'We can help you apply. Do you know where you would like to go?'

She had always known, but it seemed such a far-fetched fantasy she felt embarrassed as she told him.

'Harvard!' Mr Samuels raised his eyebrows. 'I guess no harm in aiming high, but you should apply for other colleges too. You'll need a tutor.'

That was when Mr Samuels had said he'd ask Mrs Matlock, the only resident woman on the island who'd ever been to college.

Susannah had been worried. She had no means of paying Mrs Matlock for her time, and she didn't want to tell her mother about her application. What was the point of getting her all stirred up if she didn't get in anyway?

'I am sure Mrs Matlock can work out a way you could help her out in the library in payment,' Mr Samuels had said to Susannah, as if sensing her anxiety.

Mrs Matlock had been a tutor beyond all Susannah's expectations. She adored history as well, but also was very good at math, one of Susannah's weaker subjects. The system was that she would set Susannah some tasks while the library was open, and then when it closed she'd go over Susannah's answers before they both headed home for dinner. In return, Susannah worked in the library on Saturday mornings, refilling the shelves and helping Mrs Matlock organise the catalogue.

'I'm so proud of you, Susannah,' Mrs Matlock would often say, hand on her shoulder. 'Just keep working hard; you've got this.'

Her words were bittersweet because Susannah so wished her mother could say the same.

Today, Susannah had set all her study aside at exactly five.

'I've got to meet Kate,' she explained to Mrs Matlock. 'We're going blueberry picking up at Amherst.'

'It's a beautiful day,' Mrs Matlock said, picking up a stack of books left on Susannah's table. 'You deserve a break, Susannah. It's nearly the holidays, and so warm outside.'

'It's my mom's birthday tomorrow and we're making her blueberry jelly,' Susannah said, gathering her things.

'Oh, my favourite,' Mrs Matlock declared.

'I'll bring you a pot,' Susannah said shyly.

She and Kate had planned to serve the blueberry jelly with pancakes in the morning. Ever since Daddy never came back, their mother struggled with birthdays. Spent the morning on her own in bed, crying, and then a frantic afternoon cleaning up as the Olsen clan – Gramps Olsen, Uncle Karl and Aunt Marjorie – would descend on the house in the evening with fresh lobster. They meant well, but it was a strain for them all. The same stories told about Daddy. From Gramps, about how Ronald had been the best darn baseball player the island had ever known. Fishing tales from Uncle Karl; in particular, the time their father had scooped Karl out of the freezing Atlantic Ocean, saving his younger brother's life when he fell overboard.

Kate hated the visits as much as Susannah did, although for a different reason.

'They'll never let Mom go,' Kate complained afterwards. 'How'll she find a new husband when the Olsens come over all the time?'

'They're our family, Kate!' Susannah admonished her.

'But remember when Jim Hadley would come over?' Kate said.

'Didn't he just want Mom to make him some fishing nets?'

Kate rolled her eyes. 'He asked her to marry him!'

Susannah had been stunned. How did Kate know this, and why had she no idea?

'You've always got your head buried in a book,' Kate explained to Susannah. 'You never see anything going on. Even if it's right in front of you.'

Susannah remembered the times Jim Hadley had come over, about a year before. It was true, he'd brought them way too many lobsters, and had seemed to need to talk to their mother about his fishing nets an awful lot.

'Well, Mom said no, of course,' Kate said. 'And thank goodness, he's not near good enough for her – but with the Olsens always hanging round, no other man on the island wants to come near her.'

Susannah hadn't even considered their mother might find someone else. What she disliked about the Olsens' visits was their pity. 'Poor fatherless girls,' on the lips of Gramps Olsen all the time. Aunt Marjorie would bring piles of either her ancient very old-fashioned clothes which hung off them, or even worse, cast-off dresses from her own girls, which was mortifying when everybody in school knew they were wearing Lottie and Laura Olsen's hand-me-downs.

Outside the library now, Susannah stood up. That was it. She'd just have to gather the blueberries herself, although it was Kate who was bringing the containers for collecting them. However, just as she was crossing Atlantic Avenue, she heard her sister call her name. Turning around, she saw Kate running to catch up with her. To Susannah's annoyance, by Kate's side was Matthew Young, looking very pleased with himself as he carried the blueberry baskets.

There was no denying Matthew Young had matured into a very good-looking boy. Blue eyes, with tanned skin unmarked by any teenage spots, and fair hair, thick and curly. But Susannah still harboured a deep dislike for him.

'Sorry, Susie,' Kate said breathlessly as they caught up with her. 'I bumped into Matthew and we got talking.'

'You know I've got more study to do tonight,' Susannah said, giving Matthew a scowl as she took one of the baskets from him.

'But Matthew said he'd help us collect,' Kate said as they followed the path into the woods.

Susannah felt even more annoyed now. This was something she and Kate did together every year. She didn't want this boy being part of it. Kate was different when she was around boys. She could be quite giggly and silly, and it irritated Susannah because she knew Kate was cleverer than that. Why did she pretend to be dumb whenever she liked a boy?

There wasn't room for the three of them to walk together on the path, so Kate and Matthew walked ahead and Susannah trailed behind. Already, she was being excluded. With her blonde hair and big smile, Kate was one of the most popular girls at school. It felt as if ever since Kate had turned sixteen the year before, all she was interested in was boys. Susannah was just less than a year older than Kate, and yes, there were times when she wondered about boys, but while her sister attracted so much attention, Susannah was completely ignored. She knew it was because Kate was prettier, although her sister was far from vain.

'I can't wait until school's out for the summer,' Kate trilled up ahead. 'It's so hard being stuck inside when all you want to do is go to the beach!'

'Summer's our busy time,' Matthew said. 'Lobster fishing with my dad. It's when we make all the money.'

'Do you make lots and lots?' Kate giggled.

'Oh boy, it's unreal,' Matt said proudly. 'That's why I ain't coming back to school next year.'

Susannah gave the back of Matthew's head a scathing look. Typical island logic. All the boys dropped out early to lobster fish, enticed by the cash prize.

'It's a good living,' Matt continued, in his attempt to impress Kate. 'But you work darn hard, I can tell you.'

'I bet you do,' Kate said in admiration. 'Thanks for helping out today.'

'Aw, I like hanging out with you, Kate, is all,' Matt said.

Susannah narrowed her eyes as she saw him put his hand under Kate's elbow to help her clamber up some of the granite slabs.

The bushes were brimming with ripe blueberries. It didn't take long to fill their baskets. Afterwards, the three of them climbed up to the top of Amherst to the lookout point where Matt said his dad used to watch for U-boats during the war.

'Told me one time he saw one and called the number he was given. The planes came and sunk it,' he said, all proud. 'Down at the bottom of the sea off Vinalhaven, there's at least one U-boat full of dead Germans.'

'Oh, that's horrible,' Kate squealed.

'Yeah.' Matthew shivered. 'Not the end I'd want.'

The three of them sat down on the granite plateau. Kate lay back and spread her arms wide, as if to invite the sun in. Susannah couldn't help notice Matthew Young looking at her sister. She was wearing one of the Olsen cast-off dresses and it was a little too small for her. The yellow bud print was strained across her chest and was far too revealing. Susannah glanced away. Stared out to sea. Tried not to think about the way Matthew was looking at her sister.

She couldn't help herself, though. With a backward glance, Susannah could see Matthew had lain down on the rock next to Kate and was whispering things to her, which were making her sister giggle. The two of them locked in their own secret intimacy. Susannah felt awkward. She knew their mother would be furious with Kate for being so familiar with a boy, and yet she felt like she was the one in the wrong, because she was so different from Kate's friends Annie and Rachel, and all the other girls in their high school. Any of them would be thrilled to have the admiration of a good-looking boy like Matthew Young, but Susannah saw beyond his charm. There was a hardness in his eyes behind the smile which she didn't like.

Matthew said something obviously hilarious, which Susannah couldn't hear because Kate burst out laughing. But it wasn't a real belly laugh. It was a silly, girly, showy-off laugh. It made Susannah mad. She stood up all of a sudden, almost knocking over her basket of blueberries.

'Come on, Kate,' she said. 'We need to get started on the blueberry jelly. It has to set for tomorrow.'

'But it's so lovely here, with the sun on the rocks.' Kate squinted up at her. 'We've plenty of time.'

'I've got study to do.'

Kate groaned. 'You're always studying, Susie. It's boring.'

Susannah knew Kate was just showing off to stupid Matthew, because in private she'd told her how proud she was, and that Susannah mustn't give up ever on her dream of going to college. Still, her sister's words hurt her now. Why did she change so much when this boy was around?

'Why don't you go study?' Matt piped up, giving her a sly look. 'I'll walk Kate back with all the blueberries.'

'I shan't be long,' Kate promised.

'I don't think Ma will like you to—'

'I'll look after her,' Matt interrupted, and the look he gave her made Susannah feel as if he'd like to push her off the granite, right into the bottom of the sea to end up beside all those German soldier bones.

Susannah huffed, sounding tough but feeling shaken. 'Well, give me the blueberries then,' she said, snatching Kate's basket. 'I need to make a start on the jelly. And don't blame me if you get into trouble!'

She turned on her heel and stomped off, climbing down the rock towards the road. She tried her best not to care, but she couldn't stop the tears from welling up. She dashed them away from her eyes in annoyance, but they just kept falling. Kate preferred to be with a boy like Matthew Young rather than her.

Their mother was out when Susannah got home. She and Kate had planned their jelly making to time with when they knew mother was doing a dress fitting. Susannah crushed the berries into the bottom of the cast-iron pot they used for jam making, before adding water and turning it up to boil. Her tears had dried up, but she was angry now. Her sister knew she was no good at cooking. It was likely she'd mess the whole thing up without her help.

While the blueberry mixture boiled away, Susannah sat at the lacing stand, looking out of the window to watch for Kate. The sun was still high in the sky, light stretching on until late in the evening. Susannah opened the window, breathed in the sweet scent of summer, and listened to the crickets chirruping. It was rare she had the house to herself, and the place felt strange and empty. She pulled her library edition of *Moby-Dick* out of her school bag, and placed it on the lacing stand, opening it up to where she'd left off. She spread the pages with her hands. The stand was just the right height for reading. Now she had her book, she was no longer alone. She dived into Melville's world, immediately under the spell of his story.

It was the smell of burning blueberries, sticky and sweet, which roused her. She hopped off the chair, and ran into the kitchen. Luckily, the berry mixture had only just seemed to start to stick to the bottom. She glanced at her watch. She'd been reading for nearly an hour and still no Kate. She felt a nervous flutter in her stomach. Maybe she shouldn't have left her up on those granite slabs with Matthew Young?

Susannah took out the strainer and tried to remember how they'd made the jelly last year. Cheesecloth. Four layers went in the strainer, which she balanced in a bowl before spooning in the blueberry mixture. Now it had to sit for about thirty minutes. She went back into the front room and sat down at the lacing stand, looking out of the window yet again. But there was still no sign of Kate. Just as she was thinking of going to look for Kate while the jelly mixture thickened, she saw her mother coming up the road. Oh hell, what was she going to tell her about Kate?

Her mother was in a good mood as she came in the door, carrying her sewing bag in one hand like a doctor with his medical kit.

'What a joy it is to work on Hannah Weaver's dress,' her mother said, her eyes gleaming with delight. 'Her father is sparing no expense. It's such a pleasure to be able to make bobbin lace for the detail rather than all those darn pool table nets!'

She put down the bag, and sat down at the lacing stand opposite Susannah.

'Such good people, the Weavers,' her mother said. 'They insisted on giving me a little glass of whisky to set me on my way home. And Rachel is growing up to be such a pretty girl, isn't she?'

'Yes,' Susannah said, closing her book. Susannah particularly disliked Rachel Weaver, who was always bragging about her father's big leisure boat and all her rich friends from Connecticut who came to stay in their hotel every summer.

Her mother unpinned her hair, and let its blonde tresses cascade over her shoulders. She looked younger tonight than she had in years.

'They're having a dance soon for all the summer visits, and you and Kate are invited!' she said happily. 'Isn't that just swell?'

The idea of going to Rachel Weaver's summer dance did not appeal to Susannah in the least, but there was no point telling her mother that.

'So what's that I can smell?' Her mother gave Susannah a knowing smile. 'Is Katie in the kitchen, working her magic?' She got up and went towards the kitchen.

'It's a surprise!' Susannah exclaimed, trying to stop her mother from going in.

Her mother turned and smiled again. 'Sure it is,' she said. 'So sweet of you girls.'

Susannah followed her mother into the kitchen. She hadn't noticed what a mess she'd made until now, when she saw all the spoons and bowls placed about the table.

'I'll clean up,' she said. 'I haven't finished yet.'

'But where's Katie?' her mother asked.

Susannah didn't even consider telling her mother the truth. If she knew her youngest daughter was on her own with a boy, she would be furious – and most likely blame Susannah for leaving Kate behind on Amherst.

'She's taken some blueberries over to Aunt Marjorie,' Susannah lied. 'She'll be back soon.'

'So did you make this on your own, Susannah?' Her mother gave her a curious look.

'Yes,' Susannah said, pouring the strained mixture back into the iron pot and measuring out sugar.

'Well, I sure am impressed you remembered the recipe on your own,' her mother said, taking an apron off the peg and handing it to her. 'You'd better put this on, darling. Blueberries make the darnedest stains.' She put the apron on over Susannah's head and tied it tight around her waist. 'You're a good girl, Susannah,' she said, kissing the top of her head.

Susannah felt terrible. All she did was lie to her mother. Not just about where Kate was, but also about her own life. Her plans for Harvard. All those secret hours in the library with Mrs Matlock. She was almost tempted to tell her right then. Her mother was in such a good mood. But then it was so rare, especially the night before her birthday. Susannah didn't want to darken her mother's humour.

'You carry on there,' her mother said, returning to the front room. 'I've got some more lacing to do.'

Susannah turned the heat back on the hob and stirred the jelly mixture, watching the sugar dissolve. If Kate didn't come home soon, their mom would get suspicious. What if she decided to call over to Aunt Marjorie?

It wasn't until the sun was beginning to sink below the horizon, the sky seeping rose and the sea splattered pink, that Kate finally came in the back door.

'Why were you so long? Mom's been asking where you were,' Susannah hissed.

'What did you tell her?' Kate said. Her eyes were glittering and her dress was all rumpled.

'Said you brought some berries over to Aunt Marjorie,' Susannah said, disgruntled. 'She'd better not ask her about it tomorrow afternoon.'

Kate shrugged, seeming not to care.

'I had to make all this jelly on my own,' Susannah continued, ladling the mixture into jars.

'What a great job you've done, Susie!' Kate said, twirling around the kitchen.

'That's not the point,' Susannah said. 'You shouldn't stay out so late at night. Not on your own with a boy.'

'He's not *any* boy, he's Matthew Young,' Kate said, clutching her hands to her heart. 'And he says it's me he likes the best. Imagine, Susie,' Kate continued, turning to her with stars in her eyes. 'Matthew Young wants me to be his girl!'

Susannah's heart sank. She should never have left her sister on Amherst Hill with Matthew Young, because now it was too late.

Matthew already had Kate's heart trapped, just like one of his lobsters.

Chapter 9

Susannah

August 1957

The preparations had been going on for weeks. Kate was obsessed with Rachel Weaver's summer dance. Carrying on as if they were going to a ball in, say, Boston, or some other big city they were never going to get to.

'It's only just a social on the island,' Susannah kept reminding Kate.

'But there's going to be a band,' Kate would respond. 'They're coming from Portland. And dancing. Don't you want to dance to a real band?'

'I guess.'

But in truth Susannah did not enjoy dances. They'd only been to a couple organised by the church. She'd hated the small talk amongst all the women, and worst of all, having to wait for a boy to ask her dance. It always made her feel such a loser.

She knew the reason her sister was so excited was because she had a date. Matthew Young. Kate was besotted with him. Kept going on about his long legs, blonde wavy hair like a Viking and his dreamy blue eyes. Susannah had tried for her sister's sake to like Matthew, but despite his wholesome good looks, there was something about him that made her suspicious. He was always perfectly polite to her, but she could sense the dislike was mutual. He knew Susannah was her sister's protector as the eldest. He didn't like the fact that she and Kate were so different and that

Susannah wasn't taken in by all his flirting. Too bad. The only reason Susannah was going to this lame dance was to stick by Kate's side and make sure Matthew Young didn't take advantage of her. Most of the boys had left school already to make a living as lobster fishermen, but Susannah wished her sister could fall for someone with a different kind of future. Did she want the same life as their mom? Waiting and watching the sea, praying for the safe delivery of her man every day? And then a war comes along and takes him anyway? Susannah longed to get on the ferry and never come back.

It was the first time they'd been allowed to attend a dance which wasn't organised by the church. But their mother seemed so taken in by the Weavers. Besides, she'd made Hannah Weaver's dress for the occasion.

'As long as you're chaperoned,' she'd said to Kate, as her youngest daughter jumped up and down in glee.

'Oh yes, of course, Matthew says his brother Silas will accompany Susannah, so we can all go together.'

Susannah's heart sank. She loathed Silas Young even more than Matthew. Couldn't stand the thought of people thinking he was her date.

'Say, why don't you go, Mother?' Susannah ventured. 'I could stay here.' She would rather tackle her mother's lacing jobs than go on a date with Matt's oily brother, Silas.

'Susie!' Kate wailed, pinching her arm. 'Don't be such a bore!' And, in an undertone: 'I'll have no fun if Mom comes.'

'What a crazy suggestion.' Her mother looked at Susannah, eyes wide with incredulity. 'You have a date. You can't let the boy down.'

Susannah knew exactly what her mother was thinking. If her girls married into the wealthiest lobster fishing family on the island, she was set into old age. She'd have all her family around her. They could all spend the rest of their days on this rocky outpost, protected and imprisoned from the world outside. Susannah had felt like screaming, but instead she crossed her arms, clenched her jaw.

'We've no dresses to wear.'

Susannah spent most of her time in denims on the island. For school she had a hand-me-down circle skirt and twinset from the Olsens, and for the summer, capri pants. The same went for Kate, apart from the fact she hated wearing denims and had a couple of print day dresses like their mother.

Kate had looked crestfallen at the mention of their dresses. 'Is there anything we can fix up, Mom?'

For the first time in years, a real smile graced their mother's face. Despite hating the idea of having to go to the dance, it cheered Susannah to see her mom happy for once.

'I have an idea,' she said, looking excited.

Kate had been obsessed with looking at advertisements for prom dresses in the magazines the library sometimes got in. She'd happily sit for hours while Susannah worked away, flicking through the fashions, trying to distract Susannah. But now all her research came to fruition. Their mom asked Kate to draw the dress she'd like to wear.

Frilly, fussy and romantic, with a circle skirt and full petticoat.

'What about you, Susannah?'

She'd shrugged her shoulders. 'Not as fancy, I guess.' She didn't care a bit what she wore, as long as it didn't encourage Silas Young. Though she doubted there was much danger of that. All the boys liked Katie because she was so pretty, but Susannah was too skinny and with too many freckles. She also wore glasses.

She thought Kate's dress design looked like a big poof. It was also going to be impossible for her mother to afford to buy the material to make it. Frankly, Susannah would have been happy turning up in pants and saddle shoes. The latter was the only fashion item she did crave.

But their mom, it appeared, was as enthused about Kate's dress as Kate herself. The sewing machine was in use almost non-stop – if not by their mom, then by Kate. To Susannah's surprise, their mom decided to turn her old wedding dress, a pale ivory flocked organza, into Kate's party dress. Working away at her lace stand, she made reams of lace net petticoats to build the body of Kate's skirt. The whole outfit was accessorized with a pair of pearl studs and a pearl choker that their mom had been given by their father when they married, and a pair of ballet pumps dyed teal blue. Kate made herself a teal blue purse out of an old cushion cover. The only purchases were a ribbon for her hair in matching teal blue, bought on an outing to Rockland with their mom, where they also bought thread for the dresses, and new stockings for the girls.

As for Susannah's own dress, the week before the dance, their mom insisted on measuring her so she could make adjustments to one of her own old good dresses. Susannah dreaded the outcome. She'd only ever seen her mother wear day dresses in tiny floral prints, and a winter suit of beige wool. But it seemed their mom had secrets in the back of her island wardrobe, for on the day of the dance she presented Susannah with a little black dress.

'Mom, where did this come from?' Kate asked in astonishment, as she picked up the dress and held it against Susannah.

'My honeymoon,' their mother said, looking nostalgic. 'We went to Boston, you know. A girl needs at least one cocktail frock.'

Boston! Susannah was astonished. She'd assumed her mom had been nowhere.

'It's perfect for you!' Kate squealed with delight.

Susannah could feel the colour rising in her cheeks. The truth was, she loved the dress. It was much more subdued than her sister's frock, but it suited her perfectly. Her mom had added a black lace collar to conceal any bare flesh on her chest. There was a black clutch purse, and a pair of their mom's old black ballet pumps to go with the dress. Kate presented her with a green ribbon for her hair, bought with her own in Rockland.

When Susannah put on the dress and looked in the mirror, she could hardly believe her eyes. The neat, womanly contours of the black dress made her look older. She liked the way the dress made her feel. More powerful.

There was no need for coats. It was a warm June night, but Kate had a length of organza left over from the wedding dress as a wrap, while their mom handed Susannah a finely knit black stole.

'You made this, too?' Susannah asked, incredulous.

'Sure, honey,' her mom said, tucking a strand of Susannah's loose hair behind her green ribbon. 'It's an important night for my girls.'

The dance was walking distance away, but the Young brothers turned up for their dates in their father's Buick. Kate was fizzing with excitement – all soft focus golden curls, floating on organza as they got into the vehicle. Their mother waved them off. Susannah watched her standing on their threshold, arms crossed. It seemed as if she was sending her girls off to war.

'Say, you look swell,' Silas said to her. He was driving, but Susannah caught his appreciate glance in the rear-view mirror.

'I thought you might come in your denims!' Matthew teased.

Susannah scowled at the back of his head, but when he turned round he had eyes only for Kate.

'Oh my, you look so pretty, Katie.'

Kate giggled with delight, which irritated Susannah further.

It was the biggest dance of the whole summer and the cause of much excitement on the island. It wasn't just islanders, but lots of holiday folk who attended the Weaver hotel event. The two communities were otherwise quite separate. Most of the islanders were poor, whereas the summer visitors were usually wealthy from Portland, Boston, or even as far away as New York. The truth was the islanders needed the summer visitors to boost their incomes, but resented their presence on the island, choking up the roads in their big cars and eating the best produce in the store.

As soon as they were through the door, Matthew whisked Kate onto the dance floor. Susannah followed Silas to the drinks table, where he dutifully got them each a cup of fruit punch. No liquor was allowed. They stood awkwardly together, watching their siblings dance.

'They sure do like each other,' Silas said.

Susannah took a sideways look at Matthew Young's elder brother. Silas was fair too, but his features were somehow not as heroic as his brother's. A smaller nose, upturned, which might be cute on a girl but didn't fit in with his broad cheeks, and a low forehead. His skin was also more ruddy than his younger brother's, like all the lobster fishermen. A rough burnt shade between red and brown from all the hours he spent out on the sea.

'So I near got enough saved up now to build my own house,' Silas was saying, into the awkward silence.

'Good for you,' she said, failing to conceal the disinterest in her voice.

'You know we own a whole lot of land on Vinalhaven don't you?' Silas boasted. 'I want to build my house a little in from the sea, protect it from the damage of nor'easters when they hit the island every winter. Though I also want to build on one of the islets too. Have my own private island.'

'That so?' Susannah said, taking a sip of her punch as she surveyed Hannah and Rachel Weaver's group of fancy friends from New Hampshire.

'And you know I'm not just a fisherman,' Silas said proudly. 'I'm a hunter too. Best place for deer is inland.'

Susannah had an unpleasant memory of Silas' slingshot in his trouser pocket that day at school years ago, when she was sure he'd shot down the poor seagull. She hated the idea of him hunting deer, too.

'I'd hate to live inland,' she declared. 'In fact, the only tolerable way to live on Vinalhaven is by the sea. I think if I were to live in the hinterland, surrounded by granite and forest, I'd suffocate.'

'Well, that's just plain stupid talk,' Silas said, looking at her as if she was the oddest girl he'd ever laid eyes on. 'I'll take you up there some time,' he said enthusiastically. 'Then you'll see how peaceful it is.'

'Thank you but no, I really don't care to see where you want to build your house,' Susannah said tartly.

'You could sure use some manners, Susannah Olsen,' Silas said, raising his eyebrows and taking a big gulp of his punch.

More couples joined the dance floor as the Portland band took it up a notch. Susannah dreaded Silas asking her to dance. Her attention was caught by one couple: clearly summer visitors by their attire. The girl had black hair, as shiny as a beetle's shell, and was wearing a red polka dot dress with a full skirt. As she danced, the skirt lifted, revealing layer after layer of petticoats, and slim legs in tiny black slingbacks. The girl's lips were painted scarlet and she was throwing back her head and laughing as she danced. Susannah was transfixed by her gaiety. To this girl, the island dance was just one jolly night on her summer holidays. Maybe tomorrow she would leave the island for another year, back to her big house, an urban life full of culture.

Susannah was so lost in her fantasy, she didn't notice Silas' hand on her arm. Before she could resist, he was leading her towards the floor. Kate waved over at her, grinning madly. No way. She couldn't dance with this guy. But before she could stop him, he had one hand on her waist and was waltzing her on the dance floor. Susannah had danced many, many waltzes around the kitchen at home with Kate. Their mother had first taught them when they were little. Turned the radio up loud and clapped her hands as the two girls twirled faster and faster, breathless and swept away by their perfect rhythm. But now Susannah kept tripping over her feet, stepping on Silas' toes. Thank goodness she was wearing ballet pumps and not heels. But it was just too intimate to be that close to Silas Young. She could smell the faint whiff of fish under his scent of soap. He had clearly scrubbed himself a thousand times, his skin was so raw-looking on his cheeks, but the smell of the fisherman still lingered in every pore of his skin. Every time she tripped, she could sense annoyance build in his body, his grip even tighter on her hands. She wanted to scream at him to let her go; it felt as if they were two clumsy bears waltzing around the dance hall. Everyone could see how ridiculous she and Silas were.

A flash of Kate in Matt's arms, shimmering with delight in her pale organza as if a fairy princess. Her sister was completely ignorant of Susannah's embarrassment. Not one dance, but two and then three; on and on Silas took her around the dance floor, and not one other boy stepped in and asked to dance with her. Every other time Susannah looked over at Kate, she had a new partner, although Matthew managed to get rid of them in between each dance.

At last, Silas tired of dancing. Susannah excused herself, saying she needed to powder her nose as Silas loped off to the drinks table for some more punch, the bulge of a liquor bottle in his pocket. She knew full well he'd be tipping the whisky into his fruit drink like all the boys did.

Pushing open the terrace doors of the Weaver hotel, Susannah stepped out into the soft summer night, breathing out a massive sigh of relief. Thank goodness she'd escaped for a few moments. The sky was filled with stars, surrounding a narrow crescent of silvery new moon. She searched for the true steady glint of the North Star, beckoning to her. She didn't know why, but just staring at the North Star gave her hope. Made her feel she had possibilities, a future beyond the rocky shores of Vinalhaven.

She wished she could go home right now, but she couldn't leave Kate with Matthew Young. She had to mind her sister, even if it meant putting up with Silas.

The terrace door opened and out tumbled Rachel Weaver, along with one of her New Hampshire guests. A boy with clean-cut features, and expensively dressed in contrast to Silas.

'Oh, hello, Katie's Susie,' Rachel said, her eyes glittering. She'd clearly been drinking. 'What are you doing hiding out here?' Before waiting to hear Susannah's reply, she continued. 'This is Arthur Gravell of the Gravells of Vermont.' She swung her arm dramatically, indicating the young man, who smiled at Susannah. His eyes, too, were squinting with alcohol.

Susannah had never heard of the Gravells of Vermont, but politely thrust out her hand. Arthur shook it with limp fingers, looking her up and down and making her feel cheap without saying anything.

'So, Susannah, this will interest you because Arthur is at Harvard, and that's where you want to go, right? That's what Katie told me.'

Susannah coloured with mortification. How could Kate have divulged her secret to Rachel Weaver? Especially since their own mother didn't know.

'No, no, that's not true,' Susannah denied.

'But Katie said you don't want to find a husband, you want to go to college,' Rachel said, her tone sickly sweet.

'I wouldn't recommend it,' Arthur told her. 'Harvard's not a place for women.'

Susannah felt a flare of outrage at his comment. 'What do you mean?' she said, her voice low with annoyance.

'Why, it needs such focus and dedication to undertake studies at Harvard,' he said glibly. 'Girls are too easily distracted. They don't have the aptitude.'

Rachel cuddled up to Arthur. 'So what are we good for, Arthur?' she said.

'Well, taking care of the men,' Arthur said happily. 'Behind every great man, there's always a good woman.'

Susannah didn't dare herself to speak. She almost preferred Silas to this arrogant prig. At least Silas didn't think he was better than her.

'There have been many great women who didn't need men to prop them up,' she snapped at Arthur. 'Joan of Arc, Queen Elizabeth I, Catherine the Great, Amelia Earhart…'

'Oh Lord, do stop, Susie, we don't want a history lesson *now*,' Rachel laughed, as Arthur continued to look down his nose at her.

As Susannah turned to go back inside the hotel, she heard Arthur commenting to Rachel.

'What an odd girl.'

It made her feel self-conscious all over again. Why did she always have to stand out?

By the time she returned to the dance, things were winding down already. The lights were brighter, and red-faced Silas was swaying by the drinks table, looking cross.

'Where you been?' he slurred. 'It's time to go.'

In their father's Buick, the Young boys took the girls for a ride to what they considered to be the best spot on the island.

'You've got to see the view of the harbour, Katie,' Matthew said, steering the car with one hand while his other arm was round Kate's shoulders as she sat in the front with him.

The car sped along the dark road, the silhouettes of trees lining either side, headlights every so often illuminating one of the island's white wooden houses.

'Don't you have to be up early lobstering?' Susannah spoke up. She was squashed next to Silas in the back of the Buick, who was so drunk he was lolling against her. All she wanted was to get back home to her own bed.

'Oh, we don't have to go out tomorrow,' Matthew replied. 'It's Sunday, and my family is real religious. It's our day of rest.'

Why had she even asked that stupid question? She still remembered hot summer Sundays with her daddy before the war. He hadn't gone out to fish on a Sunday either. Him filling up the paddling pool with the hose, and she and Katie tumbling in, a mixture of fear and delight, knowing he might splash them. Susannah clenched her stomach tight. Would their lives be different if they still had a father? Certainly, these two boys might not be so liberal in driving them out of town up the hill to their favourite lookout point.

'Hey, watch out!' Susannah shouted out as Matthew continued to drive up onto the granite slabs and off the road. He slammed on the brakes right at the edge of the rock. They were parked on an overhang, overlooking Vinalhaven harbour.

'We do this all the time, girl,' Silas said to her, putting a sweaty hand on her black dress. It felt like a hot brick burning through the material to her knee.

'Just look at that view, would you?' Matthew said to Kate, and Susannah watched with dismay as she saw her sister let him tuck her under his arm.

'Why would you drive on the granite?' She turned to Silas. 'It's plain dumb and dangerous.'

'Just because…' Silas began, the words trailing off as he looked at her, a little cross-eyed.

'We can make our mark.' Matthew turned to her tires mark the rock.'

'We were here!' Katie said gleefully.

What was happening to her sister? Susannah didn't like it one little bit.

'Scoot over, won't ya?' Silas said, putting his arm around her. Again, she got the faint whiff of fish underneath his soapy scent, and now whisky on his breath. Her stomach swelled and she felt rigid and awkward.

'I've never seen the view from here before,' Kate said, leaning into Matthew.

'Ain't it beautiful, baby?' Matthew said.

Susannah watched them like a hawk, despite Silas attempting to pull her into him. She felt as rigid as a flagpole.

'I believe Vinalhaven must be the most special place in the whole world,' Kate breathed. 'I never want to leave.'

'Me too,' Matthew said, kissing Kate's neck, and putting his hand on her lap.

'It's our kingdom, ain't it, Mattie?' Silas spoke up next to her. 'We got so much land,' he said, slapping a wet kiss on Susannah's cheek. She shifted away from him, feeling herself stiffen with dread. Before she could think straight, Silas had turned her head to face his and started kissing her on the lips, pushing his tongue into her mouth. She started in shock, trying to pull away.

'Hey, hold still, will ya?' Silas said as he paused, clamping her arms to her side.

'Get off me!' she hissed, looking over at Kate in desperation, but her sister was deep in kissing Matthew and oblivious to her own discomfort.

'God, you're frigid,' Silas said, slapping his mouth back on hers, releasing his hands from her shoulders to hold her head in place. She pulled back, clashing her teeth against his lips.

'Ouch!' he complained as she shook him off and opened the car door. 'What you doing?' he asked her, looking shocked.

She ignored him and walked over to the passenger window. Kate was wrapped in Matthew's arms. This was all wrong. These boys were taking advantage of them.

She tapped on the window of the car. But Kate clearly didn't hear her, and although Matthew opened his eyes and looked at her, he continued to kiss Kate. Susannah banged on the window again until Kate heard her, and was forced to break the kiss. She rolled down the window.

'What are you doing out of the car?' her sister asked her.

'Come on, let's go,' Susannah said. 'Mom'll be expecting us.'

Kate looked at her, wide-eyed. 'It's too far to walk back home.'

'Get back in the car, for pity's sake,' Matthew said in exasperation. 'We'll bring you home, alrighty?'

Susannah shook her head. 'Only if Kate gets in the back with me.'

'But I want to sit up front with Matthew,' Katie argued. 'It's not often he gets to drive me anywhere.'

'Well, I don't want to sit in the back with him,' Susannah said, glaring at Silas.

'He's only a little drunk,' Matthew said, leaning over Kate. 'Just give him a dig in the ribs if he annoys you again.'

Susannah crossed her arms, frowning.

'Relax,' Silas said, lolling on the back seat and patting the place next to him.

Reluctantly, Susannah got back in beside him. As soon as they took off down the road, Silas began to kiss her again. But as she tried to push him away, this time Kate leaned over and gave Silas a slap on the knee.

'Leave my sister alone, Silas,' she said to him, giving him a stern look in the rear-view mirror.

'But Matthew told me we're on a double date,' Silas wheedled.

'Well, my sister clearly doesn't want to be, so leave her alone,' Kate said, putting her hand on Matthew's knee as he drove them. 'Tell him to leave her be, Mattie.'

'Yeah,' Matt said, looking at Susannah in the rear-view mirror so that only she could see the mockery in his eyes. 'She clearly thinks she's above us island boys.'

'She's not like that, Mattie,' Kate said to them. 'You're just different, right, Susie?'

Susannah nodded glumly, hunched in the corner of the back seat away from Silas.

Back home, Kate pleaded exhaustion and went straight up to bed. Susannah could smell the whisky on her breath and knew she was avoiding being caught out.

'How was the dance?' her mother asked her.

'Fine,' she said tightly. Her mother looked crestfallen, clearly picking up on her negative tone. She returned to her lacing table, head bent over her work. In the curve of her hurting back, the weariness of movements, Susannah saw all the years of disappointment.

'It was great, Mom,' she said forcing herself to sound happy. 'Really. You should have seen Katie. Everyone was saying how pretty her dress was.'

'But what's wrong with Katie? Why did she run up to bed without telling me anything?'

'She was dancing all night long, Mom. She's tired.'

'But she was so excited. I've been waiting all night for her to tell me every single detail.' Their mom paused from her lacing. 'Did she and Matthew dance together?'

'All night, Mom, like I told you. All the boys wanted to dance with Katie. Every other dance, she and Matthew were together.'

Her mom flushed with delight as if she'd been the one dancing. 'What about you? Did you have fun with Silas?'

Susannah chose her words carefully. 'He's not much of a dancer,' she said. 'I'm not sure we're suited.'

'Oh dear, well never mind that,' her mom said, clearly more interested in Kate's date. 'And do you think Matthew Young is serious about Katie?' She dropped her lacing things and looked at Susannah.

'Yes,' Susannah said reluctantly. She couldn't lie to her mom. 'He sure does like her.'

Her mom clasped her hands. 'Well now, wouldn't it be a fine thing if those two made a life together?'

Susannah couldn't agree less. 'Don't you think Katie could do better than Matthew Young?' she asked her mom.

'In what way?' her mom said, not understanding as she frowned at her. 'He's from the biggest and most respected lobster fishing family on the island. Matthew's father fought in the war. His grandfather fished alongside Gramps Olsen. Who could be better than Matthew Young?'

'He's left high school already,' Susannah ventured. 'He's not even graduating.'

'Well, he doesn't need to, does he? He's set for life with the lobster-fishing. He'll be able to provide well for our Katie.'

'He's just a bit...' Susannah hunted for the right word. 'Rough.'

'Rough?' Her mom's voice rose. 'Do you mean ignorant? Maybe you should remember your father never graduated either. He was a rough fisherman too. Are you ashamed of him?'

'No, of course not!' Susannah protested. 'He was different.'

Her mom sighed. 'Your problem, Susannah, is pride, and I don't know where you got it from.' She shook her head. 'But if you're not careful you'll end up an old spinster.'

'That suits me fine, Mom,' Susannah snapped back, unable to hold her temper. 'I'd rather be on my own for the rest of my life than married to Silas Young!'

It was on the tip of her tongue to tell her mother about her aspirations for Harvard. But what if she never got in? She couldn't bear her mother's 'told you so's if she didn't make it.

Upstairs, Kate was lying with her back to her in bed, the patchwork quilt fallen on the floor. Susannah could see she wasn't sleeping yet, but she didn't say a word as she got into her own bed. She was exhausted from the whole night and just wanted to sleep.

'My head keeps on spinning and spinning,' Kate said as soon as Susannah turned off the lamp.

'Did you drink some of the liquor Silas brought?'

'Just a little, Susie,' Kate said. 'Why didn't you have some? You might have enjoyed yourself more.'

'Well, he never offered me any!' Susannah said. 'Though I wouldn't have touched it if he had.'

'You're always so serious, Susie,' Kate sighed. 'Silas is okay. He just really likes you is all.'

'He's an ignorant drunk.'

'So what? Those boys work damn hard. It's okay if they have a drink now and again.'

'What's so great about Matthew Young, anyways?' Susannah felt herself getting angrier.

'I love him!' Kate declared.

'Don't be so dramatic. That's just plain dumb.'

'I love him and I'm going to marry him. You just don't understand, Susie.' Kate's tone softened as she sat up in bed. Susannah could see her shadowy silhouette outlined against the window in their room. 'You got to understand: I want a good husband and to have babies. Make a family. That's something real and safe. Why don't you want that, too?'

Susannah had always known she and Kate were different. She wanted her sister to fulfil her dream. But not with Matthew Young. That's what she wanted to scream at her lovesick sister. Silas was a slobby drunk, but Susannah almost preferred him to Matthew. There was something as cold as the Atlantic Ocean, deep inside Matthew. She didn't like him one bit. And he couldn't know the real Kate, because she was always pretending to be a silly, giggly girl around him. He couldn't love Kate as she did. Her sister was way more than a pretty face. Even the way she'd got Silas to leave Susannah alone tonight had shown that she was strong-willed, and able to stand up to the older boy. Kate gave their mother so much support every day. It was as if her younger sister had stood in to replace the lost husband, helping their mom meet all her lacing deadlines, and work out how to cook on such a tiny budget. Susannah floated above all of the day-to-day struggle her sister took on with their mother. She knew it wasn't fair, but her passion for studying consumed her. Kate accepted Susannah's dream, although she didn't understand it, and Susannah knew that without Kate always covering for her she would have had no chance of even considering applying to Harvard.

'Just promise me you'll be careful,' Susannah whispered to Kate. 'Don't get into any trouble with Matthew Young.'

'Of course not!' Kate sounded shocked. 'You should know I'd never do something like that!'

They lay in silence for a while before Kate spoke again.

'I just love the way he kisses me,' she breathed out. 'I feel like I'm in a movie.'

Susannah couldn't help thinking about the horrible kisses Silas had given her. How they had felt aggressive and not close to romantic. Deep down, she did want to be touched, and admired too, but she'd never met any boy who made her feel that way. Would she ever?

Chapter 10

Emer

15th October 2011

Emer left Susannah in her study, typing away. Even the rhythmic clickety-clack of the typewriter sounded annoyed with her. Despite Susannah having backtracked and agreed she could stay after Emer had stupidly spilt her coffee on those papers, it was still clear Susannah would rather she wasn't there. Emer couldn't help wondering whether if Rebecca had hired her, Susannah would have been so resistant. She felt Susannah's constant disapproval of Lynsey and wondered if somehow it coloured how Susannah treated her.

Best to leave Susannah on her own for the moment. Really, there was nothing much for her to do. She'd cleaned the whole house top to bottom the day before.

Emer slipped out of the front door, grabbing her bag on the way. The early morning sun was now concealed by a light blanket of shifting clouds. She felt the odd drop on her cheeks but the rain held back, the air fragrant with fall – fading geraniums, crisping leaves on the sidewalk, the faint salty tang from the ocean. Apart from the odd pick-up truck passing her by, all was quiet. As she wound her way down the hill, past all the quaint wooden houses of Vinalhaven, she was astounded yet again by how perfect her surroundings appeared. If the houses weren't painted white, they were bright shades of blue, green, yellow, dove grey or even red. The gardens were well tended, and the trees fulsome and golden.

She had never seen so many white picket fences. The houses, though smaller, were similar to those in Quincy in Boston where she'd lived with Orla and Ethan, but in other ways Vinalhaven was so different. A miniature, storybook version of old America. One she was certain her sister would have loved.

But now, after her argument with Susannah, Emer felt like she belonged here even less than when she'd arrived a few days ago. She was tempted to head right to the ferry terminal and hop on the next boat back to the mainland. But that would be running away, which she had done before. She knew it would make her feel even worse to do that.

Of course she couldn't go right now. Her things were at Susannah Olsen's house. Besides, she had nowhere to go. Even so, she found herself heading out of town towards the ferry terminal. On her left was a wharfside row of stores and business, fishing tackle shops and a yoga studio side by side. She spied a small diner.

Emer sat down by the window and sipped her mug of black coffee. Susannah had completely overreacted when Emer knocked the coffee over her papers, but then Emer's own reaction had been so pathetic. What would Orla have done? Charmed Susannah, of course. Everyone warmed to Orla. Their personalities were so opposite. It should have been Orla who was the caring nurse, and Emer the dedicated artist, not the other way around. Really, Emer couldn't think of a soul who didn't like her sister. She'd been furious with her stepmother when she'd made that comment at Orla's funeral: *only the good die young*. They'd only just buried Orla, and were walking back to the limo when she'd said it. Emer had been in a kind of cold, shocked trance the whole day. Unable even to shed a tear. As if she'd been outside of her body. But Sharon's remark had inflamed her.

'Your sister's with your ma now, Emer,' Sharon had continued, 'and they're with the angels.'

Emer had wanted to punch Sharon in her big, fat, pitying face. What a condescending cow! What good was it to Emer to know her mam and her sister were with the angels? Did she even believe in angels? But now, weeks later, Emer had to admit there was some truth in Sharon's words. Her sister and her mam had been the good ones. Emer and her dad the bad – well, the selfish – two in the family. Her mam had brought out the worst in Daddy, as if her humility ignited his pride. At least Sharon was a match for him. It had been a source of great amusement for both sisters to see their dad running around Sharon whenever they visited them in Boston. Complete role reversal. At times it had made Emer cross though. Why couldn't Dad have been that attentive with their mam? Taken her out for meals? Brought her on sunny holidays in expensive resorts?

Orla drew out the best in Emer. She'd brought all the families together at her wedding to Ethan. Made sure everyone got on. Over a couple of awkward Christmases back home, Orla had smoothed things out with Sharon, helped Emer accept their dad would never give them the support they craved.

'He's just not able,' Orla had told Emer. 'Let him go.'

When Emer had come home exhausted from the hospital, guilty for snapping at patients, unable to stop herself from being too clinical, Orla reminded her she had to have boundaries.

'I couldn't do what you do, Em,' she'd said. 'I'd be in bits every day. You're special.'

Yes, she wanted to believe her sister was with the angels, because in some small way it meant Orla was still with her, inside her head, giving her endless advice.

What should I do, Orla? Give me a sign.

She took out her mobile phone, considered calling Lynsey. But what should she say? *Your aunt is too difficult. I'm taking the next ferry off the island.* Where would she go then? Back to Ireland?

The thought of having to move in with her dad and Sharon was enough to make her put the phone back in her pocket. She'd have to stick with Susannah.

The door of the diner opened and she looked up to see Henry, the restaurant-owning sculptor. As soon as he saw her sitting in the window, a big grin spread across his face. He came right over and sat down next to her as if they'd arranged to meet all along. It reminded her that since Lars had tried to call her the day she'd arrived on the island, he hadn't sent her one voicemail or text. Maybe he'd finally given up on her? She tried to push the thought to the back of her mind.

'Hey! How you doing?' Henry asked her. 'Mind if I join you?'

Why not? She'd no one else to talk to on the island.

'Sure,' she said.

The waitress came over and he gave his order. 'Crab roll with fries, Shirley, please. And my usual coffee.' He beamed at Emer. 'Say, you want something to eat?'

Shirley shook her head, giving Henry a long face. 'She's one of them vegans, Henry! Ain't nothing she can eat.'

'What about some home fries?' Henry suggested. 'Shirley makes the best on the whole island.'

Emer succumbed to temptation.

'Say, how's Susannah getting on?' Henry asked, as soon as Shirley went off to fill their orders.

Emer bit her lip. She wanted so much to talk to someone who'd known Susannah before she got sick. 'I think she's in a lot of pain, to be honest,' she said.

Henry nodded, as if she was confirming what he already knew. 'Guess that comes with the cancer, right?'

'I'm trying to persuade her to take some of the pain-relief medication she's been prescribed, but she won't. Says it messes with her head. She's every day either at the typewriter or reading books.'

Shirley came over with Henry's coffee. He poured in cream and sugar before stirring it several times.

'But I can see she's suffering, and she's very… irritable,' Emer added.

'Sorry to hear that,' Henry said, looking right into her eyes. Today the brown of them was almost amber. Emer felt herself blushing. 'She's always been a bit of a fierce one,' Henry added as their food arrived.

'How do you know Susannah?' Emer asked Henry.

'Well, I mean most folk know each other on the island,' he said. 'It's a small community, you know, and Susannah was our town librarian for years. Like I told you before, I used to go to her reading group as a boy.'

'Oh yes, I forgot,' said Emer.

'But I was also friends with Lynsey before I left for art school and she went to Salem,' he said.

'Oh, right.' Emer was surprised. Henry looked to be in his thirties, and Lynsey was a woman in her late forties, perhaps even early fifties. She had to be at least ten years older than him.

'We used to hang out in The Sand Bar sometimes, when she came home to visit from Salem, and after I'd been fishing with my dad.'

'You're a fisherman too?' Emer asked.

'Used to fish when I was a boy, like all the men in my family,' he said. 'But the life wasn't for me. I hated it. Put my father in an early grave.'

'I'm sorry,' Emer said.

'It was Lynsey who said I should go study art,' he said. 'Don't think I would have had the confidence to learn to sculpt without her encouragement.'

Emer looked down at Henry's hands as he tucked into his food. They still looked like working men's hands. Broad and rough. She guessed sculpting could be as tough on them as fishing.

'Have you heard of the artist Orla Feeney?' she asked him, still looking down at his hands.

'Maybe,' he said. 'Name's familiar. Who is she?'

'My sister.'

She was tempted to confide in him, tell him about Orla, and how the art world had lost such a great talent but it was too hard to speak about her in the past tense.

'Say, why don't you help Susannah with her typing, whatever it is?' Henry spoke up. 'With the two of you working on it she'd get through it faster.'

Emer doubted Susannah would ever let her near her writing again. 'She has this ancient typewriter. I don't know how to use it.'

But Henry clearly thought his idea a grand solution and continued to persuade her. 'Do you have a laptop with you? Yes? Well, do it on that. It'll be easier than the typewriter and you can save it.'

'She told me it's private stuff,' Emer said.

Henry shrugged his shoulders.

'You can only offer,' he said. 'If she's in that much pain, she might let you. Then you can find out what exactly it is she's typing.' He winked at her.

Emer still felt resistant. 'But that's not really what I'm here to do.'

Henry leant forward across the table, waved one of his fries at her. 'You're here to help, aren't you? She's your patient. Getting dug into all her paperwork is the only way you'll get to give her some relief.' Henry popped the fry in his mouth.

'I suppose I could suggest it to her,' Emer said, almost as if to herself. It had taken a stranger to point it out to her. Her role now was to help her patient in whatever way it gave her ease. Totally different from her job as a nurse in the hospital.

Henry sat back and crossed his arms, looking pleased with himself. 'And as your reward on afternoons you need a break, I'll take you for a little hike while Susannah has a nap. How's that sound?'

Emer's initial response was to say no. She couldn't help thinking of Lars, but then she thought of Susannah's cross face and all those lonely afternoons and evenings in her house where there wouldn't be that much for her to do apart from cook and clean, and to keep an eye on Susannah's pain management.

'Oh, that's very kind of you, but really, you don't have to do that.'

'Well, what about I'd like to?' Henry insisted. 'There are so many beauty spots on Vinalhaven, but you need a vehicle to reach them and a guide to know the best trails.'

He was so warm and friendly. Where was the harm? As long as she made it clear, they were just friends. She could do with a friend right now.

On the way back from the market store, it began to rain. The wind had picked up and the rain lashed into Emer as she struggled up the hill with her bags of shopping. She hadn't intended to leave Susannah for so long. The anxiety began to build inside her. What kind of nurse was she, to walk out without even telling her patient where she was going? She'd been gone for hours. The chat with Henry had felt so good. Which had confused her further. Talking to Henry made her miss Lars even more.

After Henry and his husky, Shadow, had driven off, she'd spent way too long in the market store, excited by all the vegan possibilities, and had spent a fortune on all sorts of treats: olives, hummus, seaweed snacks, chips and vegan ice cream.

It almost felt as if the darkness of the rain outside had perme-
ated through the walls of Susannah's house. Emer stepped into
the gloom of her new home, switching on the lamp in the hall,
immediately noting the quiet. Susannah was no longer typing.
She knocked on the door of her study. No answer. She knocked
again and softly pushed the door open. No Susannah. The room
appeared to be in great disarray. Papers balanced everywhere in
piles, books opened up and littering the floor. Shutting the door,
Emer went upstairs and knocked on Susannah's bedroom door,
but she wasn't in there either. She searched the whole house and
it was quite clear Susannah was nowhere to be seen. But the town
was so small: there was only one food market, and not much
else. If Susannah had been there, surely they would have passed
one another on the road? Moreover, Susannah's pick-up was
still parked outside. She must be walking distance away. Emer
looked out into the gathering dusk. The rain was even heavier
now. Where was Susannah?

This was her fault. Maybe the old lady had gone looking for
her? She pulled on her boots and coat, and braced herself for the
elements again.

Outside, she was pushed back down the hill by the wind.
Susannah could have gone to look for her back down at the ferry
terminal. Just as she was going to take a turn to the right, she saw
a small road to the left she hadn't noticed before. Leaves were
twirling off the trees. One landed on her boot. It was exactly the
same shade of red as her sister's hair.

Something told her to take the turn. She walked down the
little road, arriving at the entrance to a cemetery. As soon as she
walked into the small field of headstones, she could see a figure
bent in the wind, standing before one of the graves. It was her
patient. Head tucked into her chest, her coat flapping open like
two big black bird wings.

Emer called to her, but either Susannah didn't hear her, or she was ignoring her.

Emer was soaked through as she pushed through the wind and rain. She put a hand on Susannah's shoulder.

'Susannah, I've been looking for you everywhere!'

But Susannah was transfixed. Staring at the gravestone in front of her.

Kate Young
Beloved wife, mother, daughter and sister.
1940 – 1966

She'd been young. Only twenty-six years old. The same age as Orla when she died.

'Are you okay?' Emer asked Susannah. 'Is Kate your sister?' She remembered Susannah saying that Rebecca's mother Kate had made the quilt. The same young woman she had looked at in the photograph on Susannah's desk that morning.

Susannah suddenly whipped around, yelling at her with blazing eyes. 'What are you doing here? Why are you always spying on me?'

Emer felt stung by her hostility, but she controlled her emotions. Despite the older woman's fury, Emer could see her face was wet not just with rain, but with tears.

She's frightened, Emer heard Orla tell her. *Help her.*

'I was worried about you,' Emer said in a firm voice. 'Your niece employed me to look after you, and whether you like it or not, that's what I'm going to do.'

Susannah looked as if she'd slapped her in the face, opening her mouth only to close it again without saying a word.

'Now, you're coming home with me before you catch your death.' The words were out before she could stop them.

Susannah gave a cheerless laugh. 'Well now, we wouldn't want that, would we?' she said bitterly. 'I am staying right here. You go before you catch *your* death.'

'I'm not going anywhere,' Emer insisted.

The two women commenced a stand-off, but the wind was battering into them. Emer could see Susannah shivering with the cold. With her coat open, the rain had drenched her sweater. Emer was worried she was going to get pneumonia.

'Please, Susannah, come home with me.' Emer held out her hand.

Susannah ignored her, turning her attention back to the headstone. She put a blue hand on the wet marble.

'I'm the only one who looks after Kate's grave. Rebecca comes when she visits, but it's not that often. Lynsey never comes down here. Imagine that? Her own mother.'

Emer didn't know how to respond to that. 'Maybe it upsets her too much?' she ventured gently.

Susannah harrumphed. 'I don't think those girls remember their own mom. No matter how much I told them about her.'

'Were you older or younger than Kate?' Emer asked Susannah.

'I was the eldest,' Susannah said. 'I should have gone first.'

'Me, too,' Emer said, offering Susannah her hand. 'I'm the eldest of two girls, too.'

'Ah, at last… Something we have in common,' Susannah said, gruffly, but undeniably interested at last, letting Emer lead her away from the grave across the muddy grass. Emer was horrified by how cold Susannah's hand was. Wet and clammy, shaking, too. She put her arm around her and helped her as they stumbled in the rain back across the cemetery.

Back home, Emer helped Susannah undress as quickly as she could. There was no time for propriety. Susannah's teeth were chattering non-stop and her eyes had a feverish glare already. The worst thing would be if she got an infection when her immune system was so compromised. Having been so defiant, Susannah now succumbed to Emer's care. The trip to the cemetery seemed to have completely spent all her energy. Emer rubbed her down with a towel, and helped her into a clean nightdress before getting her into bed. She took her temperature and, as she suspected, the older woman now had a fever.

'What were you thinking, going out in that rain?' she admonished her gently.

'I wanted to talk to Kate,' Susannah said in a frail voice. 'You've a sister, you understand.'

'Yes, I know,' Emer said in a quiet voice.

She couldn't say it out loud yet. That she used to have a sister.

'What's her name?' Susannah asked her.

'Orla,' Emer said, her voice hoarse with emotion.

'Pretty name,' Susannah whispered, closing her eyes.

Chapter 11

Susannah

October 1958

The ferry left Vinalhaven just as the sun was rising, with a pale distant orb of moon still in the sky. The first few rays of warmth and light washed over Susannah as she stood on the small deck area, and tried to see past the bridge of the boat to the terminal. Kate was still waiting for her departure, hugging her sides in the early morning chill. Susannah waved and Kate waved back again as the ferry left the harbour, pushing out into still waters. It was the calm before the storm. A nor'easter was predicted, coming from Canada and due to hit the island in the evening. Susannah felt a twinge of worry about her mom and Kate, but they'd lived through enough nor'easters just the three of them. The wailing of the wind around their house always made Susannah feel something bad was coming. One year the neighbours' chicken house had been thrown by the wind into their garden. She and Kate had found the chickens hiding under their porch. They hadn't laid eggs for weeks after that.

Susannah watched Kate walk right to the edge of the harbour, take her red scarf from her neck and wave it like a banner. She unwound her own blue scarf and did the same thing. Tears pricked her eyes. It hurt so much to leave Kate. She felt like she was abandoning her and yet she couldn't stay. Kate often talked about how she imagined their island was part of a magical kingdom apart from all the rest of the world. She believed time was different on Vinalhaven with all the seasons at different paces. The slow measured breath of snowfall, the heat and race of summer, long endless days of steady rain, and the sudden fury of a storm. Nature was their queen and they were all subject to her whim. There was an island part of Susannah. She could never deny it. A deep wish to hide away in their house. A whole life could be spent in such a way. Look at her mom. Afraid even to take the boat to Rockland for the day. But Susannah pushed against this desire to retreat, because even more powerful was her need to be a part of a bigger picture, to learn and to connect. She'd always known she was different and if she didn't leave now, she might never understand why.

It had taken her weeks to build up the courage to tell her mother. After the thrilling day when the letter of acceptance had arrived at the library and she and Mrs Matlock had actually hugged, Susannah had put off telling her mother.

'You really need to speak to her,' Mrs Matlock encouraged Susannah every time she called into the library. 'I'm sure she'll be proud of you, Susannah. I mean, you got a full scholarship too!' Mrs Matlock beamed.

'I couldn't have done it without your tutoring,' Susannah said.

Mrs Matlock's wide smile took years off her face. In those bright blue eyes, Susannah saw the young idealistic student who had also gone to Harvard so many years before her.

'It was my pleasure, Susannah,' Mrs Matlock said. 'Just promise you'll write to me.'

Susannah had immediately confided in Kate too, and the two sisters had danced around their bedroom. Her sister's advice had been different from Mrs Matlock's.

'Tell her closer to the time,' she'd said. 'Then it'll all be organised and she can't stop you.'

*

Finally, just two weeks before the academic year was due to begin, Susannah could postpone telling her mother no longer. She waited until they were eating Sunday dinner, right after church when she was hoping her mother was feeling the most generous in spirit.

'Mom, I've got something important to show you,' Susannah said, her voice shaking with nerves as she handed her mother the letter from Harvard.

'What's this?' said her mother, putting down her knife and fork.

Kate gave Susannah an encouraging smile while their mother read the letter.

'How long have you known about this?' her mother said, placing the letter down on the table, and giving Susannah a hard stare.

'I only just found out, a day or two ago,' she lied.

'Well, how come it's dated for nearly three weeks ago?' her mother said, her cheeks flushing with annoyance. 'Why would you do something like this behind my back?'

'But Mom, we should be proud!' Kate exclaimed. 'Susie is going to Harvard! Imagine! It's so amazing.'

Susannah would never forget the look of disappointment on her mother's face.

'But that's not what a girl your age should be doing,' she'd said. 'You should be looking to get married and start a family.'

'I can come back and do that after college,' Susannah tried to placate her, although in her heart she had no intention of getting married and having children. If she said this out loud, her mom and even Katie would be shocked.

'There's plenty of time for all of that,' Kate had backed Susannah up. 'Mom, this is going to be a wonderful adventure for Susie. And she's so clever, she got the scholarship too!'

Tears began to well in their mother's eyes. 'Why are you doing this to me? Leaving us all alone.'

'We'll cope, come on now, Mom,' Kate said as their mother pushed her plate of food away. 'Matthew can come over any time we need. There's Gramps Olsen, Aunty Marjorie and Uncle Karl. We're not alone.'

Their mother got up from the table, leaving her dinner unfinished. She picked up the letter again, waving it at Susannah. 'You should have asked my permission first,' she said to Susannah. 'What daughter does this behind her mother's back?'

'I knew you wouldn't let me if I asked you,' Susannah said.

'Absolutely I wouldn't,' her mother said. 'What kind of future will you have if you go off on your own to a big city like Boston? No man on this island will want you when you come back full of notions.'

'I don't care.' Susannah could feel herself getting angry. 'I don't want any of the men on this island. They're all thick and ignorant.'

'Oh, Susie, that's not a nice thing to say.' Kate spoke up. 'What about Matthew? He's not thick and ignorant.'

Susannah bit her lip despite wanting to tell Kate exactly how little she thought of Matthew.

'Why can't you be normal, like Katie?' their mother asked her. 'What's wrong with you? Every girl wants to get married and have babies.'

'But I don't, Mom!' Susannah took a breath. 'I am going to Harvard no matter what you say.'

'It's Susie's dream,' Kate tried persuade their mother. 'She's worked so hard for it.'

But their mother was shaking her head, fury blazing in her eyes as she slammed Susannah's letter down onto the kitchen table.

'You're just like your father. Selfish! I begged him not to leave and he did it anyway,' their mother complained. 'He didn't have to volunteer!'

The two sisters locked eyes in shock. Their mother hadn't spoken about their father in years, and before that it had always been in glowing words. They had grown up thinking he was a hero.

'What do you mean, Mom?' Kate asked in a small voice.

'He didn't need to leave Vinalhaven,' their mother ranted. 'He had a family to look after. There were plenty of young single men who were willing to fight. But Ronald was a show-off, just like you, Susannah. Had to go and prove himself to the world.'

The bitterness in their mother's tone was something they'd never heard before.

'So I guess you're going anyway,' her mom said, her face tight with fury. 'But you don't have my blessing.'

'I don't need it!' Susannah shouted back, feeling protective of her father's memory.

Her mother gave her a hard slap across the cheek. Susannah felt the wedding ring dig into her flesh, a stinging burn to her face. Kate gave a small scream in surprise.

'Don't ever raise your voice to me again,' their mother said, her voice flinty with anger. 'You're no better than me and don't you forget it.'

'I don't think I'm better than you,' Susannah retorted, but their mom had stormed out of the room. The sisters heard her stomping all the way up the stairs and banging her bedroom door.

Kate gave a long whistle. 'I've never seen Mom so mad! Are you okay?'

Susannah nodded, pressing her hand to her hot cheek. Now her initial flash of anger had died down, doubt had begun to creep in. 'Maybe I shouldn't go? It's upsetting her so much.'

'But you've worked so hard,' Kate said. 'All those afternoons in the library with old Mrs Matlock. I would have died of boredom!'

'But what about you, Kate?' Susannah was nervous about leaving her sister. Kate was completely besotted with Matthew Young and Susannah was worried things would get too serious while she was away.

Kate took both Susannah's shoulders in her hands and looked right into her eyes.

'You are going to Harvard, young lady, if I have to put you on the boat myself!'

Since that day, there had been an uneasy truce between Susannah and her mother. A cold politeness, which was almost worse than the anger. Several times, she'd nearly relented and told her mom she'd stay after all. But Kate wouldn't let her. Whenever Kate wasn't on a date with Matthew, she was at the sewing machine making herself new clothes. Susannah had never worried about her own wardrobe before but now she couldn't help thinking she might look shabby at Harvard. Telling herself it didn't matter one bit how she looked, Susannah spent most of her final two weeks in the library, trying to prepare for college by reading every single history book on the shelves, and avoiding her mother. One afternoon just before closing, Mrs Matlock sat down next to Susannah.

'Have you found somewhere to live yet?' she had asked her.

Susannah shook her head. 'I've enough saved up for a room the first week but I need to find a job and lodgings pretty quick. My scholarship doesn't cover everything.'

'There's a family I know,' Mrs Matlock said. 'My sister-in-law's niece is married to a professor at Harvard. They've two boisterous young boys and I think they're looking for help with them in exchange for lodging. Would you like me to write to them?'

'Oh yes, that would be fabulous!' Susannah said, relief sweeping through her. She had been so worried about where she was going to live. Frightened she'd have to give up her dream because of it. 'Thank you so much, Mrs Matlock,' she said, flinging her arms around the librarian, much to the older woman's surprise.

'Well now, dear, don't you worry, we'll get it all sorted for you,' Mrs Matlock said, pushing her glasses up the bridge of her nose. 'I don't mind telling you I shall miss you a great deal, Susannah.'

'You've been so kind and helpful, Mrs Matlock; I owe you so much.'

'Not at all,' the librarian said, her eyes shining with emotion. 'Do call me Ivy, though, won't you? You're an adult now!'

The night before her departure, Kate had dragged Susannah upstairs to their bedroom after dinner. She was all giddy and excited.

'We're going to pack your things together,' she declared, dragging their father's old suitcase down from the top of the wardrobe.

'That's not going to take too long, then,' Susannah said gloomily, aware of how sparse and boring her wardrobe was.

She was beginning to feel anxious. It was stupid. Everything was organised. She'd timed the ferry to meet a morning bus which would take her all the way to Boston South Station. From there, Mrs Matlock had told her to take the subway Red Line T. On a piece of paper, she had written down directions to the Whittards' house in Cambridge. If Susannah left on the seven o'clock ferry tomorrow morning, she should arrive at her destination by late afternoon. But it wasn't the journey which was worrying her. Although she was still cross with her mother, she didn't want to leave with the way things were between them. Ever since the slap, her mother had behaved as if she hardly existed any more, as if she'd already left.

Kate began pulling things out of their wardrobe.

'Now, I really don't know what a girl should be wearing at Harvard this season,' she mused, giving her sister a cheeky grin and making Susannah laugh despite all her anxiety.

'What's all this?' Susannah asked as her sister revealed her new hoard of clothing.

'Well, what do you think I've been doing at the sewing machine these past two weeks?' Kate declared. 'Only making sure you look swell in the big city!'

'Oh, Katie.' Susannah felt emotion rise up inside her. 'I thought you were making them for yourself.'

'First up though is the black dress Mom made you,' Kate said, pulling it out of the wardrobe. 'It's perfect for any cocktail parties you might be attending.'

'I'm a freshman at Harvard, not a faculty wife!' Susannah pointed out.

'Yes but one day you might well be the wife of an academic, just like Jo in *Little Women*,' Kate said, carefully folding up the black dress and placing it in the case. 'There are going to be so many potential suitors. Mind you don't be falling for any foreign boys and get whisked away to England or Australia!'

'No fear of that ever happening.'

'I hear those Boston winters are as harsh as here on the island, so I've made some adjustments to Granny Olsen's wool suit,' Kate chatted on.

Susannah remembered their mother wearing the suit once during a particularly bad winter. It had looked hideous on her. Dark grey, heavy and shapeless.

'Oh Katie, I can't wear that old thing!'

'Hold on now, try it on, you'll see.'

Susannah pulled on the skirt and zipped it up. Her sister had taken it up and taken it in. The wool fit snugly around her hips. But Kate had worked even more magic with the jacket, tucking it in at the waist and adding front pockets, a wide collar and a belt with the extra material. The old black buttons had been replaced by big green buttons with a pattern of tiny gold leaves.

'Katie, how did you do it?' Susannah marvelled as she spun in her stockings on their bedroom floor. She felt fantastic in the suit. 'Where did you get the buttons?'

'Matthew got them for me in Rockland,' she said, looking proud. 'His mom also helped with some old bits of material and wool for other things.'

Kate laid out Susannah's new college wardrobe on her bed.

'So, I knitted you this twinset in green to go with the suit. And then a black knit sweater to go with the pants.'

All those sewing patterns Kate had received in the post had been for her! Susannah had assumed Kate had been making clothes for herself.

'You made pants for me!'

'Sure, I adapted an old pair of Matthew's.'

Susannah baulked at the idea of wearing Matthew Young's old slacks, but Kate had done a wonderful job adding feminine details: tapering them at the ankles, and putting in a waistband with a couple of tucks.

Along with the wool suit, pants and sweaters, Kate had also made a couple of blouses, one circle skirt and a lighter-weight teal blue dress. There was a navy blue scarf and matching hat and gloves. She'd also allowed Susannah's much-loved denims to go in the case, citing they were now all the rage as long as Susannah turned up the ends, wore a white shirt and tied a scarf around her neck.

'I'm afraid you're going to have to go in your old coat,' Kate said. 'Ran out of luck finding you a better one.'

Susannah surveyed the colourful collection of fashion spread out upon her sister's patchwork quilt. For a moment she was so overwhelmed she couldn't speak. She gave her sister a big hug.

'You've worked so hard; oh Katie, I'm so touched!'

'Well, just come back at Thanksgiving, mind you,' Kate said, tapping her shoulder. 'It's only two months away!'

Susannah immediately felt guilty. 'What should I do about Mom?' she asked, biting her lip. 'I feel bad.'

Kate put her hand on her shoulder and looked at her with wisdom beyond her years.

'Give her time,' Kate said. 'She'll come round. Be as proud of you as I am.'

Kate was getting smaller and smaller, but she was still waving her red scarf. Susannah willed her mom to come running down the road and to the ferry terminal. Show her support. But it was just Kate on her own, no break in her loyal waving until the boat rounded a headland obscuring the harbour. She could see her sister no longer. But she felt the thread of them connected. It was unbreakable.

Vinalhaven was diminishing in the distance as they sailed through the channel alongside its rocky coastline, with slabs of granite, tiny crescents of sandy beach and deep green pine tree forests all the way to the edge of the land. Susannah crossed to the other side of the boat and looked ahead of her. Her heart was sore from her mother's rejection, but she was determined to make her proud one day. When she was a success, surely her mom would understand she'd made the right decision? What girl could turn down a Harvard scholarship?

The sun had risen now, the horizon deep pink, seeping into the perfectly blue sky. There was a whisper of distant moon fading slowly as they ploughed through the gentle island waters, mist curling off the surface. Further out to the sea the water became choppy with tiny cresting waves. The boat began to roll a little and it was a comforting motion. Susannah sat down on the bench. It was cold but she didn't want to go and sit inside. It was packed with islanders, all of whom would want to quiz her on her journey. Everybody knew she was going to Harvard but still they all wanted to hear it from her lips. She closed her eyes and listened to the chug of the ferry's engines and the call of the seagulls above. She thought of the day her father must have left to fight in the war. How he must have been feeling, sitting on the same ferry, maybe watching the sun rise as well, listening to the gulls, and tasting salt on his lips. Surely he would have been even more afraid than she was? Had he an inkling one day he might not return? Probably not. But maybe her mom had. Susannah saw an image in her head of a young mother standing at the ferry terminal, holding the hand of one little girl with red hair, and carrying in her arms a little blonde baby girl. Watching the love of her life sail away. No wonder her mom hadn't come down to the harbour to say goodbye. For a minute, Susannah understood, and forgave her mother. But just as quickly she became angry again. This was different. *She* was different. Her mom was always going to try to hold her back, but Susannah wasn't going to let her. Not ever.

Chapter 12

Emer

16th October 2011

In her sleep, Lars came to her. Without fail every night, he took her in his arms. Brought her back to their passion, despite all the daytime hours she spent suppressing it. Their love-making had felt as inevitable as the turn of the seasons, as right as nature itself. And yet in the cold clarity of morning regret, she was filled with shame. She had let her sister down because of her desire for Lars. She could never make up for it now.

'Where were you?' her father had berated her as she'd run into Orla's hospital room. His eyes were rimmed red, his nose dripping with his tears.

Those moments she could never forget. Her body still humming with Lars' touch, so alive and vital, and yet right before her was her sister, pale and unmoving beneath the white sheet. Ethan was still sitting by the bed, holding Orla's hand. He looked up at Emer, his face ghostly with shock.

'Her hand's still warm, Em,' he whispered. 'But she's gone. They said she's gone.'

Emer had collapsed on the chair next to Ethan, put her arm around him, and tried to take some of the weight of his grief, but her head was spinning with denial. This was some kind of nightmare. It couldn't be true. None of it. They'd been told the prognosis was terminal weeks ago, but still she'd hoped for a miracle. Despite the fact that she worked with cancer patients every day of her life, she had never given up, because sometimes there *were* miracles. Patients came back from the brink of death. Could Orla have just slipped into a coma? But when Emer looked at her sister, it was clear Orla was no longer present. Her body just a shell. It possessed likeness, but it was not her sister, not the talented young Irish artist everyone else knew. She had already left.

'She was asking for you,' Sharon said, wiping her eyes with a tissue.

The words lanced Emer like a blade in the heart. She had promised she'd be with Orla all the way. Hold her hand and be strong for her. Make sure her sister wasn't scared. But she'd panicked. She'd put her needs before her little sister's at the most important hour of their lives.

'We were trying to call all night,' her father said in a shaky voice. 'But you never picked up. She went so sudden-like, in the end.'

'It was very peaceful,' Sharon tried to console her.

She wanted to jump up and slap her stepmother. How could the passing of a young woman in her prime ever be peaceful? There was no peace in it at all. Orla was supposed to have it all. A long and happy marriage, children to care for her in her old age, paintings and paintings hanging on all her walls. She would never travel the world or be acknowledged as the gifted artist she was or have a baby or take her kids to the seaside for a picnic. What was left in her wake was a devastated family and her husband Ethan, heartbroken and on his knees.

'She said she'd love me always.' Ethan turned to her with swimming eyes. 'Em, how can I live now?'

He fell into her arms, sobbing, and she held him tight. In all the months and weeks of Orla's illness, Ethan had never shed a tear in front of them. Always staying upbeat, joking with the nurses to make Orla laugh, never speaking about the end. Orla had confided in Emer, she'd felt it a strain sometimes. She wanted to talk to him about her death.

In Emer's sleep every night since her sister's funeral, Lars came to her, but so did Orla. She was still alive and Emer had to find a way to save her. She was running the hospital corridors searching for the right cure, hounding specialists. Hope blazed through her dream as she raced to beat cancer for her sister's sake.

Emer woke shivering, with the sensation of her phone vibrating on her lap. She had no idea where she was, only that she was freezing and sitting on a chair. What she did know was that her sister was dead and she'd only dreamt she was still alive. Despair washed over her. Where was she? She looked down at the flashing screen on the phone. It was Lars calling her. It hurt too much to talk to him. She'd sent him a text message telling him it was over just before she'd left Boston. How could it ever be right between them after what happened?

Her eyes adjusted to the light. She realised she was of course in Susannah's bedroom in the house on the island. She sat bolt upright, looked over at the bed and could see the hump of a body under the covers. In a panic, she rushed over. How could she have let herself nod off? Light leached in from under the curtains. It was clearly morning again. She must have been asleep for hours. What was wrong with her? She'd never been so lax when she worked on shift in the hospital.

She felt Susannah's forehead, but to her relief it was a normal temperature, and she was breathing steadily. Even so, Emer wasn't taking any chances. Going downstairs, she rang the number of the medical centre in Vinalhaven which Lynsey had given her, asking if one of them could come out and take a look.

'Sure,' said the friendly voice on the end of the line, 'but we're physician assistants. You're as qualified as us. If you think it's serious, we can get her on a plane to the mainland.'

'No, it's grand,' Emer said, just imagining how mad Susannah would be if taken off her beloved island.

She made herself a cup of coffee and headed back upstairs to check in on Susannah. She was still sound asleep. She took her temperature again and left a fresh glass of water by the bed before slipping out of her room.

Her own bedroom was up another flight of stairs right at the top of the house. She hadn't even unpacked. The innards of her case were spilled upon the floor, but she didn't have the energy to pick anything up or put them away in the drawers of the dressing table. There were two single beds in the room. Old-fashioned iron frames, with very hard mattresses. Both were covered in beautiful patchwork quilts just like on Susannah's bed. One was made up of lots of patterns of red and white with heart shapes, and evergreen trimming. It made Emer think of Christmas. The second quilt was mostly in different shades of pink, with some lemony yellow flower prints to contrast. Emer had chosen the bed with the Christmas quilt. Never went for pastel shades. Nor did Orla. Her sister had always worn jewel colours – emerald green, sapphire blue, ruby red – to bring out her pale skin, red hair and blue eyes.

Emer's room was long and narrow, but her bed faced two windows set into the eaves of the house. The view from one looked down onto the boughs of the apple tree. If she leaned out her window, she could count all its red apples. She thought it must be a very old apple tree to be so big, and indeed she could see its age in the twistings of its gnarled trunk. If she lay down on her bed, the other window gave her a vista of the island, the rooftops of other houses, tips of trees, and beyond that a distant sliver of bright blue sea. She had made her escape now from real life and yet she felt entrapped already on this small island.

Emer closed her eyes, took a breath. What was it Orla always said?

Everything passes, even the darkest night.

Her phone began to vibrate in her pocket, and without even having to look at it, she knew who it was. She took a breath and answered it.

'Emer! Where are you? I've been so worried.'

His words came out in a panicked jumble and she instantly felt guilty. It wasn't his fault, and yet she felt their fledgling relationship had been irredeemably damaged by the fact her sister had died the night they first made love.

'I'm sorry, Lars.'

She saw him again in her memory. The last time they'd spoken. He'd been in his blue scrubs, and she'd been walking away from him after giving in her notice at the hospital. She'd already had her interview with Lynsey and everything had been set up for her journey to Vinalhaven. But Lars hadn't known that.

He'd followed her down the corridor and touched her arm. Forced her to turn around.

'How can I help?' he'd asked, quite simply. She hadn't been able to bear to look at the compassion in his eyes. He felt sorry for her. But she didn't deserve it.

She had shaken her head, tight-lipped, terrified she might break down and sob in the middle of the hospital lobby. A place lots of people cried, thick with suffering and loss, but she couldn't let her professional veneer slip. Not there.

'I'm here for you,' he said, touching her hand lightly. 'Please let me in.'

'I can't,' she had croaked, shaking her head at him.

'Emer, Orla wouldn't have wanted this.' He looked into her eyes, and it was all she could do to stop herself from falling into his arms. 'You won't let me near you since she passed away.'

'I should have been there, with her,' she managed to whisper.

'Emer, darling,' he said, 'it's not your fault.'

Someone was calling him. He was needed on ward, but Lars held her gaze.

'I'll call you later,' he said. 'I'll come over, we'll talk.'

But when he'd called that night, she'd already left. Said her goodbyes to Ethan and walked away from the house in Quincy.

'I went over to your house, but Ethan had gone,' Lars said on the phone now. 'The neighbours said back to New York. Where are you?'

'I'm on an island.'

'In Ireland?' he asked. 'I can take some time off. Fly over…'

'No. I'm not in Ireland. I'm on Vinalhaven; it's an island off the coast of Maine.'

'What are you doing there?'

'I've a job. I'm looking after an old lady who has pancreatic cancer. Helping manage her pain relief.'

There was a pause. Emer imagined putting her hand on Lars' heart, feeling its steady beat.

'Do you think that's a good idea, after everything you've been through with Orla?'

'I just can't be in Boston, Lars. Working every day in the hospital where she was… I can't…'

She could feel the hysteria rising in her chest and she forced it down.

'I get it.' He paused. 'I've got some time off. We could go somewhere. A place you've never been.'

'It's no good,' she said, her voice breaking despite herself. 'Don't you see? How could it ever work between us? I was with you when I should have been with Orla. She must have been so frightened and I wasn't there for her.'

'But Emer, please…'

'It's never going to work between us, don't you see? What we have will always be tainted.'

'You can't mean that?' She could hear the disbelief in his voice and it broke her heart.

'I've got to go,' she said, whispering, 'sorry,' before she cut him off.

She waited for him to ring back, but he didn't. She sat on the quilted bedspread and stared at her phone, willing it to ring, although knowing she wouldn't answer it again. But the phone remained silent. She threw it on the floor. He'd given up on her, finally. She should be relieved. She'd told him it could never work, and yet her heart was breaking all over again. She threw herself face-first on the bedspread. Buried her face in its soft contours and sobbed, clutching on to its trimmed ends. She let her grief rip loose as a loud wail escaped her mouth. She listened to her own crying, and tried to soothe herself. *Soften your hands, child.* Was it her mother or Orla speaking to her? *Let go.*

She released her hold on the quilt, but as she did so, she felt an opening in the seam and something hard inside it. She sat up and pulled the edge of the quilt towards her. Examined the seams. It was ripped. No, not ripped – the opening was too neat for that, and about the size of her hand. She pushed her hand into it and felt her fingers touch paper. She pulled the paper out and unfolded it. It was a letter, dating back to 1958 and addressed to *Dearest Katie*. Without reading the whole letter, she scanned the neat black script to see who it was from, already suspecting the answer. Sure enough, it was signed 'your sister, Susie', the capital 'S' an exuberant flourish, contrary to Emer's perception of Susannah's personality. Emer pushed her hand inside the quilt again, pulling out letter after letter. She stacked them up, putting them in date order, while managing not to read a word of the content, which was clearly private. When she'd finished, Emer thought about bringing the letters to Susannah. But considering Susannah's mental state at the grave, it was possible that these missives from the past could make her feel worse. Even so, they were her letters to her sister, and she might not even know they were there in the quilt.

Emer lifted the stack of letters off the bed, placed them on the dressing table and stared at them. What should she do? Stuff them back in the quilt? Try to forget she ever found them? Tell Susannah, and risk distressing the old lady further? Or read them herself? If she knew what was in the letters, perhaps she could work out when the best time to give them to Susannah would be. Maybe she would find out why Susannah was so defensive and bad-tempered all the time. But that would be a terrible invasion of privacy.

Emer circled the room before picking the letters up again. She took them towards the bed to stuff them back into the quilt. It would be a terrible betrayal of her position as Susannah's nurse to read them. But as she reached the bed, one of the letters fluttered off the top of the pile and onto the wooden floor. As Emer bent to pick it up, she couldn't help but read the first line, and then she was hooked.

Chapter 13

Susannah

October 20th, 1958
Harvard, Cambridge

Dearest Katie,

I am in love! Before you get too excited, it's with a place, not a person, but truly I am besotted with Harvard. I keep thinking I'm in a dream. I wish you could see how different it is here. There's all this history going all the way back. Most of the buildings are redbrick and, I've been told, are just like the houses in England from the seventeen-hundreds. Sometimes I just walk around Harvard Square again and again, breathing in all the learned minds from the past. Reminds me of when you talk about how much you love Vinalhaven, the rocks and the sea, the big skies and tall trees. Now I get it, Katie. This is my haven! The old brick sidewalks full of puddles and wet leaves are my pathway through the woods. The libraries, oh my, it's a cathedral of books. I want to read them all. I rush to the history shelves as if I'm on a first date. Climb the ladders to the highest stacks, just like you love climbing up Amherst, standing on top of the granite slabs and looking at the world beyond our island life. Harvard is like an island within a very big city, but it is a sanctuary all the same.

I'm up early every day, helping dress and get breakfast for Joshua and Nathan, the two Whittard boys. Professor Whittard is a physicist and, as you know, lectures at Harvard. The man is a genius but all the same very friendly, and his wife is so kind. But Katie, you wouldn't believe the size of their house. I think it must be at least three times the size of ours. The kitchen is immense, and they also have a housekeeper who lives in. So instead of rent, I help her out. She's a very nice black lady called Gertrude from down south. Miles away in Philadelphia, I think she told me. Well, I could listen to her talk all day, Katie. I just love her accent. She has to cook the kind of food the family like. Meat pies and potatoes and all that, but sometimes she'll make some cornbread and it's the best bread I have ever eaten. Imagine my shock when I found out she has two teenage boys of her own back home, living with her parents. Her husband died in the Korean war, so she has to provide for them all. Isn't that just so sad? I know people have it tough on the island, we're not rich like my Cambridge family, but at least mothers don't have to leave their children. I think a lot about what Mother went through to bring us up. Now we are apart I can love her better. I miss her a little, but most of all I miss you!

My favourite times are the mornings I walk to lectures. All the foliage on the trees is glorious. I feel part of the change in the seasons, because I am changing too. There are still more boys than girls in the lectures, but we girls are connected. Even if we sit apart, we acknowledge each other. Each one of us an island in the sea of male voices! It feels so special to be part of a new generation of women who are independent and have something to contribute to

academia in our own right. We are few, but we are stead-
fast! Just like our island at home, a rock of hard granite,
which no number of nor'easters could ever blow away.

Sometimes after lectures, I don't go to the library but
spend the little bit of free time I have sitting in a café and
drinking a cup of coffee. I know you might think it odd
a girl would sit on her own and look out of the window
at all the hustle and bustle of the streets of Harvard, but
I love to watch the people. There are so many different
kinds here. From all over the world; it is so wonderful. I
imagine all their homelands and the different foods they
eat and religions they follow. How I dream of travelling
beyond America and seeing the whole wide world. But
also, I love sitting in my café window, watching the
regular folk at work, driving buses, taxi drivers honking
at each other, delivery men and construction workers.
I like listening to the chat in the café, and watching all
the other students weighted down by their study books
as they rush to a tutorial or lecture.

Would you like to be here too, Katie? If you work
hard this year, maybe you could go to college too? You've
only one year left in high school, so why not give it your
best? I know you can do it. Might it be wise to stay in
on Sundays and study? I know you are keen on Matthew
Young, but believe me, there's a big world out here and
so many boys who will fall in love with you at the drop
of a hat. We could save up for you to come visit me and
I can show you all my favourite *nooks* in Harvard. The
Whittards are good people; I'm sure they'd be happy
for you to share my bed. Oh, wouldn't that be so swell?

Time now to get back to my studying (the Reformation in Europe) while sitting in my beloved library as I

write to you. But please think about your future, because
this year is so important for you, Katie. Don't let others
tell you that you're not clever enough to go to college.
I know you the best, and I know you can do it. If you
need me to talk to Mother for you and persuade her,
I'll come home, I promise, and do it at Thanksgiving.
Just write me.

Give my love to Mother, and lots of love to you too!

*

Susannah folded the letter up and put it in the envelope. She'd
post it first thing tomorrow. In her heart, she knew Kate would
no sooner apply to go to college at Harvard or anywhere else than
she would go to the North Pole. Of course, she was clever, but
she didn't work hard enough. The only shot Susannah had had
was to get a scholarship, and she had had to work day and night
the last few months to get the grades to even be considered. Kate
was too distracted by Matthew Young to study. The first letter
Kate had sent just the day before had been full of him. What
Matthew wanted was to build his own house on a tiny islet that
his family owned across the water from Lane's Island Bridge Cove.
Matthew wanted to have his own pleasure boat one day, to take
his future family out. Matthew wanted to go hunting with Silas
this season and Kate was hoping they'd be successful and bring
back a deer. *He gets so sick of fish!* Kate had written. But where
were her sister's wants in all the tales of Matthew Young? *He's so
good to me*, she wrote, describing a bracelet he had bought for
her in Rockland when he'd gone for fishing supplies. *Mother and
I are making him new nets*, she wrote, as if it was a good thing.
Susannah felt annoyed. The nets must be saving Matthew Young
a fair bit, and were another task which distracted her sister from
school. She also felt cross with her mother. Shouldn't she have

Kate's best interests at heart? But it seemed their mother thought Matthew Young a marvel.

Mom says it's great to have a man about the house again, Kate gushed. *Remember the leaking tap in the kitchen sink? Well, Matt fixed it for us! Mom was so pleased.*

Susannah closed her eyes for a moment and pictured the kitchen in the house in Vinalhaven, with the old electric stove and the big sink they'd bathed in as babies. That tap had dripped for years. It was the sound of their home. She felt annoyance at the fact an outsider had come in and fixed it, which was dumb of course, but she couldn't help it. Of course Mom and Kate didn't think Matthew Young was an outsider. They thought he was the best thing ever. She'd tried to like him, for Kate's sake. But during those last weeks of summer before she'd left for Harvard, Susannah had really grown to dislike him strongly. She didn't like the way he patronised them all, talking down to them just because they were women. She particularly disliked how he called Kate 'baby' and 'little bird', and how he addressed their mother as 'Judith' rather than 'Mrs Olsen'. Susannah was certain if there'd been a man about the house, Matthew Young would not have taken such liberties sitting down at the head of their table and eating the biggest slice of pie every night. Worst of all, he took Kate away from her all the time. Whenever Susannah had suggested she and Kate go bathing in one of the old granite quarries or picking berries again, Kate would invite Matthew too. Once, she had even asked Susannah if she wanted Silas to come and was surprised by Susannah's vehement, 'No way!' The only time they had free together was when Matthew was out lobstering. Most of the other fishermen, including Silas, went to bed at four in the afternoon so they could get up early, but not Matthew. All summer he had seemed to be fuelled on so little sleep. Kate had confided he said being with her made him feel rested, but Susannah knew it was a game he was playing. His only real competition for Kate was not another boy, but Susannah. Her theory had been proved correct when Kate had complained in her letter that Matthew wasn't spending as much time with her as he had during the summer. The darker mornings meant he needed to get to bed good and early. But Susannah knew it was because she was out of the picture. Or so he thought.

Susannah sighed and opened her eyes. She looked at the clock on the wall. It was time to go. She was babysitting for the Whittards tonight, as they were going to a cocktail party and it was Gertrude's night off. Besides, the boys had asked for her. They both loved their books and she was looking forward to reading the next instalment of *Treasure Island* to them.

Outside, the wind had intensified, sending the fallen leaves into aerial whirlpools of gold and red foliage. She buttoned up her coat, pulling on her gloves before wrapping her blue scarf around her neck. It was already getting dark and she berated herself for being so slow getting her things together. The Whittards were expecting her and she didn't want to make them late for their party. Just as she was about to cross the road, her scarf blew up into her face. She should have stopped, but she was in such a rush she stepped off the sidewalk all the same. She heard the screech of brakes and felt a strong jerk as someone grabbed her arm and pulled her back. Losing her balance, she dropped all her books on the sidewalk and fell over onto her backside. The car she had just missed walking into honked loudly before taking off again.

'Are you okay?'

She saw the girl's eyes first. So dark, almost inky blue-black.

'What happened?' Susannah asked shakily as the girl helped her up.

'Well, you nearly got run over,' the girl said, picking up her books. She was shorter than her, but Susannah could see strength in her body as she piled up Susannah's library stash. 'I pulled you back just in time.'

'Oh, thank you,' Susannah said. 'I wasn't thinking straight…'

'Yeah, lots of students get knocked down, especially round exam time!'

Susannah tried to pick up her books, but her arms felt weak and her legs were wobbly.

'Hey, take it easy, you've had a shock.'

'I've got to be somewhere. I can't be late.'

'I can help you. I'll carry your books and you tell me where we're going.'

Susannah was amazed by such generosity from another girl. A boy might help you in the same way, but then usually he'd be looking for a date.

'Say, what's your name? Mine's Ava Greenman.'

Straight dark hair with bangs framing her eyes, the same colour. Mouth ever so slightly open, smiling. Susannah had never seen a girl like her before.

It had stopped raining, although it was still gusty, which made it easier to talk. Ava was a freshman as well. Had just started a degree in law, on a scholarship too.

'No one goes to college where I come from,' she explained. 'It was like everyone was part of it, you know, when I got in. One big party when I left.'

'Where did you grow up?' Susannah asked her.

'Washington State, north of Seattle.'

'That's a long way from Harvard.'

'You're telling me. Took three days on the Greyhound bus.' Ava whistled. 'Boy was that some trip.'

'It must have been awfully boring.'

'You know, it wasn't so bad. I got to meet a lot of interesting folk and I saw a lot of scenery. Did you know the middle of America is one big plain that goes on and on and on and on…?'

Susannah started giggling. 'I've never been anywhere but here and Vinalhaven, where I was born.'

'And where is Vinalhaven? It sounds very idyllic,' Ava said as they walked in step along the sidewalk.

'It's an island, about five hours on the bus north. And then you have to take a ferry.'

'So I guess we both are from the sea, but opposite sides of the country. You're the Atlantic and I'm the Pacific.' Ava smiled at her. She had a very warm, generous smile, with perfectly straight white teeth.

'What's the difference?'

Ava shifted the weight of Emer's books to her other arm. 'Well, I'm bigger for a start, and I think deeper, and you can get very, very lost in me.'

Susannah felt herself blushing for some reason.

'But the Atlantic is wild. Big storms!' Ava enthused.

'Tell me about it,' Susannah groaned.

By now they had reached the Whittards' mansion. It felt as if the walk had gone in an instant.

'Well, this is me,' Susannah explained, pointing to the front porch.

'You live here?' Ava looked impressed.

'I look after the kids in exchange for board and lodging.'

'That's great,' Ava said. 'I'm in student halls. Women only, with a curfew of ten o'clock every single night. It's like being in prison. Still, it's better than being back home.'

'Yeah, anything is better than being back home,' Susannah said vehemently, taking the books from Ava.

There was an awkward pause. She sensed Ava wanted her to say something, but she couldn't invite her in.

'Say, would you like to go to Club 47 with me Sunday afternoon?'

Susannah had no idea what Club 47 was, but had a feeling she should. 'Sure,' she said, feeling herself blush.

'Joan Baez is playing. Have you heard of her?'

Susannah looked up to see Ava's excited expression.

'She is totally awesome. Mostly it's jazz at Club 47, but she's different. Sings about important stuff.'

'That sounds great,' Susannah said, wondering what the important stuff was.

'Shall I see you there?' Ava asked. 'Around three o'clock.'

'Sure,' Susannah said. 'Thanks again.'

'I'm glad we met!'

Ava gave her a small wave goodbye as she crossed the road and walked away. Susannah returned the wave, excited to have made her first Harvard friend.

The hall was in darkness as Susannah stepped inside the Whittards' front door. She could hear the boys in the kitchen with Gertrude, and the parents upstairs getting ready, but she didn't call out that she was back. Not yet. She held her books tight to her chest, the ones Ava Greenman had carried all the way home for her. Ava was such a beautiful girl, so unusual. Susannah could still hear her laugh. They had talked so easily. Susannah felt as if she'd known Ava all her life, not just one hour. She couldn't wait until Sunday when she'd see her again, and not only that – in a jazz club. Imagine if Kate could see her now!

Chapter 14

Emer

21st October 2011

It had taken six days of asking, six days of watching Susannah struggle with pain and fatigue at her typewriter, before she had finally agreed to let Emer help her.

'What I'm typing is very personal,' Susannah said, eyeing Emer from her armchair as she set up her laptop on Susannah's desk. 'You've got to promise not to talk to anyone about it.'

'Sure,' Emer said. 'I wouldn't dream of it.'

Susannah sank back into her armchair, looking relieved.

'It's better for me to save it on my laptop as well,' Emer said to her. 'Then we can put it on a memory stick for you and print out a hard copy.'

'That's good,' Susannah said. 'I want the girls to have a copy each. One for Lynsey and one for Rebecca.'

The blanket had slipped off Susannah's knees, and Emer went over and picked up it up, tucking it around her again. She could sense the older woman's body was tight with pain.

'Can I get you anything?' she asked Susannah.

'No, I'm fine thank you,' Susannah said, closing her eyes.

'Let me give you some medication to ease—'

'No,' Susannah said sharply, opening her eyes. 'It dulls my mind.'

'Fine,' Emer said, trying not to get annoyed by the imperious tone of Susannah's voice.

'I'm okay,' Susannah said, her voice softening. 'I appreciate your help.' She gave Emer a crooked smile, although Emer could see the discomfort in her eyes. 'You remind me of my sister, Kate,' she said. 'She was a carer, too. Always thinking of others.'

Emer thought of the letters in the quilt on her bed upstairs. She had only read three of them so far. She was trying her best not to continue, but young Susannah and her sister Kate had leapt out at her from the pages. She felt as if she'd met Kate, and she longed to know what had happened to her. She knew she should tell Susannah she'd found the letters. Did Susannah even know they were there? All the letters were addressed from Susannah to Kate. She concluded it must have been Kate who had put the letters inside the quilt. They could have been hidden for years.

Susannah put on her glasses again, and picked up one of the stack of papers on the table next to her. 'Let me explain what I want you to do,' she said to Emer.

Emer went back to her laptop and sat poised, with her fingers hovering above the keyboard.

'I have been organising all the letters my sister sent me during the time I was away from Vinalhaven,' Susannah continued.

Emer sat up with a jolt. Surely now was the time to tell Susannah about her letters to Kate, tucked away in the quilt upstairs? But she was sure Susannah would be furious with her for concealing her discovery. At least for today, she wanted to enjoy their new companionship. She'd wait and pretend to find them in a few days' time. Although, if she was honest, it was because she wanted time to read them all.

'These letters are private correspondence from my sister to me,' Susannah said. 'No one else has read them, but I want to pass them on to Lynsey and Rebecca when I'm gone.'

Emer wondered why Susannah had never shown the letters to her nieces before.

'For years, I wondered whether I should share the letters with the girls,' Susannah said, as if reading Emer's mind. 'But I've always tried to protect them from the truth about their mother and father.'

Emer felt a cold shiver down her spine at the change of tone in Susannah's voice.

'They'd lost both of their parents in tragic circumstances,' she said. 'I thought it was better to look to the future rather dwell on the past. For a start, they had my mother to deal with as well.' Susannah sighed. 'Not long after Kate passed away, my mother began to develop dementia. I think it was the shock of losing her youngest child.' Susannah shook her head sadly. 'She'd forget Kate was gone, and nearly every day we'd have to tell her she was dead. It was very hard for me, and in particular for Lynsey and Rebecca, to live with.'

'I'm so sorry,' Emer said.

'That's why I encouraged the girls to leave Vinalhaven,' Susannah said. 'Get away from all the stories and gossip about their parents, and my poor mother ranting on about it. She was in that state for years. Absolute hell for her.'

'That's terrible,' Emer said.

'My mother only died eight years ago,' Susannah said. 'Imagine all that time, every day, finding out your child has died?'

It sounded horrific. Emer hadn't liked the sound of Susannah's mother from the letters she'd read, but now she found herself feeling sorry for her.

Susannah gave a big sigh, and picked up the first letter on the pile.

'Well, let's start from the beginning again since you're putting it all on the computer,' she said. 'I've organised the letters in order. So this is the first one Kate sent me after I arrived in Harvard. It's dated October 18th, 1958.'

Susannah read the letter out in a steady voice, careful not to betray the emotion she must have been feeling as Emer began to type. Strictly speaking, as her nurse, Emer should have been advising her to take more rest, not push herself, but it was quite clear these letters were Susannah's legacy to her two nieces. As the hours passed, the older woman's intense focus on her project reminded Emer of the times she'd watched Orla painting when she'd come home from nursing college at the weekends. During Orla's Leaving Cert, when their mammy had been at the beginning of her chemo, she had let Orla take over the good room and turn it into a painting studio of sorts. Their father had given out, but Mam was right, the room was never used. Emer remembered the glee with which her mother and sister had stripped all the furniture of its plastic coverings and opened up the dusty curtains. Emptied the sideboard of glasses, plates and useless Feeney knick-knacks, before filling it with all of Orla's art materials.

Emer remembered there had been one drawer full of leaves that her sister had dried in the autumn, and flower heads she'd picked. She had been particularly obsessed with red roses and Emer could still conjure that intense perfume of drying roses from all those years ago. Another drawer had been full of stones she'd collected in the woods. Orla prided herself on her collection of witches' stones, as she called them, which were small stones with natural holes all the way through them. She used to make them into necklaces and give them to all her friends at school. Emer had liked nothing better than to curl up on a beanbag in the corner of the room after a busy week at her nursing studies in Dublin and watch her sister create – painting, making witches' stone necklaces, using all her materials from nature to create artwork. It had relaxed Emer, and often she'd fall asleep, to be woken by the squeaking and scratching of the bats in their attic. The good room would be in darkness and Orla gone. Only then would Emer go look at her sister's pictures. They were all stories, taken from where they lived. The big lime tree in the middle of a circle of faery-sprites, mist curling off the lake with the white pooka horse at its shoreline, yellow eyes staring out of the frame and making Emer shiver. The two white swans which came to nest every year taking flight above the rippling lake. Orla had told her she believed them descendants of the swan-children of Lir, flying off to the sea of Moyle after three hundred years, and now returned to their lake to sing of peace and harmony to the two sisters. The pictures had such presence, it felt as if they were alive in the good room with her. Part of her was in awe at her sister's talent, but a small part also envied it. Orla possessed something so special. Everyone in the family said how talented she was. But Emer was ordinary.

It was only when Ethan had been packing up to move to New York that he had given Emer the drawings. A whole sketchbook full of charcoal studies of her – Emer – looking out of the window of their childhood good room, and asleep on the beanbag, all those years ago. Her heart had skipped a beat and she'd given a little cry.

'They're brilliant, aren't they?' Ethan said, looking at her with big sad eyes.

'I've never seen them before,' she whispered.

Her sister had perfectly captured the essence of her. Even at the time in their lives when they had been constantly bickering, these drawings revealed that deep down, Orla had seen her. Emer was curled like a cat on the beanbag, in the manner in which she'd always slept, but it was the studies of her looking out of the window which were so telling. Her expression one of a girl who never dared to dream.

That was why she'd chosen nursing. It had been safe, and she'd loved her training in the Mater Hospital in Dublin. Really had believed she was going to stay in Ireland forever. Her mam had always said she was a little homebody. But when their mam passed away, Orla had gone to teach English in Croatia and her dad had started seeing Sharon, Emer had felt completely at sea. She was still single, having never managed a proper relationship with anyone.

When Orla met Ethan crewing yachts along the coast of Croatia and curtailed her European trip to live with him in Boston, for the first time, Emer considered leaving Ireland despite the fact she was still at nursing college. Their mam had been born in New York to Irish parents, who'd moved back to Dublin soon after, but this meant both sisters had been able to get American passports before they were eighteen.

'It's a waste not to take advantage of it,' Orla persuaded her. 'After you finish your nursing degree, you can come for a month or two. Go home if you hate it.'

After graduating, Emer had got a job at the Mater Hospital in Dublin, worked there for a couple of years. But she'd missed Orla badly, and in the end had gone out to join her. She'd only been planning to work at Mass Gen for two or three years. Return to Ireland and pick up where she'd left off at the Mater. But then Orla got sick and Emer wanted to support her. She stayed through all the rounds of chemotherapy, and celebrated with Orla when she went into remission. They planned a trip to Mexico together for the November. But in August, Orla started feeling sick again. The cancer was back. This time it had spread to her lymph nodes. It was everywhere. In Emer's mind, her sister's cancer had been a black cloud which had never gone away, billowing toxic in Orla's body.

It was also during August, at the worst time of her life, that Emer had first met Lars.

Had he been the one? As Emer continued to type, listening to Susannah read out Kate's letters, she became immersed in the romantic aspirations of Susannah's younger sister. Kate clearly believed in the one. Matthew was her true love, as she kept telling Susannah. But despite saying nothing to her, Emer could detect a tone in Susannah's voice whenever Matthew was mentioned in one of Kate's letters. It was clear Susannah had not liked Matthew. Did she blame him for her sister's early death? What had happened to them?

Chapter 15

Susannah

November 6th, 1958
Harvard, Cambridge

Dearest Katie,

Sorry I've missed our weekly letter exchange for two weeks. Back home on our island, I was always trying to make time go faster. How many long, boring walks did I take up and down Amherst Hill, staring out to sea and waiting for my life to start? Well, it has started at last and it's going at such a speed.

You asked about the Whittard household in your last letter. Every day is busy in this family, but I am very happy in my little room in the eaves of their very big house. Katie, it's an absolute mansion with such a big garden you can't see the end of it! They are good people. Professor Whittard can be a little aloof, but he is after all a very clever man, and mostly his head is in all his theories and important calculations. Really, I can't imagine. You know I am an historian and science has always confused me somewhat. The boys are boisterous, of course. Nathan is eight, and Joshua ten years old, but they are good boys and in the main do what they are told. They both love books and stories and I am enjoying reading them all our old classics at bedtime. Their favourite is *The Call of the Wild*. I was a little worried the story would be too adult for them, but the boys loved it. The idea of the story being told from the point of view of a dog really appealed to them. When I read it again, I was struck how the story mirrors all the research I have begun on European witch trials. Like Buck, the dog in *The Call of the Wild*, the women accused of witchcraft were those who didn't fit in. They wanted to run with the wolves, Katie. But society (the other dogs) wished to destroy them.

My lecturer is from Norway and she's a woman too! Her name is Hanna Anberg, and I think when I am her age I would like to be just like her. She wears these fabulous Norwegian sweaters with brightly coloured patterns on them. Oh, you would love them, Katie. I keep meaning to build up the courage to ask her what the patterns are called and where I might get one for you. Dr Anberg has studied all over the world. Norway, of course, but also she has studied at Oxford in England, and written a paper on Matthew Hopkins, who was a terrible witch-hunter at the time of the English Civil War. She also lived in Florence in Italy to research witch persecutions, in Munich in Germany, and in Edinburgh in Scotland. She's a sort of witch trial detective with a mission to explode all the myths and get to the truth of why the witch hunts happened. She's here at Harvard researching the persecutions in Salem. Remember we did them at school? It's fascinating, and I know this is just one of my courses in the whole of the history degree, but I am already certain I'm going to write my final papers on something to do with witch trials.

Okay, I guess you're pretty bored by now! And really all you want to know about is Mrs Whittard and all her pretty clothes, right? Boy, she really does have a lot of them! Every week there's a social, whether a cocktail party or a dinner, and Mrs Whittard (her name is Jean but I always call her Mrs Whittard) dresses up in a new frock every time. Her family must be wealthy because I don't think her husband's salary could stretch to all her furs and silks. I think her most spectacular outfit was a gold sheath dress she wore with high-heeled shoes in gold satin, a gold purse all sparkly, and so many jewels it was blinding. It was a bit much for me. But I do like her rhinestone-studded housecoat. She got the idea from this television programme called *I Love Lucy* with a funny actress called Lucille Ball in it. (The Whittards have a television, Katie!) Well, she wears this black rhinestone-studded housecoat, which has capri pants as part of it, and a turban on her head. It looks super, Katie. Now that would suit me perfectly. When Mrs Whittard put on her housecoat, Professor Whittard didn't like it all. I heard him say to her he couldn't see her legs and it wasn't feminine enough!

But best of all is Gertrude. It's like she understands how you're feeling without you having to tell her. Sometimes I do get homesick. Yes, I do! I miss you so much and she always knows without me saying it. Gets me to sit down with her and have a glass of milk and one of her cookies, and play a game of gin rummy after the boys have been put to bed.

But now I come to the most exciting part of my letter, and the reason I've been bad at letter writing. A friend of mine called Ava, who literally saved my life one day (I will tell you the story when I come home for Thanksgiving) has introduced me to place called Club

47, where we've gone the last two Sunday afternoons to listen to music. Both times another student called Joan Baez sang and played her guitar. Oh, she is quite incredible, Katie. At first I didn't like her so much. Her voice is very high and it can really get inside your head, and I'd never heard music like it – Ava says it's folk – but then I started listening to all the words and they were so powerful. She writes about how it is to be a woman in a man's world, and she doesn't care what anyone thinks of her! At Club 47 I've met lots of young people who want to change things in America for the better. Give black people like Gertrude equal rights to white people. It's so important, Katie, don't you think? I never really thought about it until I came to Harvard but I had never seen a black person before until I arrived in Boston. Everyone on Vinalhaven is white. Why do you think that is? Maybe it's just because the black people don't want to live there?

Write back soon, do, dear sister. I'm keen to hear how your last year at school is going. I am sorry I upset you in my last letter going on about college. You're right, just because it's my dream, it doesn't have to be yours. We do all have different talents. But Katie, I was thinking, what about coming to Cambridge when you finish school and working in one of the stores? Wouldn't that be swell? I could get a job in a coffee shop near college and we could get our own place. You could learn all about fashion in the store, and make clothes at night. We could sell them! There is so much opportunity, really, Cambridge is the place to be right now. I want to share it with you so much.

*

November 16th, 1958

Ava was waiting for her on the sidewalk and together they went down the steps into Club 47. The past two Sundays Susannah had skipped dinner at the Whittards' to meet up with her new best friend. Ava had opened her world up. Not just to the new folk music, which Susannah loved with a passion, but also to the injustices going on in her own country every single day. If she was going to make her study of witch trials relevant, she had to acknowledge this truth. As soon as she'd told Ava her interests, her friend had asked her if she'd read or seen the play *The Crucible* by Arthur Miller, about the Salem witch trials.

'The whole play is an allegory for the McCarthy trials,' Ava told her.

Susannah was embarrassed to admit not only had she not read *The Crucible*, but she didn't know what the McCarthy trials were.

'I guess you would have been a kid when they went on; my dad told me all about them because he had friends working on the sets in Hollywood and they told him about writers and directors who got blacklisted,' Ava told her. 'It was a very aggressive campaign led by a senator called Joseph McCarthy, accusing people of being communists.'

'I know about the communists,' Susannah had said. 'I mean, that was a real threat.'

Ava cocked her head on one side. 'You think? Really?'

Susannah was shocked but also a little excited by Ava's brazenness. What if they were overheard? They could be accused of anti-American talk.

'In my opinion, it suits the government just fine if they make people scared of communists, and black people, and women even,' Ava said. 'That's how they keep us down!'

At Club 47, the girls drank red wine, smoked cigarettes and listened to Joan Baez's political ballads. Ava had lots of friends, girls and boys, and both Sundays after the music they all headed off to one of the coffee houses and talked until late into the night. Some couples got together, but that wasn't the most important thing about hanging out. Susannah loved it. She was listened to by boys, not because they wanted to date her, but because they thought she had something interesting to say.

She had tried to communicate her excitement at her transformation to Kate, but when her sister wrote back, she didn't seem to understand any of the new experiences Susannah described. In response to Susannah's idea that she come to Cambridge and work in a store, Kate told her she couldn't leave their mom all on her own on the island. This made Susannah feel guilty, although Kate reassured her she didn't want to live in the city.

> *We're different, Susie, remember. I need to be on the island to be happy,* Kate wrote to her. *Walking in the woods is my socialising, the trees are my friends, and listening to the sea as it laps against Lane's Island Bridge Cove is my music. I don't need to be in coffee houses or clubs to be happy. And wearing something pretty I've made for Matthew is enough dressing up for me. Please don't worry. I am content here, and excited to soon be done with school.*

Susannah had planned to go home for Thanksgiving, but the Whittards asked her to help Gertrude because they had family visiting.

'We were going to hire help,' Mrs Whittard told her, 'but Peter thought you might be glad of a few extra dollars.'

Susannah couldn't turn down the money. She needed every cent for her new social life with Ava.

'Are you going home for Thanksgiving?' Susannah asked Ava. She was going to be flat-out at the Whittards' all day, but if Ava was around, maybe they could meet up later in the evening? Ava gave her a funny look.

'It's not a date my family celebrate.'

'Oh. Why?' Susannah thought every American celebrated Thanksgiving.

'I'll tell you about it another time.' Ava shrugged. 'But no, I'm going to be here.'

Thanksgiving, November 27th, 1958

They arranged to go for an evening stroll. The moon was full, but it was terribly cold. Susannah hadn't even thought about the consequences of walking in such cold without being able to dive into a coffee house. But all their regular places were closed for Thanksgiving.

'I think it's going to snow,' Susannah said to Ava.

'How'd you know?'

'I can smell it!'

Ava gave a quick laugh. 'Doesn't snow much on Puget Sound.'

'I can tell by your coat!' Susannah put her arm around Ava to stop her from shaking.

'We have to find somewhere warm, else we'd better go home.'

'We could go to mine,' Ava suggested. 'My roommate has gone home for Thanksgiving and most of the girls are away. We could play records.'

The girls linked arms and made their way across Harvard Square in the stark brittle air. Susannah fell in step with Ava. She had never felt so close to anyone else before, not even Kate.

In Ava's tiny room, Susannah marvelled how two girls managed to share such a small space.

'Rosie isn't here often,' Ava explained. 'Her parents have an apartment in downtown Boston and she stays there a lot.'

Susannah sat down on Ava's bed, while her friend put on a record. Woody Guthrie, one of her folk heroes.

The two of them sang along together, beaming at each other.

'We sound like two screeching cats!' Ava laughed.

'Speak for yourself.' Susannah nudged her.

Ava caught Susannah's hand in hers. Wrapped her fingers around it. The mood changed instantly. Susannah's breath shortened, and she was aware of every muscle in her body tensing.

'I've never met a girl like you, Susannah,' Ava said to her.

'Sure you have!' Susannah brushed her off, feeling heat rising to her cheeks. 'I'm very average.'

Ava shook her head. 'Well, you know Miss Susannah Olsen, that just isn't true.' Ava let go of her hand. 'Let me turn the record. The B-side is just as good. '

She got up off the bed, and Susannah instantly felt bereft. All she wanted was to hold Ava's hand again.

She watched Ava as she lifted the record off the turntable. She was wearing a red sweater and a plain black skirt and stockings. No shoes on. Her hair was loose and fell in a long stream of ebony down her back. Susannah felt an ache throughout her whole body. Ava was the most beautiful person she had ever seen. She looked away, out of the window of the tiny room.

'Oh, it's snowing! Ava, come look.' Susannah knelt on the bed, pointing out of the window.

Ava jumped onto the bed next to her, and the two girls looked out at swirling snowflakes. How quickly it blanketed the trees and houses, the cars, the whole street in virgin snow, falling thick and fast.

They sat in silence, watching winter's magic unfurl before them.

'I will never forget this moment,' Susannah whispered. 'It has to be the best in my life so far.'

'Me too,' Ava whispered back.

They turned to look at each other. Ava's dark hair was thrown into contrast by the falling snow outside her window. Her dark eyes even darker against the white.

'You can't walk home, the snow is already too thick,' she said. 'You'll have to telephone the Whittards. Tell them you're staying with a friend tonight.' She sat back on the bed, crossed her legs. 'There's a telephone in the hall downstairs.'

'Okay,' Susannah said, her heart beginning to race again.

'But before you do, let's dance!' Ava slipped off the bed and turned up the music. She held out her hand and without thinking, Susannah took it.

Chapter 16

Emer

26th October 2011

It was their third afternoon hike together. Henry had promised to take Emer to his five top places on Vinalhaven in ascending order of preference. On their first afternoon together, they had walked the two-mile loop trail in Huber Preserve, crossing wetlands to walk up a slope with views overlooking Burnt Island and Penobscot Bay, both a giant's hop from the shore. Another afternoon, while Susannah had her rest time, Henry brought Emer to Starboard Rock Sanctuary. She had been entranced by the views from the cliff top. Interlacings of land and sea, dramatic outcroppings of granite and canopies of huge spruce trees. Henry's third favourite place on the island was the Watershed Preserve, a little further inland and a few miles north of the ferry.

'What happens when we get to number one?' she'd asked him.

'Well, the time after we'll take my boat to North Haven,' Henry said, grinning at her. 'I know a great restaurant there. Not as good as mine, but nearly!'

'You've got a boat?' she said, feeling a little clench of nerves in the pit of her belly, and ignoring the mention of a restaurant. Had he just asked her on a date? Were these hikes dates?

'Sure, every man needs a boat on Vinalhaven, fisherman or no.' He pushed his hand through his thick brown hair to get it out of his eyes. It gleamed auburn and magenta in the fall light. 'It's real small. Just a dinghy with a sail, but it gets me places.'

Henry was such easy company. Emer never felt any pressure to talk, and sometimes they walked in silence as if the nature they immersed themselves in was hallowed ground. Always by Henry's side was his white husky, Shadow. On their second hike of one whole hour, the three of them walked together, the only sound the hum of nature and Shadow's steady pant. Today Henry was more talkative, asking after Susannah. Emer found it touching how concerned he was for her welfare.

'You were right,' Emer said. 'It's made such a difference, typing for her.'

'See, I told you so,' he said. 'What's she writing?'

'Oh, she's not writing anything new,' Emer said. 'She's a stack of old letters her sister, Kate, sent her when she was away at college, and she wants to type them up so they're documented for Lynsey and Rebecca.'

Henry paused, looked at her intently.

'Lynsey never told me about any letters her mom wrote,' he said. 'She was always so frustrated she knew so little about her mom and dad.'

'I don't think Lynsey knows about the letters,' Emer said, suddenly feeling awkward as she remembered her promise to Susannah not to tell anyone about them.

'Don't know why Susannah never showed them to Lynsey when she was growing up.' Henry said, sounding a little annoyed. 'When we were dating Lynsey was still really screwed up over what happened. She was only five when her mom and dad died, Rebecca even younger. Might have helped her if she'd read those letters.'

'I believe Susannah didn't want to upset the girls further; apparently her mother had dementia and kept forgetting Kate was gone,' Emer said, in defence of Susannah. 'They had to tell her Kate was dead nearly every day.'

'Oh yeah, Lynsey would tell me all about her crazy granny,' Henry said.

Emer felt awkward to be talking about Susannah and her family behind her back, but she was curious about Henry and Lynsey. There was clearly a big age gap between them.

'How long did you and Lynsey date for?' she asked Henry.

'Not long,' he said. 'Just the summer before I left for art college. But you should have seen her back then.' Henry whistled. 'Lynsey really turned heads. I was crazy about her.'

Emer felt a bit irritated. In her eyes, Lynsey was still a very beautiful woman.

'She was really there for me when my dad died,' Henry continued. 'But then Susannah got wind of our relationship and put a stop to it. I guess I wasn't good enough for Lynsey in her eyes. She said the age gap was indecent!'

Emer detected a slight bitterness in his tone.

Henry turned to her, holding out his hand to help her climb over a rock slippery with moss as Shadow ran on ahead. 'But does age really matter when it comes to love?'

She shook her head. He really did have the most astonishing eyes. In the shade they were as dark green as the pines, in the light, hazel flecked with amber and bright green.

The weather had turned mild, with sunshine warming their backs, their jackets tied around their waists. They'd parked in the gravel lot overlooking a small lake called Folly Pond. The trail led them across Old Woods Road, before entering wetlands and forest. As the ground began to rise, maple trees filtered into a dense spruce-fir forest. Even higher up, Emer saw ancient pine trees twisting out of fissures in the granite ledges, as if the roots themselves were fossilised in rock. Up they went, Henry showing her huckleberries, juniper and crowberry shrubs on their way, while Shadow foraged in the undergrowth.

On the summit of the granite dome, Henry spread his arms wide and closed his eyes. Emer did the same. Sea breezes caressed her face and the warmth from the October sun kissed her forehead. She found herself swaying, letting herself be pushed a little by the wind's gentle direction. The life of the forest floor below them flickered as shadows behind her closed eyes. She listened to the birds, unable to make out which was which, but hearing the diversity of their songs: a steady chirrup, chirrup; a lone call.

'Do you hear the warbler?' Henry whispered, as she opened her eyes to find the sun glaring at her. 'He sounds so lonely. Always searching for his mate.'

He stood as a dark silhouette, his dog on his haunches at his feet. Emer had no idea of the expression on his face.

They climbed back down the granite dome and into the woods. The trees became more sparse and they sat on a mossy rock, littered with old needles from the pine tree above, their backs pressed against its wide girth as Shadow lay at their feet. Emer imagined the deep grooves of the tree's thick bark imprinting her skin. They waited, and after a while, their patience was rewarded as giant red and blue butterflies fluttered among the grasses, before the biggest dragonfly Emer had ever seen hovered right in front of her.

Orla had adored dragonflies, and damselflies. Emer remembered summer evenings back in Ireland, swimming with Orla in Lough Bane. The two of them hypnotised by the bright blue tiny damselflies flittering above the cold water. Orla had made a painting afterwards. Emer could still picture it on an easel in the good room. A view of the lough with its golden reeds and blue damselflies. But if you looked close enough, each damselfly was a tiny fairy. To her sister, all of nature became an enchanted kingdom. Where was Orla now? Emer wasn't religious, but she'd been around death enough to believe everyone possessed a soul. This eternal essence was *somewhere*.

On the afternoon before she died, Orla had told Emer she'd seen their mother in her hospital room. Ethan had gone out for a coffee and it was just the two of them. Emer had been reading *Harry Potter and the Prisoner of Azkaban* to her sister, when Orla had reached out and gripped her hand tight.

'Can you feel it?' Orla had said to her.

Emer would never forget the expression on her face. Orla had glowed, as if all the pain and suffering had washed out of her.

'Feel what?'

'All the love,' Orla whispered. 'Mammy's here. And Granny and Grandpa.'

Emer had felt it. A thickness in the room, as if she were surrounded by a great crowd, and yet it was just the two sisters.

In her more positive moments since Orla had died, Emer reminded herself of that last afternoon. Her sister was not alone. She was with Mammy, wherever that might be.

But in her darker moments, she thought about the big box of ashes Ethan had taken with him to New York. He had offered her some of them, and she'd said no. But the day before she'd left, when he was out, she'd taken the lid off the box and looked at the grey ashes. They could be ashes of anything. The horror of their ordinariness made her turn away suddenly, and she'd knocked the box onto the wooden floor of Ethan's house. Panic consumed her. She tugged at the kitchen drawer, pulling out a big tablespoon, and crouched down scooping the ashes back into the box with the spoon. She wanted to get them back in as quick as possible but the more she rushed, the more spilled over the edges of the spoon back onto the floor. 'Oh no, oh no,' she moaned as tears filled her eyes. She tried to stay calm, work methodically, all the while speaking to Kate inside her head. Telling her she loved her. She was sorry.

Ever since, she'd been tortured by the idea she hadn't managed to scoop all Kate's ashes up and put them back in the box, or worse – and which was very likely – that mixed up now with her sister's ashes were bits of dust and grit from between the floorboards in the house in Quincy. Why did she always mess everything up?

'Hey, you okay?' Henry said to her, his face creased in concern.

She was crying and hadn't even noticed, but now the tears had started, Emer couldn't stop. She hadn't cried when Orla had died; the shock had knocked the tears right out of her. And now, weeks later, it was all coming out. Of all places, in front of someone she hardly knew.

'I'm sorry,' she managed to say, pulling a tissue out of her pocket to dam the flood.

'Let it out, that's my advice,' Henry said.

'It's just this place is so beautiful, and it reminds me of my sister, Orla,' Emer said in a broken voice. 'I told you about her before. She was a painter. Made a beautiful picture of damselflies back home one time. She would have loved it here.'

'What happened to your sister?' Henry asked gently.

'She died. Five weeks ago.'

'I'm so sorry,' Henry said, and she could hear the compassion in his voice.

'She had cancer, too. Different from Susannah's. It was very aggressive, but it was an infection which killed her in the end. She was so weak from all the chemo; she went downhill very quickly.' Emer raised her face to the sky, let the tears drip off her chin. 'She was only twenty-six.'

Henry said nothing. What could he say? There were no words in the whole world which could give her comfort. She drew her knees up to her chest and buried her face. She felt Henry's hand on her back, and Shadow pushed his snout between her arms to lick her salty cheeks.

'Oh no, Shadow, stop.' She found herself being tickled by the sensation of the dog's tongue on her skin, but the husky wouldn't let up.

'He won't stop,' Henry said. 'You're part of his pack, and he needs to make sure you're okay!'

She sniffed, using Henry's damp tissue to blow her nose. 'I'm okay,' she said. 'Sorry.'

'Don't say sorry,' Henry said. 'Emer, it's good to let it out.'

But as they walked back to Henry's pick-up, Emer felt there was a new awkwardness between them, as if she'd shown too much of herself. As they reached the parking lot, Henry turned to her.

'Emer. Do you think it's wise to be looking after Susannah, considering what you've just been through?'

'I know what I'm doing,' she said, suddenly defensive.

'I'm not saying otherwise, but you've just been through huge loss, and now you're here and in a position where you're going to experience that loss all over again.'

'I need to do this. For my sister.'

'I don't understand.'

Emer looked into Henry's kind eyes.

'I let her down. I wasn't with her when she needed me most.' Emer's chest felt heavy with all the guilt. It was hard to get the words out. 'I ran away, Henry. My sister was calling for me but I wasn't there. I abandoned her.'

'But Susannah is not your family. She's not your responsibility.'

'She has no one, Henry. I mean, Rebecca calls her every day. But Lynsey doesn't come to the island. Why don't they get on?'

'Lots of reasons,' Henry said. 'They clash on so many things. Susannah hates that Lynsey is a tarot reader. And it's hard for

Lynsey to return to Vinalhaven when she feels judged by Susannah all the time.'

They got in Henry's pick-up, and he took a thermos out of the back, unscrewed the lid and poured the contents into two cups.

'What happened to Kate and her husband?' Emer ventured. She was dying to know, but daren't ask Susannah.

Henry's whole body stiffened as he spoke, although his face looked quite relaxed. 'If I tell you this, never – and I mean never – talk about it with Susannah. Lynsey says she goes nuts when it's brought up. That's one reason why they've fallen out.'

'I promise, of course not,' Emer said, taking a sip of the hot black coffee.

'Well. The story goes Lynsey's dad killed her mother, and then he killed himself. Ran into the sea and drowned.'

'Oh my god!'

'Yeah, like I said earlier, Lynsey was five at the time, and Rebecca was only two.'

Poor Kate. From Susannah's letters, she had come across as the sweetest girl. She had been so in love with Matthew, and yet he had killed her. And as for those poor girls – how horrendous to not only lose their mother, but to know it was their own father who had taken her from them. Emer's heart welled with compassion for Lynsey, and for Rebecca, who she was yet to meet.

'Why did Lynsey's father murder her mother?'

'I wasn't even born when it happened, so all I know is what my parents told me. They thought he killed her by accident, as did most on the island.' Henry took a sip of his coffee. 'I promise you, most folk said Lynsey's dad was a good man. Worked hard for his family every day, out fishing and risking his life. Problem was, he drank too much.'

The way Henry spoke about it was a little odd, Emer thought. Even if it had been an accident, the man had still killed his wife.

'Also, there's been gossip,' Henry said, putting the thermos back together. 'Some folk here on Vinalhaven don't believe Matthew Young drowned. I've heard whispers.'

'Do they think he ran away?' Emer asked.

'Possibly, but his family never heard from him again. My dad told me he loved those little girls. Said he used to take them out on the boat on a Sunday sometimes with some of the other kids. My big sister remembers it,' Henry said. 'My dad always said he would never have left those girls.'

'So?' Emer asked Henry. 'What do you think happened to Kate's husband?'

'Well, now, I just don't know for sure,' Henry said hastily, tucking the thermos into the glove compartment. 'But there has been talk about Susannah. My dad was always saying the neighbours saw something the day Kate's body was found. My dad said it sure was strange Susannah turned up back from college on the same day both her sister was found dead and her brother-in-law disappeared.'

Emer sat back in shock. The coincidence did seem very uncanny.

Henry stared out of the car window. Reflections of dappled sunlight fell on his face, casting it in and out of shadow. 'My dad told me she hated Kate's husband, was very possessive of her sister.'

Emer felt her throat go dry. What was Henry implying?

'And one of the neighbours told him they saw Susannah in her brother-in-law's boat, out the day Kate's body was found. Course, they never told the police that. Felt the family had been through enough, but my dad was raging. Always felt justice hadn't been done.'

Henry's revelations stunned Emer. Was he really suggesting Susannah had been responsible for the disappearance of Kate's husband? Had she somehow done away with him, and tipped the body out into the sea?

Emer felt sick. She thought of Susannah at home, resting in her bed. The frail old lady who looked like she wouldn't hurt a fly. She might have a sharp tongue, and Emer might have only known her a short while, but she really couldn't believe Susannah had it in her to kill any soul, no matter how much she hated them.

'I really don't think Susannah has it in her to do any such thing,' Emer said firmly.

'You never know,' Henry said, as he started the ignition. 'I mean, *I* don't believe it, Emer. But Susannah is very strange, don't you think? She takes notions about folk. For instance, she's had it in for me since she broke things up with me and Lynsey. That's been years, and still she won't talk to me if we meet in the street.'

'Oh, I didn't know that,' Emer said, feeling a little uncomfortable as she stroked Shadow's head as he lolled in her lap.

'Yeah,' Henry said, as he pulled out of the lot. 'Like I said first time we went for a hike, best not say we're meeting, even. She really has it in for men in general.'

Susannah might be cranky, but this was a whole other side to her which Emer found hard to believe. She liked Henry, but felt conflicted about the walk she'd just enjoyed with him, or even the idea of going on another walk after all the things he'd said about Susannah. He had said it wasn't just him who thought Susannah might be guilty of actually killing Kate's husband, but most folk on the island. No wonder they had no visitors to the house.

As they drove back to Susannah's house, Emer remembered how distraught Susannah had been in the graveyard. How could you ever get over the loss of your sister when she had been murdered? But had Susannah's distress also been guilt due to her part in the tragedy? Although Emer's instincts were telling her Susannah would never do such a thing, how well did she really know her new patient? Had guilt softened Susannah with time?

As Henry pulled in at the bottom of Susannah's road, he leaned over and touched Emer's arm.

'Remember,' he said, 'being here with Susannah might not be the best thing for you right now.'

'I'm fine, thanks,' Emer said, embarrassed again by her upset earlier. 'I don't know what came over me in the woods.'

'You can't hold grief in,' Henry said. 'Otherwise, it consumes you.'

There was an edge to his voice. She realised that even after their hikes together, she still knew very little about him.

'Why don't you come by The Sand Bar tonight?' he suggested. 'There's a band playing, from Rockland. I'll buy you a beer.'

'I'm not sure, Susannah might need me.' Emer was beginning to feel it might be better if she didn't hang out with Henry any more after what he'd told her. He and Susannah clearly had a history because of Lynsey and she didn't want to get caught up in it.

'Surely she'll give you leave for one night?' Henry persisted. 'I mean, have you had one night off since you arrived?'

Despite her better instincts, Emer felt it impossible to say no.

Back in Susannah's house, Emer prepared her patient's tea, cutting a pear in half, peeling and slicing it. Susannah might only manage half the pear, but it was something at least. She felt a knot of anxiety in her chest. Henry's invitation to The Sand Bar could be viewed as a proper date. But she'd nothing fancy to wear. Only jeans and jumpers with her. What was she doing going on a date anyway? Henry had been so kind when she'd been upset today over Orla, but then she really didn't like all the gossip he'd told her about Susannah and her family. It also felt weird that he had once dated Lynsey, who was almost the same age as Emer's mother would have been if she were alive.

And then there was Lars. Where was he now? She pictured him, his blue eyes flipping her heart every time he looked at her. She hadn't heard from him since their last phone conversation where she'd hung up on him. Not one text. She'd asked him to leave her alone, but it hurt that he'd given up so easily. What she needed to do was keep away from all men. Stay in and retrieve the rest of the letters from the quilt. Her head was buzzing with all of what Henry had told her. Maybe she'd find out the truth if she read all the letters.

'Where've you been?' Susannah asked her, as Emer propped her up in bed with a couple of pillows and placed the tray with a cup of tea and the pear on her lap.

'I went walking.'

'Well now, it must have been a long way.'

'I called in and chatted with Peggy Steel, in the library,' Emer lied, immediately feeling uncomfortable for doing so.

'Well, I'm glad you're getting out and about,' Susannah said. Her humour was so much better since she'd allowed Emer to give her a small amount of pain relief in the afternoon to allow her to rest.

'There's a band playing at The Sand Bar tonight. I was thinking of going,' Emer found herself telling Susannah. 'But I shan't if you need me.'

Susannah scrutinised her. 'Of course you should go!'

'I don't even have anything good to wear,' Emer said now, wishing she'd said nothing. Really, she would rather stay in and read those letters. 'Maybe it's not such a good idea. I don't think I should leave you on your own.'

'You certainly will!' Susannah declared. 'I was always such a loner and it did me no good. You need to meet some people your own age.'

'I guess,' Emer said, feeling nervous at the thought of seeing Henry again. But then, she wanted to ask him more about his life on the island.

'Open up the wardrobe over there.' Susannah's order broke through her thoughts. 'Look right in the back of it,' she said.

The wardrobe was jammed with old shirts and coats. Emer pushed through them.

'Can you see any dresses?'

Emer saw a glimmer of white, took hold of the hanger and pulled out a dress.

'Oh. It's beautiful.'

It was fifties-style. A neat bodice, and a wide skirt of white organza with gold flocking.

'That was Kate's dress,' Susannah said, her voice heavy. 'I remember the first time she wore it.'

'I can't wear your sister's dress!' Emer protested.

'Yes, of course you can,' Susannah persisted. 'You're the same size as her. Rebecca and Lynsey are both too big for Kate's clothes.'

'But it's *your* sister's.'

'Exactly,' Susannah said. 'And that's why you should wear it.'

The dress fit Emer like a glove. Susannah made her twirl in front of her, and to see Emer in her sister's dress did seem to make the older woman happy. Again, Emer found her thoughts returning to what Henry had told her after their walk. To be in Kate's dress made her feel even closer to her tragedy. Would the letters from Kate, which she was typing up for Susannah every day, reveal why her marriage had ended so fatally?

'Well now, you'd think it was made for you,' Susannah declared.

When she looked in the mirror, Emer was astonished by the transformation in how she looked. She never wore dresses. Her going-out outfit was usually jeans and a silky top. Easy and comfortable. She rarely wore make-up. But the dress required glamour, so she ran down to the store before it shut and bought some red lipstick, mascara and black liquid eyeliner to give herself an authentic fifties makeover.

Back upstairs in her room, Emer checked the time. She had just over an hour to read more of the letters. She slipped her hand inside the quilt and pulled them all out. Neatly piling them on the end of the bed, she put to one side the ones she'd already read. Henry's talk had ignited her curiosity to know more about the sisters. She lay on her tummy on the bed and picked up the next letter, immediately entering Harvard in the late fifties.

Later, still feeling as if she was in the past, Emer went downstairs to give Susannah a final viewing of the dress. The letters had been so moving. Reading about Susannah's life and loves had touched her deeply. And in those letters, she could sense what had been going on in Kate's life. But she was still none the wiser as to what had happened on the fateful day of Kate's death.

Susannah seemed even more delighted to see Emer in her sister's old dress, and amused by her whole attire.

'Well now, you know I love the way you accessorized,' she laughed, pointing out Emer's black boots and biker jacket.

'Does it look stupid? Am I bit over the top for The Sand Bar?'

'Not at all, who cares what they think.' Susannah closed her eyes, and leant back on the pillow. 'Okay, well. Now have a good time, Rebecca. Don't be too late.'

Emer nearly corrected her, but Susannah looked so wan and exhausted she didn't bother. So what if she'd called her Rebecca? It was clear to see the cancer was beginning to really eat away at Susannah's life force and it made Emer feel sad, and guilty. She considered whether now was the right time to tell her about the letters in the quilt. Susannah had been in such a good mood, but now she was falling asleep, so very tired and weak. Emer would tell her tomorrow. In the morning. When they both had more energy.

Emer walked into town to the sound of the crickets chirruping and the sight of the sun setting over the sea. She pulled out her phone to check the time and saw a missed call from Lars. She tried to push it from her mind, but couldn't help feeling a twinge of relief. He hadn't completely rejected her.

Town was quiet enough. Apart from lights, and the sound of music coming from The Sand Bar, the only sign of life was one lone man, standing at the end of town on the part where the road became a bridge over the rushing waters of the Atlantic. The way he was standing reminded her of Lars again. He was always there in the back of her mind. As she got closer, the man moved his hand – a tiny gesture, but it made her heart catch in her throat. He turned around and she stopped dead in her tracks. At the same time, he saw her. It was Lars.

Everything fell away. The whole island slipping off her shoulders and into the Atlantic. Gone was Susannah and her story. Gone was Henry waiting for her in The Sand Bar. All she could think of, all she could see, was this one man standing before her. He was her whole world.

Chapter 17

Susannah

December 1958

It had only been a few months but even so, Vinalhaven looked different to Susannah's childhood memories of it at Christmastime. Everything appeared so much smaller than Cambridge. The houses and the harbour. The road seemed narrower, and it had not seemed nearly as long a walk to her house as she remembered yesterday when she'd got off the boat.

The quiet. It was all around her this Christmas morning as she, Kate and her mother walked across the snow-laden island to the Youngs' house. Susannah found herself missing the noises of city life: honking cars, the chatter of other pedestrians, and the occasional police siren. Most of all, she was missing Ava. Ever since their special Thanksgiving evening, they'd spent as much time together as they could. Hanging out at Club 47, or in coffee houses with other students. Susannah had never felt so alive, so in the right place. Being back home was hard. The fact she didn't belong here felt even more pronounced than when she'd left. Moreover, they had been invited to Matthew Young's family house for Christmas dinner, which was not an event she was looking forward to.

'I don't understand why we can't have Christmas at home like always,' she complained as they trudged through the slushy snow.

'It would be rude to turn down the invitation,' her mother said.

At least her mother was talking to her now. Although she still hadn't asked Susannah one thing about Harvard since she had come through the door last night.

'But they're not family,' Susannah had protested.

'Not yet,' Kate said gleefully, her cheeks rosy with cold.

Susannah's heart sank. She had really hoped Matthew Young might have tired of her sister, and found a new love interest while she was away in Harvard. But since she had been gone, Kate and Matthew had started going steady. Their mother had befriended Matthew's mother through dressmaking for her, and in return, Mrs Young had insisted they join them for Christmas dinner.

'It won't seem like Christmas without Gramps Olsen, Uncle Karl and Aunt Marjorie,' Susannah said.

'Things change,' her mother said. 'Now that Lottie's living in Montreal and has a family of her own, of course they are going to want to spend Christmas with her.'

It was hard to believe her cousin had a baby. It only seemed a few winters ago, they'd all been out carol-singing together.

The Young house was on the far side of the island from their home, right on the water's edge. The family had their own private pier and owned two fishing boats, which bobbed at ease upon the still water. The air was so bright and clear. It really was a perfect winter's day, and Susannah would much rather have been out sledding.

'Please try to be nice to him,' Kate whispered, as they were brought into the house by Mrs Young, a mousy little woman with the same blue eyes as her sons. Susannah immediately felt guilty. Kate was always standing up for her with their mother; the least Susannah could do was try to get on with Matthew.

But it was as if as soon as he laid eyes on her, Matthew was intent on goading her.

'Well, the prodigal daughter returns.' Matthew eyed her up. 'Found a rich Boston husband yet?'

Susannah ignored him, taking her place at the table. The whole family was there – Mr and Mrs Young, Matthew, Annie the sister, and of course Silas, whom Susannah hadn't seen since the awful dance. But sitting next to Silas was Rachel Weaver, of all people. Silas had his arm around the back of Rachel's chair, and it was clear they were a couple. Rachel looked different. Less plush than Susannah remembered. Her face was a bit puffy and pale, and her brown hair looked lank.

'Oh hi, Susie,' she said. 'How's Harvard?'

Susannah couldn't detect any sarcasm in her tone at all, and she was looking at her with a genuine expression of interest.

'It's great, thank you,' she said.

'Isn't it just so amazing?' Kate announced proudly. 'I still can't believe our Susie is at Harvard!'

Matthew shrugged as if he didn't care, and Silas looked at her with dead eyes, as if she were nothing to him.

'Sure, I could have gone to college if I'd wanted,' he said, which was the biggest lie Susannah had ever heard, seeing as he'd dropped out of high school before he had even graduated. 'But I wanted to make a proper living.'

'What good is a college education for an island girl?' Mr Young joined in. He had the same harsh mouth as his eldest son. His features reminded Susannah of a fox: all sharp eyes and pointy nose.

'You're the only girl from Vinalhaven apart from Mrs Matlock to have gone to college,' Rachel declared. 'That sure is something.'

'Mrs Matlock isn't a real islander,' Mr Young contradicted her. 'She came to Vinalhaven after. That woman had a privileged upbringing down south.'

Susannah really wished they'd change the conversation. She didn't like all this scrutiny.

'So, what you think you'll major in?' Mr Young asked her.

'History.'

The older man guffawed, his mouth full of food. 'Well, what's the good of history?' he said. 'I might have thought if you did nursing or law or such, might be of some value. But history?' He turned to Susannah's mother. 'Well, Judith, I can see why you were none too happy about her going off like that.'

Susannah was mortified at the idea her mother had been discussing her with Matthew's parents.

'Rosa, the gravy's gone cold.' He turned to his wife. 'Heat it up.'

'I am so sorry,' Rosa Young apologised, picking up the gravy boat.

'Please, it's quite delicious, Rosa, I don't find it too cold,' her mother said.

It felt like the longest Christmas dinner of Susannah's life. At last, the subject changed to rogue fishermen who'd been trying to muscle in on the islanders' lobster grounds.

'Those outsiders don't know who they're dealing with,' Silas said, a menacing note to his voice.

The conversation was dominated by the three men as they moved from fishing to hunting.

'Did you hear Mick Reed got shot in the leg, taking a crap in the woods?' Matthew told his father and brother, and the three men had a good laugh about the unfortunate Mick Reed. The women stayed silent, not even looking at each other. It felt so suppressed to Susannah, after all her free debating in the coffee houses of Harvard.

As Mrs Young served Christmas pudding well-soaked in brandy and cream, Silas cleared his throat.

'I've an announcement to make!' he said, standing up from the table and pulling Rachel Weaver with him, whose pale face was now streaked red with embarrassment. 'I've been working hard these past years, and got enough now to build my own house.' He looked directly at Susannah as if to say, *See what you're missing out on.* 'I've asked Rachel's father for her hand in marriage and he's said yes!'

Kate clapped her hands in delight, and Annie squealed with excitement. Everyone rushed forward with congratulations. Silas held his arm tightly around Rachel's shoulder as everyone crowded around them. There was a smile plastered on Rachel's face, but Susannah could see her eye twitching, and tears welling. She really didn't look ecstatic at all.

'You beat me to it!' Susannah heard Matthew tell his brother.

'Well, I am the eldest,' Silas said. 'I need to set the example.'

Rachel turned and whispered in Silas' ear. He gave her a look, nodded and released her. She scurried out of the room, clutching her stomach. She really did look very pale.

'Do you think Rachel's okay?' Susannah whispered to Kate.

'Yeah,' Kate said, looking solemn. 'I'll go check on her.'

Kate slipped out of the room while Mr Young poured everyone a celebratory whisky. But the two girls didn't come back. The men didn't seem to care, so intent were they on downing their bottle of Christmas whisky.

'Go see if those girls are okay,' Susannah's mother whispered to her, as she got up from the table to help Rosa Young and Annie with the dishes.

Susannah had no idea where the Youngs' bathroom was, but she could hear crying and followed the noise. Pushing the door open at the end of the corridor, she found Rachel kneeling over the toilet, crying loudly, while Kate was sitting on the side of the bath and holding her hair out of her face as she retched.

'Oh, sorry,' Susannah said, backing out of the room.

'Wait,' Kate said. 'Can you get her a glass of water?'

When Susannah had come back with the water, Rachel was sitting on the side of the bath next to Kate. Her sister had her arm around her friend. The girl had stopped crying, and her face was all red and blotchy.

'Are you okay, Rachel?' Susannah asked.

'She's fine,' Kate said.

But Rachel looked far from fine.

'What am I going to do, girls?' she whispered, her eyes wild with despair.

'You're going to do what you said before,' Kate said, her voice calm. 'You're going to marry Silas. He'll look after you.'

'But I don't love him,' Rachel said in an agonised whisper.

'Then don't marry him for pity's sake!' Susannah said, without thinking. 'He's a terrible drunk!'

'Shush, Susie, you don't understand,' Kate warned her. 'Rachel has to marry Silas. It's the right thing to do.'

'But why, if she doesn't like him…' Susannah's voice trailed off as she looked down at Rachel. The way she had her hand on the belly, and the very tiny but pronounced bump. 'Oh,' she said.

'We only did it the once,' Rachel told her, her voice passionate with defence. 'He took me up the granite slabs in his father's Buick and he had a bottle of liquor. I got a bit tipsy. Told him no, but then he called me frigid.' Rachel's voice shook. 'I didn't want him to think there was something wrong with me, so I let him.'

Susannah didn't know what to say to Rachel. Part of her wanted to tell her how stupid she was to fall for Silas' lines. She didn't, though, because another part of her felt very sorry for Rachel indeed. It could easily be Susannah herself sitting on the side of that bath, throwing up in the Youngs' toilet and facing a lifetime with Silas Young.

'It'll be okay,' Kate was consoling Rachel. 'When the baby comes, you'll be happy. You'll see.'

Susannah couldn't help glancing at her sister's stomach now, but it was as flat as ever.

'You're being careful aren't you, Katie?' Susannah turned to her sister.

'Yes, Matthew doesn't push me. He never has.'

At least that was something.

'But I think he'll propose soon,' she said, clutching Rachel's hand. 'And then we'll be like sisters,' she said to her friend.

Kate's words wounded Susannah, despite the fact they clearly cheered Rachel up. Even within two months, Susannah's place on Vinalhaven had completely shifted. She had somehow become an outsider. Rachel was even usurping her position as Kate's new sister. Susannah didn't know how to stop it, apart from give up on Harvard and stay – and there was no way she could do that. Not just because she had worked so hard to get there, but also because of Ava.

Chapter 18

Emer

5th August 2011

Emer and Lars had met at work – not on the ward or in surgery, but standing at the vending machine in the reception of the Mass Gen. She had been waiting for him to put his money in, pick an item, but all he seemed to do was stare at the rows of chips and chocolate bars.

'I can't decide what to get,' he commented, turning to her. She couldn't help but notice his eyes were the clearest blue she'd ever seen.

'This is all junk but sometimes it hits the spot.'

'I know,' he said. 'But I've lost my appetite. Bad morning.'

Emer knew not to ask further questions. They were in a hospital, after all. He slipped the quarter back into his pocket.

'Want to get some food in the canteen instead of this crap?' he said.

Just like that. They walked together into the hospital canteen, Emer in her nurse's pink scrubs, Lars in his surgeon's blue. Over lunch, Lars confided he'd lost his first patient that morning since qualifying as a heart surgeon. He hadn't expected it to hit him so hard.

'Sometimes shit just happens,' Emer said as she sipped her tea.

'So you don't believe everything happens for a reason?'

'Not when you work on a paediatric oncology ward.' She found she wanted to tell him about Orla. 'And when your sister is in the ward above fighting cancer.'

'Fuck!' Lars said. 'That's bad. How old is she?'

'Twenty-six.'

Emer told him Orla's story. Their journey with the chemo. All the positive vibes and healing energy she, Ethan and all their friends had surrounded Orla with. The raw juicing, and the Chinese medicine. The joy at the news of remission in the spring. The devastation at the return of the cancer the week before. He didn't feed her the usual platitudes, tell her Orla would pull through. Not when Emer explained how much the cancer had spread.

'I'm sorry,' he said to her. 'That is very tough for you.'

'She's all I've got.'

It became a ritual for Lars and Emer to share dinner together in the hospital canteen every night when they were both on shift. At first, they talked about Orla a lot, and work. But then the conversation broadened. Lars began to tell her a little about his family in Bergen, in Norway. How he'd come to America to study medicine and had never returned once he'd qualified.

'My father's American, my mother Norwegian,' he explained. 'They're divorced.'

Right from the first day, her attraction to him had been immediate. Even though she'd had no make-up on and was in her scrubs, she'd felt her whole being awaken in his presence. He had been up for twenty-four hours and had two days' growth on his chin, but in Emer's eyes he was the most gorgeous man she'd ever seen. If he ever touched her – a hand brushing hers as she passed the salt, their legs knocking together as they sat down at the canteen table, a reassuring hand on her shoulder when she opened up about Orla – the memory of the touch resonated throughout her body for hours. Thoughts of Lars filled her mind. Her desire for him. Her hope that he desired her. It was the only thing which distracted her from the horror of what was happening to her little sister, as Orla faded away before her eyes.

They had never even so much as kissed until she'd banged on his door in the middle of the night. Even then, Lars had tried to slow things down. Wanted her to talk to him, but her pain had been past words. She needed to lose herself in passion. It was the only way to blot out the heartache of what was happening.

'Shouldn't you be at the hospital?' he'd asked her, his hair standing on end, his eyes all sleepy.

'Please?' she'd asked him. 'Just hold me.'

Within his embrace, she had found the courage to kiss his lips, slip her hands inside his pyjama bottoms.

'Are you sure?' he whispered, no longer sleepy, but looking at her with intensity.

She had nodded, and that was how it had begun. She had drunk Lars in: no amount of kissing, caressing, love-making was enough to quench her thirst for him. All night long, their passion had bloomed beneath the covers of his bed. With Lars inside her, she was no longer lost and spinning in terror.

Chapter 19

Susannah

October 19th, 1959
Harvard, Cambridge

Dearest Katie,

Can you believe one whole year has passed since I first walked across Harvard Square on my first day at college? It feels like it was only yesterday, and yet so much has happened in this time. I am an entirely different person. I've even changed my hair since you saw me last at Christmas. Ava cut bangs into it. Not sure if they suit me, but she insists they make my eyes appear bigger.

How was your summer? Hope it got better. I was sorry to hear Matthew was sick, but good to hear he's on the mend now. Who would have thought you could get such a terrible disease from a tick? He was very lucky to have such a devoted nurse as you. I am sure you looked after him so well, as you look after Mother and me.

I know it was disappointing I didn't come home during the summer holidays, but Katie, how could I have turned the Whittards down? I couldn't believe it when they asked me to come with them to Oxford in *England!* And paid for everything! Professor Whittard had been invited to a conference with all these other top physicists and the whole family was going with him, apart from Gertrude. I asked her, didn't she want to go too? But she looked at me as if I had three heads! Told me she was getting her summer holidays with her boys back down in Philly. I felt bad then, Katie, because I'd actually forgotten Gertrude has two teenage sons. It feels like she and I are just part of the Whittard family now.

Did you receive all my letters from Oxford? I know the mail takes a long time from England to America, so some could still be on their way to you, or worse, lost over the Atlantic. I shall tell you everything when I see you next, but Oxford is the most magical place I have ever set foot in! I was in heaven to be part of so much history. The buildings are much older than Harvard's; some of them date back hundreds of years. They're not red brick as I imagined, but soft, honeyed stone, with latticed windows and small courtyards of green grass with colonnaded walkways called quads. They are what I think medieval monasteries might look like. Most of the students were away for the summer, but some still remained. You could tell who they were immediately as they cycled around Oxford city, their heads up in the clouds.

My duty was to mind Nathan and Joshua, but the boys were old enough for us to have great fun exploring the nooks of Oxford. We went to the Ashmolean Museum, after which Joshua became quite obsessed with Ancient Rome. And we went punting on the River Thames. Now, this is the kind of water activity you would like, Katie. On the river, you can see the banks on either side, and the current is gentle and the water shallow. Punting involves propelling a long rowing boat with a big stick, which Professor Whittard tried to do rather unsuccessfully. In the end, I had a go, and must admit I was a little better than he, much to the delight of the boys.

There is so much history in Oxford, Katie. Truly, it felt like every building I was taken to had been visited by a king or queen or someone of note. One evening the Whittards organised a babysitter, and took me out for a drink in an English pub! I had no idea what to drink so copied Mrs Whittard, who ordered a gin and tonic. It's very nice indeed with a slice of lemon. But what I want to tell you about this excursion is that the pub they brought me to was the one that C.S. Lewis and Tolkien drank in. Can you imagine? I could have been sitting on the same stool that the man who created Narnia sat on. Do you remember how much I loved those books when Mrs. Matlock got them in the library?

Wow, this is turning into a very long letter! I shall write again soon, but please send me news of how you are and what you're doing now you're no longer in school. I'd better race; going to be late for a lecture.

*

It had been a dream summer. The only downside of being in Oxford was that Susannah had missed Ava terribly. Ever since that unforgettable snowy Thanksgiving night, the two girls had spent nearly every free evening together. If not at Club 47, then hanging out in the coffee house where Ava now worked.

Until Susannah had gone to Oxford, she hadn't been able to put a name on what she and Ava were to each other. She knew it was something more than friendship, because of what had happened at night when the two of them shared a bed. But would she be just as aroused if a boy had touched her in the same way as Ava? Sometimes, in her chilly attic room in the eaves of the Whittards' house, she'd close her eyes and think again of Ava stroking her skin. Immediately, her heart rate would quicken, and she'd feel a softening between her legs. She'd pretend Ava was there and caress herself, unable to stop, although it was such a bad thing to do. Ava had done something to her. Freed a part of her that had been captive. As if she had been a bird locked in a room, and her new friend had opened the window, let her fly free. She wanted to experience the sensation again, and again.

In England, despite being entranced by Oxford, steeped in so many centuries of history, it had still not been enough to ease the sheer physical sensation of missing Ava. She worried all the time that when she got back, Ava would have found a new best friend to hang out with. But when she had stepped into the coffee house on the first night of her return, she had been greeted by a loud squeal of delight as Ava almost dropped her coffee pot in her rush to hug her. Susannah had spent the whole night sitting in a booth being fed coffee and cherry pie by Ava, who was giddy with joy to see her. By the time they'd got back to Ava's room, Susannah's head had been spinning, and her body buzzing from all the coffee and cigarettes.

'Stay here,' Ava begged her. 'Just tonight.'

'What about your roommate?'

'Take a look! She's gone. I have my own room now,' Ava said, sweeping her arms wide. The second little bed had disappeared and in its place was one slightly bigger bed.

'But you're not allowed visitors,' Susannah protested weakly, smiling all the while as Ava took her hand and slowly spun her around the room.

'We'll be quiet. Besides you're a girl. They just don't allow boys,' Ava said happily.

'The Whittards will worry.'

Ava wagged her finger at her. 'Call them. Tell them your friend is sick. You're staying over to look after her.'

'Now, that's a lie,' Susannah said, shaking her head at her in mock disapproval.

'It's not. I am sick,' Ava said, her face suddenly serious. 'I've been lovesick the whole long damned summer.'

Her declaration swept through Susannah like a hot wind. Ava hooked her boldly with her eye. She was challenging her. It was as if she was saying, *Leave now if you won't acknowledge what we have.* But Susannah understood, because of what had happened one evening in Oxford.

The Whittards had held a dinner party and Susannah's job had been to help the hired cook, Clara, and serve the guests at table.

'I know it's not what you usually do, but you don't mind, darling, do you?' Mrs Whittard had asked her.

Mrs Whittard had taken to calling her 'darling' recently (mostly after her third martini), and saying Susannah was like the daughter she'd always wanted. It was silly, but her words meant a lot to Susannah, seeing as her own mother still never wrote.

Dinner had been preceded by cocktails, and Susannah had circled the room with a tray of Manhattans mixed by Professor Whittard. There were six other guests: two male physicists and their wives, one couple from France, and one from Italy; and two English women, both of them academics at Oxford – Milly Agnew, a physicist, and Jocelyn Hartley, an English literature professor and published poet. Mrs Whittard had already whispered to Susannah that the women had a *special* relationship.

'They're eccentric, you know, very English,' Mrs Whittard had said to her before the guests arrived, as Susannah helped style her hair – rather uselessly, but she guessed the point was Mrs Whittard wanted someone to gossip to. 'Peter says they're a marriage in all but name. Been together years, it seems. Imagine,

Susannah!' Mrs Whittard's eyes were incredulous in the mirror. 'No children of course, but apparently they have three dogs and four cats. Very eccentric!'

'Have you read any of her poetry?'

'Jocelyn's? Oh no, not really my thing, darling. But I've heard she's very good,' Mrs Whittard said, lighting a cigarette and offering Susannah one. 'But you mustn't stare at them now, will you? We have to be open-minded and all that, as Peter says. But I guess it is a little odd, unnatural. What woman doesn't want children?'

Susannah bit her tongue. *Me*, she wanted to confide in Mrs Whittard. *Would you still call me the daughter you always wanted if I told you that?* Susannah had always known she didn't want children, even before she'd ever even thought she might not be attracted to men. Ava felt the same way. But they lived in a society which considered them not to be real women if they didn't want to have babies. Susannah knew that not wanting children was nothing to do with her loving women. It was something else. The need to mother was not one she possessed. She felt indignant she should be judged for how she felt.

While Susannah served the cocktails, she tried her best not to stare, but she was entranced by Milly and Jocelyn. The fluidity of their movements: one lighting the other's cigarette without even having to ask. To Susannah's eyes, the two women seemed so much more united than the other couples. Mrs Whittard drank too much before dinner and got a little loud, which embarrassed the professor somewhat, especially when she asked the French professor to explain to her again what astrophysics actually was 'because Peter could never get her to understand'. In response to this, the French wife began to flirt with Professor Whittard. As for the Italian couple, they were having their own personal argument all the way through dinner, as they broke out in Italian along with wild gestures every now and again. It seemed to Susannah it was Milly and Jocelyn who kept the dinner party together and on an even keel.

'So, Professor,' Jocelyn said as they were drinking their coffee. 'Who do you think will land a man on the moon first? Russia or America?'

'Well, I have to say the States of course.' The professor looked relieved to escape the flirtations of the French wife.

'I've heard they've already been doing many of the tests with female pilots,' Milly said.

Susannah pricked up her ears. This was information Ava would be very interested in.

'Yes. Apparently women are better suited to space travel. We have more stamina.' Jocelyn finished Milly's sentence smoothly for her and Susannah noticed the two women clasping hands beneath the table.

'Yes, it's true,' Professor Whittard said. 'I know about the tests. It's all happening out in New Mexico. But I'm afraid to say, ladies, it will definitely be a man who sets foot first upon the moon.'

After the dinner party was over, Susannah helped Clara clean up and wash all the dishes. She carried the trash out to the bins at the back of their rental house in Oxford. It was at that precise moment she saw Jocelyn and Milly departing for home. Milly opened the passenger side door of their car for Jocelyn, and bent down to kiss her on the lips as she got in. When Milly got into the driver's seat, Jocelyn leaned over and kissed Milly back. Susannah watched the two women kissing in their car for a long, thrilling moment before they separated and drove off.

She walked back into the kitchen, liberated. Almost felt like taking Clara the cook's wet hands and dancing round the kitchen with her. At last, she understood who she was. She'd always known she was different, had found out Ava was different too – but they weren't alone.

*

Her first night back at Harvard, Susannah told Ava about Milly and Jocelyn as they lay side by side in Ava's bed.

'You watched them kissing? But for how long?' Ava teased her.

'They looked so happy, Ava.'

'As happy as us?' Ava kissed her gently on the lips.

'They couldn't possibly be,' Susannah whispered as she kissed Ava back. 'As right now, I must be the happiest girl alive.'

That night, Ava became a part of her, as Susannah stroked her gently, listening for the slightest change in Ava's breath, releasing and pressing, spinning her fingers into the softest parts of her. Surely nothing in nature was as beautiful as her darling Ava, or as perfect? The two girls barely slept, their love-making sustaining them all night long. In the morning, they lay spent, looking into each other's eyes.

'Have you ever loved another woman before?' Ava asked Susannah.

She shook her head. 'No, you're the first. How about you?'

Ava gazed into her eyes. 'I've slept with one other woman, in my first week at college, but I never felt about her how I feel about you.'

Susannah felt a twinge of jealousy. Of course, she'd known deep down there must have been someone before her. Ava had known what she was doing from the moment, they'd first kissed.

'I thought I was doing something I shouldn't, before, with her,' Ava said. 'But when we were together first, it felt so right. How can that be wrong?'

'I know,' Susannah agreed, holding tight onto Ava.

'Let's be like Milly and Jocelyn,' Ava whispered to her. 'Let's have a secret marriage!'

'Are you serious?' Susannah's heart was in her mouth at the thought of it.

'I've never been more serious in my whole life.' Ava looked at her with stern eyes.

Susannah held Ava in her arms, feeling the beat of her heart against her chest, wrapping her legs around hers. How they fit together, as if designed for it. Ava needed to know she was serious too.

'I promise nothing, no one, will ever make me give you up,' Susannah swore.

Later, the two girls went walking. Through their beloved Harvard, and on. They walked down the leafy streets of academics to the furthest edges of Cambridge, before jumping on a bus, leaving Boston city to enter the family suburb of Newton. Long, wide streets with house after house even larger and grander than the Whittards' place. They got off the bus, continued to walk. There was no one else on the streets apart from the odd kid on their way back from school, yellow school buses trundling by. Pumpkins were already piled high on doorsteps, ready for Halloween.

Every few blocks, they came across a church. But none of them were right. Too big and grand. Too masculine. Finally, in a small park, they both stopped walking at the same time. Before them was a weeping beech tree split open, its boughs cascading glossy green leaves on either side. They could actually walk inside the tree, so they were hidden from anyone walking by. It was perfect.

Inside the hidden sanctuary of the weeping beech, they took their vows to love each other until the day they died.

Chapter 20

Emer

26th October 2011

Here he was. Right before her in Vinalhaven, the sun setting behind him, taller and more beautiful than she remembered him. She didn't need to ask Lars why he was there. She had become his compass as much as he was hers. She ran to him, and he took her in his arms, kissing the top of her head. Her cheeks were wet with tears.

'I thought I'd lost you,' he was saying. 'Oh Emer, my darling.'

They pulled away, and Emer felt herself colouring. She had publicly embraced a man in the main street in Vinalhaven. Had anyone seen her? Lars didn't care, clearly, for he took her hand and led her back along the street – but she tugged away.

'I can't,' she said. 'I have to be somewhere.'

'You're all dressed up!' he said, looking at her outfit. 'You look beautiful.'

She blushed. 'I'm sorry, Lars, that's why I have to go.'

For a moment, she thought of inviting Lars to go with her but then would it look like she was on a date with Henry? Instinct told her to keep the men apart.

'Let's just talk,' Lars tried to persuade her.

'I'm late already,' she protested. At this very moment, Henry was probably ordering her a beer.

'Please, we can't talk out here on the street. Just come to my room for a minute.' He took her hand again in his. It felt so good to feel his fingers around hers. The warmth and safety of his grasp.

'Okay,' she heard herself saying to Lars. 'For a little while.'

He led her to the inn on the harbour, then up the stairs, his hands trembling as he opened the door. All thoughts of Henry and The Sand Bar were gone as they tumbled into the room, kissing. Lars pulled back and gazed at her.

'My god, you're stunning,' he gasped as she took off her jacket. 'Where did you get the dress?'

Emer didn't have time to answer as he began kissing her again, while helping her unbutton Kate's organza gown.

Their synergy was effortless as they came together. How could she stop herself from succumbing to what felt most natural, most right? Lars unlocked her body, which had felt so cold and unloved, encased within her tomb of grief. Both of them naked, they made love on top of the bed in the inn, not even bothering to get under the covers. As Lars kissed her lips, her throat, her breasts and belly, each part of her awakened, and gave back. It had never been like this with anyone else in her life. She had wondered after their first time if she had imagined how connected she and Lars had been physically, but now she knew it was as if her body had been made for his. The sensations were beyond anything physical: it was her mind which was opening with pure rapture. He brought her to the edge, and for the few minutes they were united, guilt, responsibility, everything was abandoned to bathe in pure, erotic love.

It was only afterwards as she lay in Lars' arms, snug under the covers now, that Emer remembered Henry. She slipped out of bed and rummaged around for her purse. Found her phone. Henry had sent one text.

I guess you're not coming. Shame.

She felt a little irritated by it. How did he know something hadn't happened with Susannah? But then she had stood the poor man up. Her feelings for Lars had made her selfish yet again.

As she watched the love of her life sleeping, it all came back to her. How her need for Lars had taken precedence over Orla's need for her. In the end, she'd let everyone down. Even Lars, by bringing him into the whole mess.

She began to get dressed.

'Where are you going?' Lars asked her as he woke up, stretching his arms above his head.

'I have to get back to Susannah.'

'Is that the name of the lady you're looking after?' Lars asked her, leaning up on one elbow. God, he looked so gorgeous, it was all she could do not to get back into bed with him.

'Yes, I can't risk falling asleep here; she might need help overnight.' She put on her jacket, zipped it up.

'Emer, what are you doing here?' Lars said, sitting up completely. 'This is crazy. Come back with me tomorrow. We'll find a replacement nurse for Susannah.'

She shook her head. 'I can't go back to Boston, Lars.'

Lars climbed out of bed, wrapped the sheet around his waist. 'Then we'll go somewhere else,' he said, holding her shoulders and looking into her eyes. 'Anywhere, as long as we're together.'

'We don't deserve to be together,' she said in a small voice.

Lars gave her a long, considered look.

'Do you think Orla would want you to be unhappy, Emer?'

'Stop,' she said, pressing her fingers to her forehead as if she had a pain in her head.

'You need to let it go. It's not your fault.'

She pulled away from him. If she was too near to him, she'd want to make love, and then they would be back to the beginning of the end all over again.

'I'm existing, Lars, but it feels as if I'm not alive. From the moment my phone rang in your place that morning, what we had was destroyed.'

'You've got to stop thinking like that, Emer. It's not true.'

He came over, squatted down next to her chair. The scent of him consumed her and it was all she could do not to disintegrate into his embrace again. 'I'm sorry,' she whispered, 'but you need to leave the island. It's over.' She looked away, unable to bear the desperate look in his eyes.

'Emer, don't do this. We belong together,' he said, reaching out to touch her.

She stood up abruptly, brushing his hand away with her body. 'I don't know if that's true any more,' she said, her voice shaking with emotion.

Grabbing her purse, she legged it out of the room before he could say something else. This was how it felt to have your heart broken. As she ran down the stairs of the inn and out of the door, up the road towards Susannah's, she was in agony.

Even so, she would choose to have her heart broken again and again, if she were allowed just five more minutes with Orla.

Chapter 21

Susannah

February 15th, 1960
Harvard, Cambridge

Dearest Katie,

I have big news! It's why you haven't heard from me in over a month. Ava and I are renting our own apartment! It all happened pretty suddenly. Professor Whittard and his family are moving to Florida because he's been asked to work with NASA, the National American Space Agency. Have you heard all about that? We're racing against Russia to get the first man on the moon, and my Professor Whittard is part of it all! Imagine, maybe in the future we'll be able to take holidays to the moon – although by all accounts it's a dark, cold place with lots of rocks and craters. The Whittards told me I was welcome to go with them to Florida, but of course I'm still at Harvard so couldn't accept. I was devastated at first. Having to start all over, looking for a new family to lodge with – but then Ava suggested we get a place together. Said there was a job going in the coffee house where she works in the evenings, so I could pay for my share of the rent.

Before I knew it we were going to look at places, and everything lined up so perfectly because we found the dearest apartment not far from Harvard Square. It's small, but we love it. Up on the fifth floor, lots of stairs, but our view is wonderful: treetops and old historic university buildings. You must come visit. Oh do, please, Katie. I could show you where I go to my lectures, and all the best places. You would get to meet Ava and all our friends. We'd bring you to Club 47, and you could wear your flock organza!

It was sad saying goodbye to the Whittards. I have grown very fond of the family, especially the boys. But even sadder was saying goodbye to Gertrude. She was very upset, because where they will be in Florida is so much further away from Philadelphia, where her boys are. And she needs the work. She can't just walk out because it would be so difficult for her to get a new position. Life just isn't fair for some people, Katie. America is supposed to be a free country, but things are not equal. I feel quite stirred up about it sometimes.

I can't believe Rachel is pregnant again! Please give her my regards when you speak to her. It's so kind of you to help her out with her baby. I can't think of anything I would less like to do. You mustn't be jealous of her, Katie. My goodness, no. She must be so worn out and tired. Remember she didn't even want to marry Silas? So don't get carried away now. I know you're frustrated Matthew hasn't proposed yet, but you're so young, and there's plenty of time to think of settling down.

We have a pool table in one of the bars Ava and I go to, and it always makes me think of you and Mom at the lace stand, making the nets for the balls. Have you thought any more about dressmaking? I do believe you have inherited this talent from Mom. Can I suggest the fact Matthew hasn't proposed yet is a sign to move on?

I am sure there are plenty of gorgeous young men who would snap you up if you were available. Really think about it, Katie, before you push Matthew further. Do you really want to be a lobster fisherman's wife in Vinalhaven for your whole life? Take a good look at Rachel's situation. Do you really want what she has? There is a big world out here!

I'm due on shift now, so I shall post this letter on the way to the coffee shop. Write back soon.

*

Susannah brewed the coffee on top of their little stove. Early morning was the best time of day. The late winter sunlight cascaded through the window, dappling the wooden floorboards with shadows of new leaves and branches from the trees. Outside, the city was all fresh and new for another day. The sidewalks damp from night-time rain, the air busy with the sounds of people on their way to work or school or college. After the stillness of the dark, the motion of first light always infused Susannah with an appreciation of all she had. And she felt rich right now. Maybe not in dollars – they were both working every hour they could between studies to meet the rent. But Susannah had learnt a new lesson with Ava. Being wealthy wasn't the only thing that could make you happy. Many times, she'd believed her mother's misery was due to the fact they'd been so poor. Always struggling. She'd listened to her mother's daily moans about how hard it was to be a widow. It was unkind of her to criticise her mom, but she saw now that if only her mother had chosen to see what they did have, then they might all have been happier. And perhaps Kate wouldn't be imprisoned with her now.

Ava had been awake for a little while when Susannah brought in her coffee. She was sitting up in bed, writing a college paper, in her black silk pyjamas. The top button had undone and Susannah could see one of her breasts. She ached to get back into bed with Ava, but she knew her paper was due that afternoon and she mustn't distract her. Besides, she had a lecture herself in an hour.

The two girls lived in blissful harmony. Their domestic chores were seamlessly shared. Ava did most of the cooking, and Susannah visited the laundromat once a week with their washing. They shared the cleaning between the two of them, which wasn't much, as the place was so tiny. But it was theirs! They were living like Milly and Jocelyn back in Oxford, England, although of course none of their friends knew about the nature of their relationship. Twice, after sharing a bottle of wine, Susannah had been tempted to kiss Ava in public. Let the whole world know, because she didn't care what they thought – but Ava had counselled her not to.

'You have no idea how prejudiced people can be,' she told her. 'Believe me, I've experienced enough of it already.'

One night, not long after they'd moved in, Ava told Susannah she'd grown up on an American Indian reservation in the Puget Sound.

'You're a Red Indian?' Susannah had declared in astonishment. She hadn't even considered that might be why Ava had slightly darker skin than her. Her assumption had been that maybe there was some Hispanic blood in Ava's family, going back some way. To be honest, she hadn't really thought about it much. Ava was Ava, pure and simple. She didn't need to label her. But clearly it was important to Ava.

'Honey, calling me a Red Indian is not something I like.'

'Sorry.' Susannah instantly felt terrible. 'But how did you get to be here at Harvard?'

'With a lot of grit,' Ava replied. 'It was one of the reasons I was so attracted to you, you know. I could see you were poor, too. That you'd had to fight to be here.'

'My mom still won't ask me about Harvard whenever I see her, although Katie keeps telling me she is proud really.'

'No one leaves the reservation,' Ava said. 'That's what we're told, right from the start at school. Don't even think about going to college. But all I could think was: no way will I believe that, I'm going!'

They shared childhood stories and discovered they had both felt they didn't belong where they grew up.

'I love my family,' Ava said, 'but it's so broken. I can't be there, else it makes me feel trapped.'

'Never felt like I belonged on Vinalhaven,' Susannah confided in her. 'I was guilty all the time because I hated it. It was like a prison to me.'

'We'll we're here now, together.' Ava kissed her cheek.

'So we are.' Susannah kissed Ava back.

Chapter 22

Susannah

March 1960

As Susannah saw Kate on the harbour waving to her as the boat pulled in, she decided she would convince her sister to come back with her to Cambridge for a couple of weeks. The semester was nearly over, and Katie's only work was helping out their mother with her lacing and netting orders. Surely she could be spared? Her sister had never left Vinalhaven, apart from to take the boat to Rockland and back. She was nearly twenty. It was time.

The first hour at home was glorious. The two sisters lay on the new quilt Kate had made, sharing stories about their lives. Kate filled Susannah in on island gossip, while Susannah told her more about the coffee house and friends she and Ava had at Harvard.

'Will you come back with me for a visit, Katie?' she asked her sister.

'Oh.' Kate looked taken aback. 'I don't think we could afford it.'

'I have some money saved from my job,' Susannah said proudly. 'I can buy you a ticket.'

'Well, I don't know about Mother...' Kate began, looking uncomfortable.

'Please come back with me, Katie. I want you to meet Ava.'

They were unable to continue their conversation, as their mother called from downstairs that Matthew had arrived for his dinner.

'Why's he eating here?' Susannah said to Kate, as she followed her down the stairs.

'He's says it's too full at home, what with Silas, Rachel and the baby.'

'I thought Silas was building his own house,' Susannah said, unable to conceal her sarcastic tone.

The tension between Susannah and Matthew was palpable at the dinner table. He had put on weight since she'd last seen him, and his skin was more weathered from the sea. The whole meal, Susannah bristled with indignation that he didn't even thank their mother for the plate of stew, nor Kate for pouring him a glass of beer. Kate was all jittery, serving him like he was a king or something. Why couldn't Kate see that Matthew Young wasn't good for her?

'The coffee's cold, Kate,' Matthew snapped at her sister, as he took a sip from the cup she'd handed him. He was sitting in their father's old armchair. His tone of voice reminded Susannah of the way Mr Young had spoken to his wife two Christmases ago.

'Don't be so rude to my sister,' Susannah told him off.

'Oh, I'm sorry, Katie,' he said, his tone laced with insincerity as he looked at Susannah with loathing.

'Matthew's very good to us; how dare you criticise him?' their mother berated Susannah.

'But he was snapping at Katie for his coffee being cold!' Susannah protested.

'Quite right,' their mom said to Susannah. 'It *was* cold!' She turned to Matthew. 'I am so sorry for Susannah's *cheek*.' She turned to Kate. 'Brew another pot, dear, for Matthew.'

Matthew gave Susannah a triumphant smile. Their mom was completely taken in by him.

Susannah couldn't help but narrow her eyes at Matthew as the air sizzled with antagonism between them.

'We're so happy you're home for once,' Matthew said, his words not matching the hostility of his gaze. Kate came to sit on the arm of the chair, while Matthew put a proprietorial hand on her knee. 'We've been waiting to tell you our good news,' he continued.

Susannah felt her chest constrict with dread. She looked over at Kate, but her sister had a big smile on her face and truly looked delighted.

'Judith,' Matthew said, turning to their mother with mock deference. 'I've asked Kate to be my wife and she's accepted my proposal. I do hope you will give us your blessing.'

Their mother cried out in delight. 'But of course, Matthew!' she replied, a rare smile on her face. 'I've been hoping for this day for a long time.'

Kate leapt up from the chair and hugged her mother. 'I'm overjoyed, so excited!' she said, turning to Susannah. 'We've been waiting and waiting for you to come home so we could announce it. At last, my dream wedding!'

Susannah felt sick to her stomach. How could she not pretend to be happy for her sister's sake? But there was a part of her that believed Matthew had stored up this moment as some sort of revenge for all the times she'd tried to convince her sister to break up with him.

'Congratulations,' she said to the happy couple, knowing her voice sounded flat.

Matthew got up and took Kate in his arms, planting a kiss on her cheek. 'It's about time we started a family,' he said to her and her mother. 'How do you feel about grandchildren, Judith?'

'You must both live here,' their mother insisted. 'There'll be no room for you and your children in your parents' place.'

'Hold your horses,' Susannah tried to counsel her mother. 'Katie's not even expecting yet. They're not even married.'

But her mother ignored her, as caught up as Kate in the excitement and romance of wedding plans.

Later that night, as the two sisters lay in bed, Kate chattered on about how she was going to make her wedding dress stunning, with intricate lacing on its cuffs and hems.

'It will be the best dress I've ever made, Susie,' she declared.

Susannah felt sick to her belly. How could she persuade her sister she was making the biggest mistake of her life? She felt it to the very core of her being.

'We want to get married in May,' Kate said. 'That's the best time of year on the island for a wedding.'

'So soon?' Susannah questioned her.

'I've waited long enough, don't you think?' Kate replied hotly.

'Are you really sure, Katie?' Susannah pushed. 'You've never left Vinalhaven, never seen anywhere off the island. Don't you want to go places? Meet other people?'

'I love him, Susie!' Kate exclaimed. 'And he loves me. I don't need anything else. I want to live in this house all my life and I want to raise my children here.'

Susannah had to admit, she had never heard her sister so sure about anything before. Even so, the thought of seeing Kate marry that bully made her feel sick. She couldn't stop thinking about it on her journey back to Cambridge. How could she get Kate to change her mind?

'You have to let it go,' Ava advised, as soon as Susannah confided in her back in Cambridge. They were on shift together in the coffee house.

'She could do so much better, Ava,' Susannah said, as she sliced up the cherry pie and placed it on display on the counter.

'But you can't control your little sister any more than she can control you,' Ava said. 'What would you do if she advised you not to live with me?'

'That's different!'

'Not so much,' Ava said, as she cleaned the tables. 'All you can hope is he turns out nicer. They want kids, right? Being a dad can really change a man.'

Susannah appreciated Ava helping her see the best of it, but her gut was telling her Matthew Young wasn't good for her sister. She dreaded the wedding.

'Say, would you come with me?'

Ava stopped her cleaning. Looked at her in astonishment. 'To your sister's wedding?'

'Yes. I want to show you where I grew up,' Susannah said. 'And I want you to meet Katie. My mom too, I guess.'

'Are you sure it's a good idea?' Ava said, looking wary.

'No one will know,' Susannah said in a low voice. 'They'll never guess.'

'Okay,' Ava said slowly. 'I'd like that.'

Relief washed over Susannah. If Ava was by her side, then maybe she could endure her sister's wedding to a man unworthy of Kate's love.

Chapter 23

Emer

27th October 2011

Emer was woken by Susannah's thin cry. She immediately leapt out of bed and raced down the corridor into Susannah's bedroom. But the bed was empty. She found Susannah on the floor of the bathroom.

'It's okay,' she said as she helped Susannah to her feet.

The older woman was trembling all over. 'I don't know what happened,' she said in a weak voice. 'I never fell just like that before.'

'You're all right,' Emer said, checking her over. 'Nothing broken. Want me to help you back to bed, or in the bathroom?'

'I'm done,' Susannah said. 'Bed.'

'Why didn't you ring your bell?' Emer gently cajoled Susannah as she tucked her back into bed. 'I would have helped you get up.'

'But I was fine yesterday.' Susannah looked at her with a shocked face. 'I was strong enough. I… must have slipped or something.'

Morning light was filtering through the drapes in Susannah's bedroom. Emer glanced at her clock and saw to her surprise it was nearly nine o'clock. She'd completely overslept.

'Shall I get your breakfast for you?'

Susannah's face creased. 'Not hungry.'

'Are you in pain?'

Susannah grimaced, shook her head. 'Not too bad.'

Emer could tell she was lying.

'Make me one of those herbal teas, will you? And when you get back you can tell me all about your night out.'

Emer winced. She still hadn't replied to Henry's text. She had no idea how to explain to him what had happened last night.

In the kitchen, Emer brewed a pot of slippery elm tea for Susannah and made a coffee for herself. Although she hadn't been drinking last night, her head felt fuggy and confused. She couldn't help thinking about Lars and glanced up at the clock. There was a ferry leaving just about now. Was he on it? Her body still hummed from his touch. For a moment, she felt angry at him. How dare he come here and rip her heart open again? She had just, only just, managed to regain some kind of relief, within the daily calm of helping Susannah type up the letters from Kate and going for walks with Henry. She doubted now she'd ever get to see Henry's 'top two spots' in Vinalhaven. Lars had come storming into her new equilibrium and turned it upside down all over again.

Emer brought the tea to Susannah, who sipped it gingerly. The first time Emer had given it to her, she'd declared it disgusting, but after a bit more encouragement she'd admitted it made her feel better.

'And at least it's natural, doesn't make me dozy.'

The tea was something Ethan had discovered for Orla. One of the many remedies they'd tried to cure her cancer. It hadn't worked, but Emer still believed it had helped her sister with pain management and energy levels.

'I was thinking,' Susannah said. 'Now the mornings are darker, it's a bit gloomy and cold in my study downstairs. Shall we type the letters up here?'

'Sure,' Emer said, surprised by Susannah's suggestion. She was always so keen to get up in the morning and dress – had snapped many times, when Emer had suggested a longer lie-in, that she had plenty of time to rest when she was dead.

'We're nearly there,' Susannah said, 'aren't we?'

'Yes, I think there's only three or four letters left,' Emer said, thinking of the stack inside the quilt on her bed. She still had to tell Susannah about them, but she kept putting it off. Most likely, Susannah would ask her if she'd read them, and Emer knew she wouldn't be able to lie. She was ashamed for prying without permission, despite the fact Susannah was openly showing her the letters Kate had sent her. She'd tell her soon, she promised herself, as she cleared away the breakfast things.

After Emer had taken the tray downstairs, she came back up with the last few letters and her laptop. They worked for an hour. Susannah's dictation seemed to be faster than usual. Emer could hear a breathlessness, and a new weakness to the quality of her voice. Still, Emer was fascinated at hearing Kate's voice through her sister. Kate was describing preparations for her wedding – great details all about the dress she was making.

'Are there no letters after Kate got married?' Emer asked Susannah.

The older woman shook her head. 'No, she got too busy with being a wife,' she said crisply and looked away, clearly not wanting to talk any further.

At ten o'clock, as was usual most days, Rebecca called on the phone. Afterwards, Susannah was excited.

'She's coming home,' she told Emer, her eyes shining with delight. 'I'll see my girl again!'

Emer couldn't help feeling sorry for Lynsey, whom Susannah had never referred to as 'her girl'. She knew exactly how it felt to be the least popular one.

'I'll get up now,' Susannah said, with new gusto. The call with Rebecca had clearly given her fresh energy.

*

Emer had just settled Susannah downstairs in the front room by the woodstove when she heard a knock on the door.

'Well, I don't know who that could be,' Susannah said, a puzzled look on her face.

'I'll go see,' Emer said.

She already had a suspicion, which was confirmed when she opened the door. Lars was standing on the threshold. Her heart skipped a beat to see him again. It was all she could do not to fall into his arms.

'I found you, again,' he said, looking at her with serious eyes. 'Can I come in?'

'Who is it?' Susannah called from the front room.

'I'm at work,' Emer whispered to Lars. 'How did you find me?'

'Well, that was easy,' he said. 'I just asked in the local store and they told me who the new Irish nurse was working for and where she lived.'

'Please, Lars, I don't know what to say any more.'

'Emer, I can't just leave, not after last night,' Lars said desperately. 'We need to talk.'

She bit her lip, sensing a lump in her throat. 'Please, Lars, please don't push me.'

'Well, now. Who are you?' Susannah stood behind her in the hall. Emer felt herself freeze. She couldn't send Lars away now.

'It's a friend of mine. From Boston. Lars.'

Susannah looked at her and then at Lars. 'Well invite him in, won't you?'

'Pleased to meet you, ma'am,' Lars said to Susannah, as she waved him into the kitchen.

'It's nice to have visitors,' she said, sitting heavily at the kitchen table. 'Lars is your name, did you say? Norwegian?'

'Yes, my mother's from Norway.'

'Always wanted to go there,' Susannah said.

'Well to be honest, this island looks just like the island my mother is from in Western Norway. Really, I could be back home.'

'You don't say?' Susannah said.

What was happening? Lars was charming Susannah just as he had charmed Orla, and Emer's stepmother, and everyone he ever met in her life. Emer put on the coffee, still not sure what to say.

'Well now, Emer never told me you were visiting, else I'd have got her to get some cookies from the store.'

'Lars can't stay,' Emer said quickly. 'He's taking the next ferry.'

'Is that so?' Susannah said, looking surprised. 'But he only just arrived!'

'I came yesterday,' Lars explained. 'I just wanted to see if Emer was okay.'

Susannah cocked her head on one side.

'It's been tough for her, since her sister Orla died,' Lars continued.

Susannah jerked in her seat, and Emer could feel her eyes on her. Blazing into her. No one spoke for a moment. The silence in the room was heavy and weighted with questions.

'Well, I guess I'll let you young folk chat then,' Susannah said, standing up.

'Can I help you?' Emer said, but Susannah batted her away.

'I'm quite able to walk myself,' she said, and Emer detected a sting in her voice. She was hurt. Of course. Emer had lied to her about Orla.

As soon as Susannah was gone, Lars leaned across the kitchen table and grabbed both Emer's hands in his. 'Please, Em, please promise me you'll come back to me.'

'I can't leave Susannah; you've seen how sick she is.'

'It's not good for you to be here. She needs someone who can take care of her with none of your history. It's bad for you, and probably not so good for her, either.'

'That's not true,' Emer argued. 'I let down Orla, but I'm not going to let Susannah down. I'm staying.' She couldn't explain it to Lars, but she also felt she needed to work out what had happened to Kate.

They stared at each other across the table. Emer absorbed every tiny detail of his face. Although she would never forget him, because he was always with her in her dreams at night.

'You know that's bullshit, Emer. You're scared, I get it. But not everyone has what we have. Why would you let it all go?'

He didn't understand, and Emer sensed that no matter how many times she tried to explain it to him, he never would.

'I have to get back to Boston, the hospital,' he said, making for the door. 'But I'm here for you, Emer. All you have to do is call me.'

After he had left, she let herself cry. She imagined him waiting for her on the ferry until the last minute before it departed. The disappointment when she didn't come running down the hill with her bag, hair flying, her heart open and ready to receive his love. She couldn't do it.

Everyone leaves.

Orla had said it to her once, after their mam had died. *You love with all your heart, and then they leave you.* Mammy, Orla. Emer couldn't fall into her love for Lars because if he left her too, forever, it would destroy her, and she'd never get back up. At least now, she was clinging on by a thread. Susannah, an old dying lady, was her lifeline.

The thought of Susannah roused her from the kitchen table. She had to shake off her self-pity. Explain to Susannah about Orla. And the letters.

Susannah wasn't in the front room, nor was she up the stairs in her own bedroom. Emer heard footsteps on the floorboards. Susannah was above her, up in the eaves of the house, in Emer's bedroom.

'I'm so sorry about that,' Emer apologised, rushing up into the bedroom.

Susannah was standing at the window, staring out at the golden trees.

'No need to apologise for your visitor,' she said stiffly. 'I just wanted to look at the view from up here again.' She turned and looked at Emer coolly. 'This was our bedroom, mine and Kate's.'

Emer took a breath. 'I'm sorry I didn't tell you about Orla,' she said, her voice trembling.

Susannah frowned at her. 'Yes, why did you do that?'

'It's just it's so raw for me,' Emer said, fighting back the tears. 'She only just died last month. It's very hard to accept.'

'I understand,' Susannah said, her gaze softening as she put a chill hand on her arm. Emer could feel the bones in her thin fingers. 'Really, I do.'

Emer felt overwhelmed by the older woman's kindness. She hadn't been expecting it. 'I need to show you something I found,' she said, going towards the bed and picking up the quilt.

Susannah frowned at her, looking puzzled.

'Let me show you,' Emer said, finding the hole and pushing her hand inside the quilt until she grabbed hold of the letters. She began to pull them out, one by one.

Susannah gasped as she recognised her own handwriting. 'She must have been hiding them from *him*,' she whispered to herself. 'He wanted to read everything I sent her.'

Emer couldn't imagine how awful it would be to have to hide your sister's letters from your husband.

'Oh, Katie.' Susannah's voice broke as she took the letters from Emer.

'Would you like me to read them to you?' Emer offered.

'Have you read them already?' The older woman looked at her, and Emer felt herself colouring.

'Yes, I'm sorry. I didn't mean to, but I just couldn't help it.'

Susannah clutched the letters to her chest, and gave Emer a piercing look. 'Then I guess all our secrets are out tonight,' she said.

Chapter 24

Susannah

May 1960

It took Susannah a moment to figure out where she was. The bed was harder than normal, the sheets stiff, and there it was – the familiar scent of soap and salt. She was home again. Back on Vinalhaven, in her mother's house. They'd only arrived last night and already she ached to run away. She rolled over in her bed and looked at Ava, asleep in her sister's bed beneath the pink and blue quilt. Kate was sharing their mother's bed until tonight, when she and Matthew would be moving into the front room downstairs. While Ava had been upstairs last night, freshening up in the bathroom soon after they'd arrived, Kate had shown Susannah the newly decorated room.

'We've got new drapes, do you like them? I think the yellow is so sunny, and the room gets the morning light. And Matthew's father gave us the bed.'

Susannah sat down on the iron bedstead. She really didn't like the thought of Matthew living in her old house with her mother and her sister, but what could she do about it? She had left, with no intention of returning.

'I think it's so great of him to move in with Mom,' Kate said cheerfully. 'It means I don't have to worry about her on her own, all the way out here.'

*

If Ava had been nervous about meeting Susannah's family, it hadn't shown. She and Kate had got on from the first instant they had been introduced. Especially when Ava had shown such great interest in Kate's wedding dress. Their mother had been a little more reserved, clearly not having expected Ava to be American Indian.

'And where are you from, Ava?' her mother had asked as they sat down to dinner.

'The northwest,' Ava said. 'Place called Puget Sound.'

'What's it like?' Kate asked her.

'Not so different from here. Little islands and the sea. Though the skies feel bigger.'

'And what are you studying at Harvard?' Kate continued to gush. 'Are you majoring in history, like Susie?'

'No, I'm majoring in law,' Ava said.

'Oh boy,' Kate enthused. 'You must be even cleverer than Susie!'

'And what does your father do?' Susannah's mother continued the interrogation.

'He works in construction,' Ava said, keeping her voice light, though Susannah sensed she wasn't keen to talk about her parents. 'This peach cobbler sure is the best one I ever ate,' she said, changing the subject.

'Well, thank you,' Susannah's mother said, looking pleased.

'What kind of food are you having at the wedding?' Susannah asked, continuing the food line of conversation and steering it away from Ava.

'We're doing a cold buffet. Matthew's mom is coming over in the morning to help us make it. Can you and Ava help too?'

'No problem,' Ava said. 'What do you need making?'

'Chicken salad and dessert, so it's simple enough,' Kate said. 'Mom has already made the cake.'

'We just need to put it together,' Susannah's mother added.

'I can't believe it's the eve of my wedding,' Kate said, clasping her hands in excitement. 'You are happy for me, aren't you, Susie?'

Susannah felt Ava squeeze her hand in reassurance under cover of the dinner table. There was no point trying to stop Kate now. Her sister was besotted. The best Susannah could hope for was that she could somehow get along with Matthew, and that he would prove to be a good, kind husband to her sister.

'Ava is so great,' Kate enthused later that night as Susannah helped her set her hair for the next day. 'I'm so glad you have a good friend now I'm getting married.'

'You're still my sister, Katie. Nothing changes with us.'

Kate gave her a serious look. 'I'll have to put my family first.' She sighed, and looked at Susannah in the mirror. 'When are you ever going to meet a nice boy? I want our children to be the same ages.'

Susannah met her sister's eyes in the mirror. Could she tell her the truth?

'I'm not sure I want to have children, Katie,' she'd said.

'What? You're only thinking that because you haven't met the right boy,' Kate retorted. 'Believe me, as soon as you do, you'll want a baby all right.'

Early the next morning, Susannah watched Ava sleep. She was all she ever wanted. But how could she ever explain that to Kate?

Susannah closed her eyes and summoned their apartment off Harvard Square. All the books piled everywhere: towers of words, thoughts, knowledge. The big green chair in the window, where she'd curl up for hours, notebook balanced on her lap, flicking through her books and taking notes. She could see the sanctity of her desk now. The little black typewriter, her piles of paper, and the blue glass paperweight on top of them.

There was Ava back home. Sitting in her nook, black stocking feet on Susannah's lap, balancing a cup of coffee on her knees as she gazed out of the window. They were listening to Billie Holiday. Her powerful lyrics binding them in complicity. Over the next couple of days, they had to keep their secret safe. Susannah couldn't wait to be back at Harvard, and themselves again.

But today was Kate's wedding day. Her little sister was getting married, and it was her duty to make the day as special and as wonderful for Kate as she could. Susannah pulled the covers off the bed, and opened the curtains. She stared out of the window. The view looked across their garden to the harbour. The bay was rough, waves cresting white and choppy, with clouds racing above. It looked like it was going to rain. Maybe if there was a storm so fierce nobody could leave their houses, the wedding would not go ahead today? Susannah felt a surge of hope, and then immediately guilty. She needed to stop thinking her sister's wedding was an event to dread. She had to be happy for her. This had always been Kate's dream. She'd been so excited in all her last letters, going on and on about all the plans.

I can't wait to be his wife, she'd written to Susannah. *It's all I've ever wanted, to have my own family. Lots of babies, Susie! You're going to be the best aunty in the world!*

Ava stirred in the bed and opened her eyes, stretching and yawning.

'Good morning, darling,' Susannah whispered.

'Good morning, my sweet.' Ava smiled back.

Susannah felt better instantly. She was here with Ava, her love. This was all Kate had ever dreamed of, to be in love and to be loved. How could Susannah stop her from trying to have that? Maybe marriage would be the making of Matthew, and he would prove deserving of her sister's adoration.

The rain stayed off, and the wind dropped. It was a picture-perfect wedding day. Kate looked like a princess in her long white dress, edged with lace she'd made herself. Not a soul could help but admire how pretty she looked, glowing with pride and joy as she showed off her gold wedding band. It was a small wedding, just the two families, and some fishermen friends of Matthew. Silas watched on, bottle of beer in hand, while poor Rachel stood behind him, heavily pregnant and looking miserable as a small child tugged on the hem of her old dress. She'd put on so much weight, Susannah hardly recognised the popular and glamorous Rachel from the night of her summer dance less than three years ago. Susannah looked away, terrified she'd just seen a vision of her own sister's future.

Kate was dancing with her handsome groom, her long tresses golden beneath her veil. Sweet and wholesome. Susannah longed to take Ava's hand and dance with her love, but could only imagine the reaction they'd get from the wedding guests if they did so. Already, they'd been getting looks from Mr Young. Susannah was in a dress, sure, but her mother had complained it was too short and the black stockings were indecent. Her hair was short too – gamine, Susannah had told Kate – and she'd outlined her eyes in thick black kohl. Ava looked slightly more conservative with her long hair, but her dress was as short as Susannah's. It was more than her clothes, though, which made the islanders stare at Ava, and that made Susannah mad. She was tempted to give Ava a smacking kiss on the lips. Why not give the Youngs something to really talk about?

Ava passed Susannah a lit cigarette. She took a drag and fixed her gaze on Matthew, Kate's new husband. They'd barely exchanged words all day long. Almost as if he was avoiding her. When she'd introduced him to Ava, he had flat out stared at her, not even offering a hand or word in greeting. Susannah had been mortified, and shocked that Kate hadn't noticed his blatant hostility. Now her new brother-in-law had a high colour in his cheeks from all the drink. He was swinging Kate around and around. It was his wedding day after all, of course he was a bit merry. But something in the way he held on to her sister made Susannah uneasy. *Let her go now*, she wanted to shout out. *Can't you see it's too fast? Can't you see the worry in her eyes?* But Matthew kept on spinning Kate, and the fiddler was going faster, and everyone was up laughing and jigging, even her mother with their father's old friend, Danny.

Matthew was almost dragging Kate now, and her sister was stumbling over the hem of her wedding dress. Ava put her hand on Susannah's arm. She'd noticed too, and knowing Susannah so well, she was trying to warn her. But when Kate almost went down on her knees as Matthew tugged at her roughly, Susannah joined the throng, instinctively protective. Taking a hold of Matthew's arm, she pulled him back.

'Hey, you're going too fast for her,' she told him.

Matthew turned his eyes on Susannah. They were cloudy with the drink, dark with anger. He removed her hand from his arm and continued to dance, spinning Kate even faster. She saw her sister's pale face, knew that glazy look. Kate was going to throw up.

'Stop it, you're making her sick.' She pulled again on Matthew's arm.

He pushed her. He actually pushed her away, before springing forward, still gripping tight onto Kate's hand, and hissing in Susannah's ear: 'She's my wife now, and you don't tell me what to do. We don't want you here.'

Ava was instantly by Susannah's side.

'Say, take it easy,' she said to Matthew. 'Let Kate go for a minute. She looks a little sick now.'

'Who are you to tell me how to treat my wife? You're just a filthy *injun.*'

Susannah felt a flare of anger as Ava went very still beside her. Luckily, the music was so loud no one else had heard his insult, but that wasn't the point.

'Don't you dare—' Susannah began to say.

'Or what?' Matthew leered at her. 'What exactly will you do? I'm the master of this house now, and you and that dirty little *injun* aren't welcome here no more.'

Susannah turned in shock to Kate, but her sister said nothing in her defence. She saw the fear in her sister's pleading eyes. *Back off.* The dread she'd been feeling all day swept through her.

Ava's hand on her arm.

'Come on, Susannah,' she said gently. 'It's not worth it.'

She and Ava retreated. For the rest of the night they avoided Matthew and his drunken brother. Both of them were red-faced from beer and whisky. Susannah waited for Kate to come talk to her, but her sister didn't come near her.

For the first time in years, even her mom drank too much. Susannah and Ava had had to help her into bed.

'Such a grand day,' her mom slurred. 'Now, when will you make me as proud, Susie?'

After her mother had fallen into a loud, snoring sleep, Susannah and Ava didn't return to the party. Susannah found an old hurricane lantern in the porch, and the two of them changed into denims and went for a walk in the dark.

Susannah knew every tree, every rock of the island as if it had been etched inside her head. They walked all the way down to Lane's Island Bridge Cove, their way lit by the moon and the lamp. The bulrushes rustled in the summer breeze, and the crickets chirruped like crazy. At the cove, they sat on one large rock together, sharing a cigarette and staring out to sea.

'Well, that was real bad.' Susannah finally spoke. 'I'm sorry, Ava.'

'Don't be,' Ava said. 'I'm sorry, too. For your sister. She deserves better.'

'I know,' Susannah sighed. 'She's been stuck on that heel for years. I really hope he treats her right, but after what we saw I just don't know what to think.'

'It was the drink,' Ava reassured her. 'I've seen some good men turn bad because of drink. But when they're sober they are the best, kindest souls you'll ever meet.'

'Problem is, I don't think Matthew Young is good sober or drunk.'

When she and Ava returned to the house, the wedding party was still raging in the garden, but they retired to their beds, falling asleep to the sounds of the fiddle and the men's drunken singing. It was hard not to think about Kate. Their whole childhood, they'd been inside each other's pockets. Knew every inch of each other's experiences. But now Kate was charting unknown waters, and Susannah couldn't go with her. In fact, it was best she forgot all about it right now.

Susannah woke at first dawn. They hadn't closed the drapes the night before, and the early morning summer sun blazed across the room. She must have only been asleep a few hours, but she felt suddenly alert. She heard a door slam downstairs. Getting up and looking out of the window, she saw Matthew staggering across their garden, bottle in hand. She slipped out of bed, glancing at Ava, mouth open, and clearly in a deep sleep.

As she crept down the stairs, she heard crying. The door of Kate and Matthew's room was ajar, and looking through the opening, she could see her sister curled up on the bed.

'Katie, what's wrong?' Susannah got on the bed with her. The sheets were all over the place. Her sister was bawling. 'It's okay, honey, tell me what happened.'

Her sister calmed down slightly, bringing the sheet to her face to dry her eyes. 'Nothing happened. That's precisely it.' She hiccupped. 'I've been waiting all night, Susie, for him to come home. It's our wedding night for Christ-sakes!'

'He's very drunk,' Susannah ventured.

'I know!' Kate wailed. 'He left me on my own all night and when I told him I was upset, he got so mad with me.'

'Did he hit you?' Susannah didn't know why she asked this particular question first. An instinct, maybe?

'No, of course not,' Kate retorted. 'But he's so angry now, and it's all my fault. I should have gone to sleep. Waited for him to sober up. What does it matter if he's drunk? He was celebrating.'

Her sister wasn't making much sense. One minute berating Matthew, and the next minute blaming herself.

'Hey.' Susannah put a hand on her arm. 'Take it easy.'

Kate hiccupped again, wiped her face dry, and took a breath. 'I'm fine, honest, Susie.'

Susannah had to say it now. Else she'd never forgive herself. 'If, you know, the marriage isn't… consummated, well. You could get an annulment,' she ventured. 'Come with me and Ava back to Cambridge, Katie.'

'What do you mean?' Kate looked at her in confusion.

'Just that. I'm worried for you, Katie. I don't think Matthew is a kind man.'

Kate sprang back as if Susannah had burnt her. 'I love him! And he loves me! Are you crazy, Susannah? We just got married. I want to be with him. I don't want to live in Cambridge. I would hate it!'

'But he's not good to you.'

'Yes, he is, he is!' Kate cried out. 'I shan't have you saying those things about him. Stop it, Susannah! Just because you're jealous, don't be mean about my husband.'

'I'm not jealous!' Susannah felt her blood begin to boil. 'I'm just trying to help.'

'Well, you're not. Just leave me alone. How could you suggest such a thing?'

'He's cruel, Katie, and he's ignorant.'

'Shut up, will you? Just get out, now!'

Susannah stormed out of the room and up the stairs. She and Kate had never ever fought before. Her sister had said terrible things to her. It dawned on her: Matthew Young had finally won. She'd lost Kate. Would she ever get her sister back?

Ava was still fast asleep. Susannah slipped into the narrow bed beside her. Put her arms around her love. Just to feel the rhythm of Ava's breath calmed her. She felt Ava stir, and then turn, opening her eyes, looking at her questioningly. Susannah put her finger to her lips and Ava smiled. She kissed her on the lips, and Ava kissed her back. They undressed each other under the covers between kisses, slipping out of their pyjamas, and pressing their naked skin against each other. Susannah felt the thrum of Ava's heart against her breast. It felt as if she breathed in Ava's love, filling her belly right from the pit of her stomach through her chest and throat so all she wanted was to exhale kisses all over her. The sun bathed them with glorious warmth as the two girls entwined. Ava snaked down Susannah's body, and caressed her with her lips as Susannah raised her arms above her head, letting the sheets fall from them onto the floor of the bedroom completely forgetting where exactly it was they were.

'Susie!'

Kate's voice sliced through their passion like a blade. Ava rolled off her, and Susannah sat up with a jerk to see her sister in her bride's nightie, staring wide-eyed at her and Ava, naked upon her childhood bed.

'Oh my god!' Kate whispered. 'What are you doing?'

Chapter 25

Emer

27th October 2011

After Emer had read all the letters to Susannah, it was dark.

'Are you tired?' she asked Susannah. 'Do you want to go to bed?'

'No, I'm just too agitated,' she said. 'All those letters have stirred up so many memories, and regrets.'

'Let's think of a way to help you relax,' Emer said. 'How about a bath? Or would you like me to wash your hair for you?'

Susannah agreed to a hair wash, and the two moved to the bathroom. 'What happened to your young man?' Susannah asked, as Emer brushed her hair. Susannah was sitting on a stool, with a pillow behind her neck.

'He had to go for the ferry, remember?' Emer said, checking the temperature of the water.

'Shame,' Susannah said. 'I liked him.'

She tipped her head back over the sink and closed her eyes. Emer wet her hair, massaging shampoo into it until it lathered. Susannah had such soft skin, and her features were so fine and elegant. Within the space of just under three weeks, Emer had come to know her face and body so well.

After rinsing her hair, Emer wrapped a towel around Susannah's head, folding it into a turban, and helped her up. They went downstairs to the front room, where Emer set Susannah up on the couch in front of the woodstove.

'Would you like me to style your hair?' she asked Susannah.

Susannah looked up at her in surprise. 'Okay, but make me a cup of that disgusting herbal tea first.'

Emer gently removed the towel and dried Susannah's hair with it. When it was wet, her hair was the colour of the granite she saw everywhere on the island. Emer combed it out. Susannah's hair was surprisingly thick, and straight. It was cut to just the nape of her neck, and framed her face neatly. Emer took up her styling brush and hairdryer.

'I haven't had my hair styled in years,' Susannah said. 'Ava used to do it. My friend – you know, from the letters.'

'Well, I'm not really much good at it. I used to do mine and Orla's hair when we were teenagers. Hers was so wild and curly, it was impossible to manage. But then it changed.'

'I used to have long hair when I was at Harvard,' Susannah said. 'With bangs.' She raised her hand to indicate. 'Straight across, just below my eyebrows. Then Ava cut it real short for me. We all wore thick black kohl to make ourselves look like cats.' She sighed. 'Ava always looked so amazing.'

'Do you see her any more?'

'No, we lost contact.'

Emer could hear the catch in Susannah's voice, but Susannah said no more on Ava, and remained silent as she dried her hair. The stone grey hair began to lighten as it dried, turning to silver, so many tiny variations of the shade, all sparkling in the firelight. Emer admired the shine of it. Really, it was so beautiful. Why did older women feel they had to dye their grey hair? She'd always been afraid of getting older, of wrinkles, grey hair. But looking at Susannah, what she saw was a beautiful woman, and in all the fine lines of her face, the story of her life. It was inspiring. And Emer felt sad that at this time she was alone. No family with her, and no friends. Just a random nurse.

Emer turned off the hairdryer and put the brush down. Susannah looked up at her.

'Were you and Orla close?' Susannah asked her.

'Yes,' Emer whispered, trying but failing to hold back the tears.

Susannah didn't move to console her, but her voice was kind. 'My advice is allow yourself to grieve. Cry if you have to. Don't mind me. When Kate died, I wailed the house down.'

'What happened?' Emer ventured, dabbing her eyes with the sleeve of her sweater. She remembered all the gossip Henry had passed on. How could anyone possibly think Susannah could hurt another soul?

Susannah flinched. 'Not sure I want to tell you anything about that. It was too long ago,' she mumbled. She leaned back against the couch. 'I guess, it might help me somewhat to tell you,' she said, eventually. 'It's like I lug it round with me every day. The weight of what happened to my sister.'

Emer sat down on the other end of the couch and hugged her knees to her.

'Don't let that happen to you,' Susannah said. 'Let her go, because if you do not, you'll just drown in your loss.'

'I feel so guilty,' Emer whispered.

'It wasn't your fault your sister died, Emer,' Susannah counselled her. 'She had cancer. But Kate's life was taken from her by her husband. I should have protected her.'

Emer could see Susannah's whole body trembling. She leant over, pulled the blanket up over Susannah's knees, and tucked it in.

'And then there was Ava,' Susannah moaned. 'I will never forgive myself.' She turned to Emer again, her eyes flashing. 'Don't think you can let your true love go. Listen to me: I saw how it was between you and that young man today,' Susannah said.

'It's over between us,' Emer said.

'It's never over,' Susannah insisted.

Chapter 26

Susannah

July 3rd, 1960
Harvard, Cambridge

Dearest Katie,

It's taken me several weeks to get the courage to write to you. But the silence from your end has upset me. I need to explain what you saw the morning after your wedding. I believe I know you the best, Katie, out of everyone in the whole wide world, and this is why I feel you will not be judgemental or narrow minded. I also wonder – did you not, for a second, have an inkling? I never liked boys. I never hid that from you.

What I share with Ava is a love so deep and special, it goes beyond the boundaries of friendship. It is spiritual, intuitive, all-consuming, and it is physical too. Ava and I are not alone, Katie. There are other women who feel the same way we do. Some of them never get a chance to be their real selves. They are trapped in marriages with men, to conform with society's rules. But why persecute those who are different? Didn't Jesus say *Blessed are the persecuted for theirs is the Kingdom of Heaven?*

But it's a sad truth that prejudices run very deep in this country, even here at Harvard and in academia. Ava and I need to be very careful and keep our love secret. All our friends and colleagues believe we are best friends and roommates. This is why I am asking you not to tell anyone, not even Matthew and especially not Mother, about what you saw. I was so hurt by your reaction, Katie.

Why did you refuse to talk to me for the entire day before we left? Was it because of Ava and I? Or was it to do with our argument before?

I was only offering you a way out because I thought you wanted one. I want you to be happy. That is the most important thing of all. Please write to tell me how your new married life is? I can't bear the thought of my sister angry with me.

*

Susannah clutched the letter to her chest, running up the stairs two at time. By the time she burst through the door of their apartment on the fifth floor, she was out of breath and could hardly speak.

'Hey, what's up?' Ava said, looking up.

She was curled up in her favourite corner of the room, on the green chair reading Susannah's battered copy of *The Ballad of Sad Café* by Carson McCullers.

'She wrote back,' Susannah gasped. 'At last!'

She tore open the letter from Kate, her heart tight with anticipation. It had been nearly five months since the wedding, and Kate's silence had been driving her wild with guilt. She should never had said those things about her new husband. It had been plain dumb of her. Susannah had been terrified she'd lost Kate for good.

'So what's she say?' Ava asked her, putting her book down.

'Dearest Susie, I am sorry you haven't heard from me in so long,' Susannah read aloud, sitting down at their little table. *'Married*

life keeps me busy, and Mother needs more and more help with the lacing. Her eyesight has gone very bad. What with looking after Matthew and making nets, I've very little time to write.' Susannah paused to shrug off her jacket. Picking up the letter again, she continued, *'I won't lie, Susie, I was very shocked when I walked in on you and Ava. It's very hard for me to understand. But I love you so much, I will try, I promise. Your secret is safe with me of course. All I want for you is happiness as well, and this is why I'm concerned. Do you not want to have children one day, Susannah? I do like Ava. I think she is a great girl. And I have never seen you so happy. I guess our life on Vinalhaven was one which never fit you right. I like to imagine you at Harvard some days, Susannah, when I look out the window across the harbour, all those miles of sea and land between us. But, sister, always we are connected. I would never break our bonds, even for Matthew.*

'I am sad it is clear you don't like him. Please can you try to understand how I feel about him? It is the same as what you feel for Ava. My love for Matthew fills me right up and I couldn't bear to be without him. You did not see the best side of him on our wedding day. He was nervous and drank too much. But he is a good man, provides well for me and Mother, and he will be a good father.

'I can't wait to get pregnant, Susie. Every day, the hope for it consumes me. A baby will bring us all together, don't you think?

'I have to go now. Time to cook the dinner as Matthew will be home soon. He has such a tough life out on the sea every day in all weathers. You know how dangerous it can be. The least I can do is make his life at home easy.

'Say hello to Ava from me!'

Susannah put the letter down on the table and took a breath.

'Well that's good isn't?' Ava asked her, getting up from the green chair.

'I guess,' Susannah said. 'But why do I feel so flat?'

'Because she's tolerating us, not accepting us,' Ava said, wrapping her arms around Susannah's shoulders and kissing the top of her head.

'Is there a difference?'

'Yes, a big one,' Ava sighed.

'She'll understand, one day,' Susannah said. 'She has to, because she's Katie. She's my sister.'

Chapter 27

They had fought as children. It was hard to believe it now. As adults, she and Orla had been so close. More than sisters: best friends and confidantes. But when they were little, their different personalities had clashed. Emer couldn't even remember what they'd fought over. But she did remember terrible, vicious fights. Hair-pulling, kicking; Orla even bit her once. Another time, she knocked out Orla's front baby teeth. Their mother had been driven demented by the two girls. Because she was the eldest, Emer felt as if Orla got away with more than her. Orla always started crying when they were getting told off, so that Emer received more of the blame. She remembered feeling so furious with Orla. Running out into the garden after her and screaming, *I hate you! I wish you were dead!*

How could she have said such awful things to her own sister? How could she have been so angry with her? In her heart, Emer had to admit she'd always been a bit jealous of Orla. She was the favourite. The prettier sister, better at singing, dancing, and all sports. Emer was the bookish one. Boring.

Things had calmed down a little when they were teenagers. Apart from the fact that Emer had to hide all her good make-up and lock her wardrobe. She didn't mind the fact that Orla 'borrowed' her stuff, it was that she either never returned it, or returned it damaged. Emer's favourite dress crumpled on the floor, or put in the wrong wash. Her lip glosses stuck with bits of grit, the end of her eyeliner pencil blunt. No apology, ever.

For a couple of years, Orla had gone through an emo-goth thing, only wearing black and getting her nose pierced. Their dad had gone mad, but their mam had said it looked good, and bought Orla a little silver stud for her nose.

'I might get my nose pierced too,' she'd announced, much to the horror of both girls.

Orla was just so cool. Everyone wanted to hang out with her at school. Boys were drawn to her. Orla had her first boyfriend way before Emer. Lost her virginity before her, too. Emer remembered Orla ringing her in Dublin, and telling her in excited whispers how she and her first boyfriend, Sean, had done it in the back of his father's big Audi.

'It's not that big a deal,' Orla had told her. 'I don't know why there's so much fuss over it.'

'You did use protection, didn't you?' Emer asked her. Always the older sister.

'Of course, I'm not thick.'

Emer always associated Orla's dark phase with the time preceding their mother's cancer. The once sunny little girl turned taciturn, monosyllabic. Spending hours in her room with Sean, playing morose music and then painting on her own in the good room. Orla had been obsessed with graphic fiction, and horror. Even as an adult, Orla had still loved horror movies. Something Emer found very hard to understand. She hated any hint of horror. Wasn't there enough frightening, dark stuff in real life? She didn't want to fill her head with zombies, devils and poltergeists.

As soon as their mam got sick, Orla dropped the whole emo thing, spending more time in the good room painting. She was in her final year in school, and Emer had already left home for nursing college. When she looked back now, those months with their sick mother had become a sort of blur. Emer had come home every weekend to help, but it had been so intense and exhausting. Often, their dad would have gone off drinking in the pub with his pals, unable to cope with his wife's sickness. Orla was with their mam on her own, trying to keep her positive. Was that when Orla's personality had transformed? In her fight to save their mother? She dropped all the black clothes, along with Sean, and wore colour again. Sat in the bedroom with their mam for hours, reading to her. Painting the view from the window, while their mam slept, just to keep her company. No wonder her Leaving Certificate was such a disaster.

Emer had never asked her sister how she must have felt when she'd been told she had cancer too. Had she believed she could beat it? Or had the experience of watching her own mother die from the disease right from the start made her feel hopeless? Emer had been angry. Wasn't one loss in a family enough?

They had told each other everything. All their feelings, and fears. It was this which had tortured Emer during her sister's final weeks. For everyone else, Orla had put on a brave face, but with Emer she'd told her how very frightened she was. Emer would wake up in a cold sweat every night, just thinking about how her sister must be feeling. She'd told Orla about Lars as a distraction. To lighten the conversation.

'I met this cute guy at the vending machine downstairs. We went to the canteen together.'

'Oh yes? Tell me more.' Orla had broken out in a smile.

Every day, Emer would tell Orla a little bit about her and Lars' chat. Her sister had insisted she invite him up to her ward so she could meet him.

Really, Emer had been surprised. 'Are you sure you want to meet someone new? In here?'

'He's not new to you,' Orla had said. 'Besides, he's not going to be shocked. He's a medic. Seen it all.'

Emer had been so nervous about introducing Lars to Orla. She needn't have worried. They had hit it off immediately. Lars noticed the stack of graphic fiction by Orla's bed, and revealed his passion for the medium.

'What's your favourite comic book of all time?' Lars asked Orla.

'Oh I love so many! *Watchmen*, *Wonder Woman* and then there's *Persepolis* and *Maus* which are totally different,' Orla declared.

Lars also got on really well with Ethan, the two of them discovering a mutual love of sailing, as they sat either side of Orla's bed and talked about boats.

'I love him!' Orla had said to her, as soon as the boys had left the ward to go get coffee.

'Orla's amazing,' Lars had said to Emer the next day, as they'd eaten lunch together in the hospital canteen.

She could have been jealous at how easily Orla and Lars had hit it off, but of course, she wasn't. Ethan was Orla's soulmate. They could have been the perfect double dates. If only. If only.

Chapter 28

Susannah

August to October 1960

Susannah and Ava worked as many shifts as they could in the coffee house over the whole summer. Long, lazy evenings were spent in Harvard Square, listening to all the new folk singers who'd turned up in Cambridge. There was a sense they were part of something important. A change in the spirit of America, and a desire from all the young liberals to tear down old prejudices.

Ava was getting more and more involved in the civil rights movement for American Indians.

'It's time people stopped thinking American Indians can't help themselves,' she told Susannah. 'Or that we need to become like white Americans. Adopt your society.'

Susannah was proud of Ava's passion and her involvement in some of the protests she went on, although sometimes it meant she was away for nights on end. She also was ashamed of how ignorant she had been of American Indians, all the different tribes and their history until she'd met Ava. She had been aware of some tribes from Maine, but knew very little about them. It hadn't been covered in school at all.

'I've never asked you what tribe you're from,' she admitted to Ava one evening, as they were sharing cigarettes, sitting outside on the stoop. 'Why have you never told me?'

'I was raised to be careful whom I told,' Ava said, inhaling deeply and letting smoke plume from her nose. 'My skin is quite fair. I can get away with not looking American Indian.' She sounded sad. 'My parents instilled a fear in me to reveal who I really am.'

Ava took up one of the chalks left lying on the sidewalk from kids who'd been playing hopscotch earlier. She drew a small leaping salmon on the sidewalk.

'That's one of our symbols. We are a coastal nation. My people from the Swinomish Tribal peoples of the North West,' she said. 'Like I told you the day we first met, I am from the Pacific.'

Susannah couldn't believe how many different tribes there were, and had been, in America.

'Do you speak Swinomish?' she asked Ava.

'Sadly not.' Ava shook her head. 'My dad speaks very little. But we were forced to learn English in school, and in his day if he spoke his own language he was beaten.'

Susannah felt so ashamed of her white American heritage. 'I know there were American Indians where I come from.' she said. 'The Abenaki people. But where are they now?'

'They got decimated during the colonisation. Disease was the worst offender,' Ava told her.

Susannah was so proud of Ava's commitment to her cause. Sometimes she was almost a little jealous. Wished she were American Indian. It would give her purpose. Once, when she'd admitted this to Ava, Susannah had been surprised by how angry Ava got with her.

'Do you realise how patronising that is?' she said. 'You have no idea how privileged you are, being a white person. I know there are prejudices against women, but there is no comparison to being a black woman or an American Indian woman.'

'But it's just you have such purpose,' Ava said. 'Such vision!'

'And so do you!' Ava berated her. 'Your historical research is a study of witch persecutions. How relevant is that right now?

Rather than wish you were one of us, you can use the fact that you are listened to as a white person to help us.'

The hot, sticky summer in Cambridge burnt out into busy fall days back at college. Ava was swamped by all her law studies. After the summer of protests, she was even more determined to qualify as soon as possible and become a civil rights lawyer, with emphasis upon rights for American Indians. Money was always an issue for the two of them. As well as their coffee house jobs, which provided them with free food and coffee, Susannah took on private tutoring in Newton for the kids of wealthy banking friends of the Whittards. But despite always being on the run, and some weeks the two of them scrimping to get together enough dollars for cigarettes, Susannah had never felt so happy. Ava's love and patience was a constant presence. She was also doing well at college. Dr Anberg had put her forward for a tutoring position in the history department once she'd delivered her dissertation. She had chosen her topic and was very excited. It was an assessment of the causes of witch hunting in Europe in the sixteenth and seventeenth centuries, with particular focus on Scotland and Norway.

Three weeks after the letter from Kate in October, another one arrived in the post before Susannah had even had a chance to reply.

Dearest Susie, I'll keep the letter brief but I'm so excited I need to tell you right away. I'm pregnant! I took the ferry to Rockland and went to see Dr Redfern yesterday and he confirmed I was with child. Due next June. We are all so happy – Matthew and I, and Mom. It has really picked her up. Write soon! Regards to Ava.

Susannah's heart had dropped a mile. She should be happy for her sister. It was what Kate had always wanted. But a voice inside her head said something else.

Now she's trapped forever.

She realised the final piece in her happiness would have been if Kate had come to Cambridge and never gone back to the island. Been as free a bird, as she was. But as much as Kate couldn't change Susannah, Susannah could never change her sister. Try as she might, Susannah would never accept Matthew was a good match for her sister, but she'd tolerate him for Kate's sake, and for the baby.

Chapter 29

Emer

28th October 2011

The night after Lars left, Emer dreamt about Orla being alive again. This time, Orla was in a boat in the harbour at Vinalhaven, preparing to set sail. Emer was standing at the wharfside, calling to her to come back.

'You're very sick,' she shouted at her. 'I have to make you better.'

But her sister laughed at her, hoisted the sails. 'Come with me,' she called back. Orla had wanted to go sailing in so long, and she wasn't coming back even if Emer was too frightened to get on the boat, even if she had cancer.

Emer woke filled with panic. She had to get her sister off the boat. Time was running out; she had to save Orla. And then the cold realisation. It was too late. She was already dead.

The sun had just risen as she got out of bed. The sky outside her window was a flat, pale grey, making the foliage look even brighter and more glorious. Fall was nearly over, the colours giving an intense final flare before winter set in. How would she find the dark months on Vinalhaven? Susannah had told her they could be cut off for days if an extreme nor'easter came in with snow. Would she be able to endure the loneliness and the cold? How would Susannah fare?

A lone pick-up drove by past the house. It looked like Henry's, and Emer instantly felt guilty. She still hadn't replied to his text. Why did she always screw everything up?

*

Later that day, Susannah asked Emer if she could light the fire in the woodstove in the front room and read to her.

'I feel like revisiting some of my books,' she told Emer. 'You have a very pleasing reading voice,' she complimented her.

'Oh well, one of my many talents,' Emer said, happy to be of use.

Susannah's front room was filled with books. Row after row of packed bookshelves, with an array of titles from old classics, to hardback volumes of history and trashy paperback crime novels, which, Susannah was hasty to point out, belonged to Lynsey. It was the history books Susannah wanted Emer to read to her. At first, Emer thought she'd be bored. She'd never been interested in the past that much. But now she felt herself drawn into the subject matter, pausing to ask Susannah questions if she didn't quite understand.

'You're a good teacher,' she told Susannah, after Susannah had explained to her what the Reformation was and why it had happened.

From her letters, it was evident Susannah had adored her life at Harvard. Emer was mystified as to why she hadn't pursued her academic career, rather than live as a recluse on a remote island off the coast of Maine.

'You know so much,' Emer said. 'Did you ever teach in a university?'

'No,' Susannah said. 'I would have needed to study more, got an MFA. And I had to raise Kate's girls.'

'But you could have gone back, when the girls left home?'

'I couldn't leave Vinalhaven. It was my mother who kept me here. It's not that many years ago that she passed away.'

'I'm sorry.'

'Don't be, she lived to the great age of ninety-six years old. By the end, she had dementia so bad it was a relief when she was finally gone.'

The letters Emer had been typing up from Kate to Susannah all these weeks had been dated until just before she had got married. Not in one letter was there an indication of any problem with Matthew. However, there were five years from 1961 to the year of Kate's death without any correspondence between the sisters.

What had happened to Kate's marriage?

'What happened between Kate and her husband for him to kill her?' Emer now asked Susannah, unable to contain her curiosity any more.

The older woman gave a big sigh. Shook her head. 'He was a bully and a brute,' she said to Emer. 'Beat her up on the regular, I'm sure of it. But in those days, no one batted an eye.'

Susannah looked at the flames leaping inside the wood stove.

'I don't know exactly why, but I suppose it was one of his beatings gone too far. I think he killed her by mistake.'

On her walk into town later, Emer found herself imagining how things would have been for Susannah all those years on Vinalhaven, bringing up her sister's daughters on her own in the aftermath of such a terrible tragedy. Her heart went out to her. Susannah had given up so much to look after Kate's girls. Not just her career, but clearly Ava, too.

In the food store, Susannah scoured the shelves for something she could cook for Susannah, whose appetite was pretty non-existent. Anything fatty, or too heavy, gave her terrible pains in the stomach. Emer settled on some tofu, which she would stir-fry with some spinach and noodles, hoping she could coax Susannah to eat something. She had got dreadfully thin and Emer was worried when Lynsey and Rebecca arrived they'd be upset and shocked. But that's how it was with cancer. Emer closed her eyes, and despite the fact she'd promised herself she'd only remember bonny Orla, she had a flash of her sister in her last days. How gaunt she'd been. From the day she'd been diagnosed again, Emer hadn't taken any pictures of her. She'd wanted to remember healthy Orla, not sick Orla.

She walked around the market store in a daze now, not really present but partly in the past. Reliving those last weeks with Orla. As she turned the corner into the next aisle, before she knew it she'd walked slap-bang into Henry. She hadn't seen him coming at all.

'Hey! How are you?' Henry said. He gave her a big smile, which took her aback completely. He seemed very relaxed and certainly not annoyed with her.

'Oh hello!' Emer said, her throat drying up. 'I'm so sorry about the other night. Someone turned up at the last minute from home.'

'Ireland?'

'No. Boston.'

Henry stood smiling at her, clearly waiting for her to say more. 'Your boyfriend?' he asked.

'No,' she said, taken aback by how personal the question was. 'Just a friend, but they arrived as I was leaving… and, well, I should have texted.'

'It's okay.' Henry shrugged. 'You missed a good night. Should have brought him with you.'

'Yes, I should have,' she said, nodding, but thinking the opposite and imagining just how awkward that would have been.

They stood in silence for a moment. Emer really wanted to get away from him. It was odd, the way he was so cool about being stood up.

'Well, I'll see you around,' she said, drifting away.

'Say,' he called after her. 'Want to go for another walk tomorrow? To my number two spot?'

She found herself saying yes. She didn't really want to, but she couldn't think of a good excuse. *So this is what island life is like*, she thought as she walked back to Susannah's house. *Impossible to be anonymous.* Henry had known her friend was a he, so she guessed the whole island must be aware of Lars' visit. Sure, they probably all knew she was shacked up in the inn with him for a couple of hours. What did it matter? But she was confused. Why would Henry still want to hang out with her when she'd so clearly rejected him?

Chapter 30

Susannah

July 15th, 1961
Vinalhaven, Maine

My darling Ava,

Every day I miss you more and more. My first thought every morning is of you, and my last. I think of you in bed asleep. I think of you making coffee. Or getting dressed, brushing your hair, putting on lipstick. I think of you about our busy life in Cambridge. How are our coffee house regulars? Did Charlie get his book published at last? What's happening with Sam's record? And college. I can see you in my head, running across the square, trying to carry all your heavy law books. How did your exams go? I know you will have aced them. You're going to be the best and most beautiful lawyer! So proud of you.

I promise, I'll be home soon. Katie had such a difficult birth and Mom hasn't been well either. They've really needed my help with Lynsey. She's so adorable, but she does cry a lot, Ava. Oh my god, for something so small I can't believe how much crying there is in her. It has Katie very tired all the time. She feeds for a little time, falls asleep, but wakes up again only an hour later and wants more milk. Mom told Kate she should give her a bottle, but Katie is trying to breastfeed. I do love my new little niece but the whole experience has made me even surer I don't want to have a baby. It's so much work for such a small helpless little thing. However, I might be writing all this now, but once I hold Lynsey in my arms and get her to fall asleep, it's all worth it. I do love her!

As for my brother-in-law, things are a little tense, I guess. The night Lynsey was born he went out with his brother and got very drunk. But that's what new fathers do, isn't it? And he wasn't abusive or rude when he came back, just fell on the couch and snored the house down. Missed going out to fish his lobster the next day, which put him in bad form, and he complained none of us women woke him up. But I didn't know what to do, Ava, and Katie and Mom were preoccupied with the baby. When Lynsey cries and Matthew is home, he tells Katie to get her to be quiet all the time. But sometimes it's impossible to get Lynsey quiet and this makes Matthew very irritable. I tried to explain how difficult it was for her.

'She's the mother,' he snapped back. 'That's her job. Mine is to get a good night's sleep so I can feed all you women.'

'Katie lost a lot of blood when she had Lynsey,' I told him. 'She's very worn out and needs rest.'

He didn't like me saying that at all. Me talking about 'women's stuff', as he calls it.

'I don't want to hear it. Women give birth every day. Look at my mother. She had my youngest sister Annie and was up the next day baking bread for the whole family.'

'Every woman is different,' I tried to explain.

But the man is so dense. Honestly, Ava, why has my sister chosen to lumber herself with him for the rest of her life?

Now he has taken to going to The Sand Bar every afternoon when he comes back from fishing, which gives us some peace from his complaining for a few hours. But then when he comes home at four o'clock in the afternoon to sleep, Kate and Mom get in a right state if Lynsey isn't napping or is making too much noise. I have taken to bringing my niece out at that time in her baby carriage to escape Matthew's drunken ranting. We walk along the main street and all the neighbours stop and admire how pretty she is. Sometimes I might call into the library and have a chat with Mrs Matlock, who is such a dear.

When I return, my brother-in-law has passed out in the bed, and my poor sister is washing all the mounds of dirty diapers while Mom is trying to do her lacing. I walked in the door yesterday afternoon, and it really hit me how different the mood in the house was from when I was a girl. Back then, it had been my mother's house. An island woman and her two island girls. My mother might have been sad and lonely, but she did give us freedom to roam the island and explore. I know I've always been a disappointment to her, but the important thing is she let me go. But now, my old home feels like a stranger's house. It belongs to Matthew Young, and he lords it over all of us. He holds my sister prisoner. She doesn't see it herself, but truly, I've never seen her so miserable. It breaks my heart. I tried to talk to Mom about it, but she puts it down to baby blues.

And the truth is, Ava, the reason I've stayed so long to help with Lynsey is that I am afraid for my sister. Bruises on her arms, which when I ask her how she got them she makes a lame excuse, like she banged her arm against the door, or fell over.

'I don't think Matthew Young is a good man,' I tell my mom.

I believe she understands. I see it in her face, but she won't admit it. After all, she pushed Katie into the marriage.

'Your sister has made her bed, Susie, and now she has to lie in it.'

What can I do? Katie will tell me nothing about what happens between her and Matthew in private. Every time I suggest he is a bully, she gets angry with me, and defensive. I guess it's time for me to come home, my darling. I will be back soon.

*

She had taken Lynsey on a glorious summer walk around the island. It had been a perfect afternoon, and Susannah had enjoyed the warmth of the sun on her face as she pushed the baby carriage down the road and along Main Street. The leaves rustled in the trees, some fluttering to the sidewalk in the breeze, a lush green trail all the way into town. Today, instead of going to the library, she took a turn that brought her up a hill to a viewing point of the bay and harbour. Taking Lynsey out of the carriage, she held her close to her chest, wrapping the blanket tight about her, although the air was warm.

'This is your childhood kingdom, darling,' she told her baby niece.

Lynsey blinked, and indeed she tipped her tiny chin as if trying to catch a view of the big wide open Atlantic ocean. The serenity of the blue waters of Vinalhaven harbour, and all the little islands dotted all the way out to the ocean. Susannah remembered the time she'd 'borrowed' an old rowing boat from the harbour and had taken Kate out in it. She'd been nine and Kate seven at the time. Susannah had wanted to go on an adventure. See what was beyond the island. Follow in their father's footsteps. But the boat had had a hole in the bottom, and they were hardly out of the harbour before they began to sink. Susannah had tried to stay calm, but Kate got frightened and began to scream. Luckily one of the summer visitors had been sailing into the harbour and came to their rescue, but not until both sisters were up to their waists in water. Ever since that day, Kate had refused to go out any deeper than up to her knees in the ocean. She'd only paddle by the shoreline, or in the granite quarries inland which they used as bathing pools in the summer months. She couldn't swim for that reason. Hated going on boats. It struck Susannah as extremely odd that she would choose to marry a man who spent his life on fishing boats.

'When you're a big girl, leave this island,' Susannah whispered into Lynsey's little shell ear. 'Leave and never come back.'

As soon as she stepped into the house, Susannah knew something was very wrong. The same feeling as when a bad nor'easter has just blown across the island. Devastation and uneasy calm.

She called out for her mom and her sister, but there was no answer.

Looking out of the window, she saw her mom in the garden, standing at the white picket fence and staring out at the ocean. Leaving Lynsey still asleep and tucked up in her carriage, Susannah ventured outside.

'Mom, are you okay?'

Her mother turned to her.

'Too much shouting,' she said, her face pale, as she put her hands over her ears. 'None of my business.'

'Where's Katie? Is he asleep?'

Her mother shook her head. '*He* indeed! Every woman should have a man. What's wrong with you, Susannah?'

Susannah ignored her mother, and ran back into the house, searching for Kate downstairs in the kitchen and knocking on the door of her and Matthew's bedroom but there was no answer.

Eventually she found her sister upstairs in her own bedroom, their childhood bedroom, curled up in a foetal position on the bed. Susannah ran over to her.

'Katie, what's wrong? Where's Matthew?'

'Out,' Kate whispered.

She looked like she'd seen a ghost. Susannah knew something was terribly wrong because she didn't even ask for Lynsey.

'What happened? Please, Katie, tell me?'

Her sister sat up in the bed. Her breasts had leaked through her shirt. Any minute now, Lynsey would wake up crying for her feed.

'He said I'm disgusting,' Kate whispered. 'But he is stuck with me. I'm his wife and I need to do my duty.'

'What did he do to you?' Susannah whispered in horror.

'Tell me, Susie, what's it like when you make love with Ava?' Kate asked, her eyes wet with tears. 'Please, tell me how it feels?' Kate gripped her hand tight.

Susannah closed her eyes for a minute. 'Oh, Katie, it's the most wonderful joy I've ever felt.'

Kate nodded, tears beginning to fall down her face. 'I don't feel joy when Matthew and I are together.'

'I'm sorry, darling,' Susannah said, stroking her sister's soft blonde curls. 'Please tell me what happened?'

'I told you,' she said quietly. 'I had to do my duty as his wife, but he got angry with me. Because… he couldn't…' Kate sobbed. 'He said it's because I'm disgusting.'

Susannah took her sister in her arms and cradled her head in her hands. 'It's okay,' she said. 'Everything will be okay.'

But in truth she had no idea what to do.

At that moment, Lynsey started crying downstairs. 'I'll go get her,' Susannah said. 'Your little girl needs you.'

After Lynsey had been fed, changed, and put to sleep in her crib in Kate and Matthew's room, Susannah persuaded her sister to let her wash her hair. While their mother laced at her stand, Susannah filled the old tin bath with pot after pot of boiled water. As she bathed Kate, gently massaging her head and neck, their mother began to sing one of their old childhood songs.

They were all on alert for sounds of Matthew's return, but it was Saturday night, and Susannah was certain he would be out all night, especially after what had happened earlier. She wasn't sure what to do. How much could she interfere in her sister's marriage?

Just when they had all begun to relax, they heard the front door slam open. They all sat in anxious silence as Matthew appeared in the doorway, gripping the handle as he swayed to and fro. Susannah had never seen anyone so drunk before. He said nothing at first, as if taking in the scene of the sisters and their mother in harmony. But Susannah saw a dark glint in his eye, as his mouth twisted into a cruel smile.

'What's going on here?' he asked. 'Why are you naked in the kitchen for all to see?' He addressed Kate, ignoring Susannah and her mother as if they didn't exist.

Kate stumbled out of the bath, grabbing the towel off the chair. Her whole body radiated fear.

'Leave her alone,' Susannah said, standing up, hands on her hips.

'Or what?' Matthew said, dismissing her, before grabbing Kate by the arm. 'Where's my dinner?'

'We thought you would be out all night,' Kate simpered. 'But I can make your dinner now, darling. Of course. Won't take me long.'

'I'll help,' their mom said, putting down her lacing and taking a pot out of the cupboard. 'You put your feet up, Matthew, and we'll have some potatoes and fish cooked up for you in no time.'

Matthew narrowed his eyes.

'What kind of useless wife are you?' he roared at Kate. 'To have no dinner on the table for her husband when he's out risking his life every single day?'

'Keep your voice down. The baby,' Susannah said.

Matthew turned on her. 'Did you just tell me to keep my voice down in my own house?' he yelled at her. Immediately, they heard Lynsey crying from across the hall.

'Don't antagonise him, Susie, please,' Kate begged as she went to go for the baby. But Matthew grabbed her by the arm on her way out of the door.

'I come first,' he demanded. 'You have to feed me first.'

'But the baby is crying; she's hungry, Matthew. Mom and Susie will get your dinner.'

'It's *your* job. Let them give the darn baby a bottle.'

'Her name is Lynsey and she's your daughter!' Susannah suddenly flared, pushing past him out of the door to get to her niece, who was screaming at this stage.

Lynsey was red in the face by the time Susie picked her up. 'Come on, darling, hang on now, Mommy is coming.' She jigged her up and down, so that her screams subsided into hiccups.

Any minute now Kate would come in, Susannah reassured herself. Matthew would hardly stop his wife from feeding her own baby. But to Susannah's horror, Matthew thundered into the room after all and yanked Lynsey out of her arms. Lynsey began roaring again.

'Give her back!' Susannah yelled at him.

'She's my daughter,' he declared.

Kate ran into the room. 'Matthew darling, please, she needs to be fed,' she said, her voice trembling. 'Give her to me, come on now.'

'Fine,' he said, offering Lynsey to Kate. Her sister quickly took her in her arms and unbuttoned her shirt to feed her.

'Not in here,' Matthew said, pushing Kate out of the door. 'No man wants to see his wife looking like a milking cow.'

Susannah could feel herself trembling with rage. She had to get away from this hideous man, but when she went to follow Kate out of the room, Matthew stood in her way.

'Let me by,' Susannah said.

'I know your dirty little secret,' Matthew said in a low hiss.

Susannah felt her chest tighten, a shiver down her spine. 'Get out of my way; you're drunk.'

'In case you didn't know, as Kate's husband I read all her mail before she does, although she's so dumb she doesn't notice.' He gave her a nasty smile. 'I especially read every single one of the foul letters from her sister about her filthy *injun* lover.'

The air was suddenly thick with threat. Susannah felt her mouth go dry. 'That's none of your business.'

'It is so,' he said. 'As the head of this family it's my responsibility to ensure my wife isn't corrupted and to look after all of your moral values. And Susannah, I find yours lacking.'

'You're a monster,' she hissed.

Quick as a flash, Matthew slapped her across the face. She stepped back in shock, and as she did so he punched her in the mouth and pushed her on the bed.

'I think we both know what lesson it is you need to learn,' he said, flipping her over on her stomach so that her cries were muffled by the bedclothes. She tried her best to fight against him as he pulled her skirt up. She could taste blood in her mouth as she tried her hardest to clamp her legs shut. *Please, God, please someone help me.* With his knee digging into her back, he pulled her legs apart.

'I own Katie, and I own you. This house, your whole family,' he said as he pushed his fist up her and she gasped in shock at the pain of it. 'Is this what your girl does to you?'

She writhed, and screamed into the mattress. Fought with every fibre of her being, but she had no way of stopping him.

'Now feel how it is for real.'

He tore into her and she screamed with horror, her whole being shattering with her head buried in the bedsheets. Matthew kept thrusting and thrusting and all she could think of was a wild beast and how she wanted to kill him, pummel him with stones. At last he called out, 'Katie!' in a completely different tone of voice, almost like a mother calling for her child, and collapsed on top of her. She felt his seed leaking down the inside of her leg and she wanted to be sick, but she lay quite still until she heard the steady rhythm of his sleep. Carefully, so as not to wake him, heavy with pain, she slipped out from the bed.

She fled upstairs to her bedroom, shaking all over, trembling with shock and pain. Took her sheets and wiped down her legs, before throwing all her things in a case. She'd no idea where she was going. There was no ferry until the morning. But she'd sleep outside rather than stay in this house one more minute.

She went tumbling into the kitchen with her case, and Kate gasped when she saw her cut lip, smarting cheek.

'We've got to go now, right now, while he's sleeping.'

Kate's eyes filled with tears. 'Oh, Susie, I'm so sorry he hit you. But we can't leave; where would we go?'

'Katie, please, he did more than hit me.'

There was an uneasy silence in the kitchen.

'Well, what do you expect, talking back to him and antagonising him the whole time?' Their mother spoke up.

Susannah looked in her horror at her mother.

'He'll be sorry, I'm sure,' Kate placated her. 'It's my fault. He'll be better when the baby doesn't cry so much, when I'm more able—'

'He raped me!' Susannah screamed at her mother and sister, appalled by their lack of outrage.

'No, I can't believe it.' Kate shook her head, unable to meet her gaze. 'He wouldn't do that. Don't say such a lie, Susie.'

'More likely you led him on,' their mother interjected.

'Oh my god!' Susannah wailed.

'Sit down, now, come on.' Kate tried to calm her down. 'It'll be all right. I'm so sorry. Please don't be angry.'

But Susannah had never felt such fury at her mother, nor so frustrated at Kate. 'I'm leaving right now. I'm not spending another moment in this house, ever!' she shouted at them. 'Come with me now because I'm never coming back.'

'It's late, there's no ferry!' her mother argued with her. 'Have you lost your senses, you stupid hysterical girl?'

But Susannah couldn't bear the betrayal of her mother and sister any longer. She fled out of the door of the house. It was a chilly summer's night, but she didn't care. She ran all the way to the ferry terminal building. Thankfully, the waiting room door was open. She found a corner and cowered in it, half-expecting one of her family to hunt her down. But no one came.

At first dawn, she got on the ferry to Rockland, swearing she would never return. No matter what.

Chapter 31

Emer

29th October 2011

Henry had driven her to the other side of the island to the Perry Creek Conservation Area. Emer had met him at the diner on the wharfside, right after Lynsey arrived to visit Susannah. As soon as Lynsey had seen her aunt, and they'd given each other a cool hello, Lynsey had ushered Emer into the kitchen.

'Why didn't you tell me she's so bad?'

'But she's stable,' Emer protested. 'Doing well.'

'She's got so *thin*.' Lynsey said, and she looked upset. Emer had seen this so many times. When you were with someone every day you didn't notice the changes, but the shock for others who had perhaps not seen their loved one for weeks was devastating.

'Thank god Rebecca's coming on Friday,' Lynsey said. 'It won't be long now.'

Emer was shocked by her bluntness, but then Lynsey reminded her of Susannah. She'd obviously inherited her direct manner from her aunt. Strange they were so alike and yet didn't get on.

'Are you okay to stay with her today?' Emer asked. 'She'll not want to take any pain relief until the afternoon. She needs a little help now getting into bed.'

'Sure,' Lynsey said. 'You deserve a day off. What you doing?'

'A friend's taking me for a hike,' Emer said, careful not to mention Henry's name as she was not sure how Lynsey would react.

*

Fall at its splendid finale. The foliage a breathtaking expression of burning colour – red, umber, gold, green, yellow, brown. As she and Henry walked the many trails of Perry Creek, the essence of the island hit her. This ancient rock with its rugged coastline, surviving the wild Atlantic – so vulnerable, and yet resilient. It clung on to the edge of the coastland, just like all the hundreds of other little islands dotted all the way along Maine's boundary with the ocean.

At first, they walked in silence, taking it all in and following Shadow as the husky trotted ahead. At the parking lot, there'd been a sign to keep dogs on a leash, but Henry had ignored it. They had parked at the northern edge of the preserve and were making their way to Perry Creek through glades of hay-scented ferns: amber, gold and yellow. They'd already seen deer running away through the woods, and squirrels busily collecting nuts for winter.

'If we didn't have Shadow with us we'd see more wildlife,' Henry said to her. 'You might catch a glimpse of a hare, or some otter by the creek.'

They climbed up some rocks, rising above the treeline. The view was staggering. The blue ocean swayed before her, and views of North Haven island across the bay, and Vinalhaven to the east and south.

'My god,' she said. 'It almost beats the west of Ireland.'

'Almost?' Henry questioned her, an amused look on his face.

'Well, nothing is quite like the west,' she said as they sat down on the rock and shared a bar of chocolate.

'You'll have to take me one day,' he said.

His words hung in the air, unanswered.

Dusk was beginning to descend as they drove back across the island. Emer's legs were sore from all the walking, but she felt good. It was soothing to be in nature, to stretch her body and feel space all around her.

'Are you hungry?' Henry asked her. 'Would you like to come back to mine for food?'

'Well, I should get back to Susannah,' Emer said, hunting for an excuse.

'But you told me Lynsey's there overnight,' he said. 'Don't you think you need a proper break?'

'I suppose.' She was unsure though. Would Lynsey cope on her own if there was a medical emergency?

'I've made pumpkin and pecan pie,' he said. 'It's my speciality every fall.'

Emer did want to go back to Susannah. Check in on her, and talk more with Lynsey. But then, she didn't know how to say no to Henry.

'Okay, for a little bit.' She gave in. 'I'll just give them a call. Let them know I'll be back later.'

'I don't think you'll get network here. Call them from mine.'

Henry drove along the island road, pulling in by a small cove. He parked the car, but Emer couldn't see a house anywhere, just a small motorboat moored to a little wooden quay.

Henry opened his door and let Shadow jump out.

'My house is on its own islet.' He indicated the boat. 'We need to take my boat there.'

Emer immediately felt tense. The last thing she wanted to do was get into a small boat.

'Maybe I should go back; it's late.'

'It's not far, literally a few minutes by boat.'

She didn't know what to say, embarrassed to admit she was scared of boats.

He helped her in, and Shadow jumped in next to her. She held on to the fur at the husky's neck as they took off across the water. Sea sprayed her face and she tasted salt on her lips. Her stomach swelled with the motion of the water as they sped across the bay.

It was a new moon rising, as the daylight leached from the sky. The whole bay glittered, and the ocean glinted in the distance as they approached Henry's tiny little island, all dark pines with a flagpole and the American flag fluttering on it. Would it be safe to return on the dark water? She guessed Henry had done it a hundred times before.

The house was hidden behind the pines. Shadow ran on ahead, a white ghost dog in the dusk. 'Careful, it's a bit slippery on the wet stones,' Henry said, taking her hand to help her along the rocky trail. They came to a clearing, within which stood a small wooden house.

'It's so quaint!' Emer said, glad to be off the boat. And it was: it seemed like a fairy-tale house in the woods. But as she looked at it in the fading light, she couldn't help thinking of Hansel and Gretel. She shook herself. Henry was hardly a witch.

'Built it myself,' Henry told her proudly as they climbed the steps to the porch. 'My father started it, but he died with it unfinished. So I took over.'

Inside, the house was filled with beautiful things. Emer was quite taken aback. She had been expecting a cluttered, rather messy bachelor's pad like Lars' apartment in Boston. But Henry had clearly spent a lot of time and effort creating a little haven. The walls were covered with art. Not just traditional landscapes of the sea and boats, but more contemporary pieces. He pointed out a couple of his own sculptures. They were all soft contours and smooth edges, naked bodies entwined or creatures of the island. A fox, and an otter. He'd used island granite for most of them. She liked them.

The main room had a large glass porch, facing out onto the pine woods and the sea. Henry turned on the lamps and the room was filled with a warm glow, outside immediately dark. She walked around, looking at the art, and then her heart stopped.

'Oh my god!'

'What is it?' Henry asked, all concern as she turned to him, her eyes wide with incredulity.

'That's one of Orla's paintings.'

She pointed with shaking finger at a small mixed media piece. She remembered Orla making it, just before one of her last exhibitions. It was of the woods back home in Ireland. Giant moths fluttering around the light emanating from a broad oak tree. Orla had called it *The Light House*.

'You're kidding?' Henry said. 'I bought that last year. Went to the exhibition with friends in Boston.'

'How insane! I can't believe the coincidence,' Emer said, staring at the painting. Had Orla just sent her a sign?

Henry poured them each a large glass of red wine, before popping his pie in the oven.

'Won't take long to warm up,' he told her, putting out a selection of nuts and tortilla chips on the coffee table.

'How long have you lived here?' Emer asked Henry as she sipped her wine. It tasted of blackberries and dark cherry, and she felt herself relax even with the first mouthful.

'In this house, five years,' he said, sitting next to her on the couch. 'Before that, on the island, in my family home all my life. I mean, I left to study art in New York, worked in restaurants making my way up the ladder too, but I always knew I was coming back.'

'Do you not find it lonely?'

'A bit, lately,' Henry said. 'But my girlfriend, Mandy, lived here with me until six months ago. We broke up.'

'Oh, I'm sorry,' Emer said, embarrassed she'd put her foot in it.

'Yeah, that was pretty bad,' he said. 'She cheated on me and ran off to another man on the mainland.' He took a big gulp of wine. 'But I'm over it now.'

The last thing Emer wanted was to get into a therapy session about a bitchy ex-girlfriend. It had happened to her too many times before. She changed the subject. 'I still can't believe you have one of my sister's paintings on your wall!'

'I know, it feels like more than a coincidence, don't you think?' he asked her, putting a hand on her knee.

'I guess,' she said, wondering whether to shift her knee. Not sure if she wanted him to touch her or not.

Maybe he sensed her wariness, because he got up. The aroma of pumpkin pie had filled the room, sweet and spicy. Emer's stomach groaned. She was very hungry.

'That pie should be ready. Don't worry, it's all vegan,' he said. 'Made sure of that. I've got oat cream too. Want some of that with it?'

Had he planned all along to bring her home for pie? She suppressed the idea: it made him seem a little presumptuous. He was being sweet, that's what it was. To think ahead like that, just in case.

The pie was amazing, melting in her mouth. She ate two slices, along with another glass of red wine. She hadn't enjoyed food in so long, not even all those vegan snacks she'd bought in the store when she first arrived. Since Orla had died, she'd been eating to live, not for any kind of enjoyment. It had felt wrong to have any kind of pleasure. It dawned on her. That was why she and Lars were doomed: because she couldn't allow herself the intense pleasure that came from being with him. Even though just thinking about him made her feel such longing for his touch.

'So, are you single?' Henry suddenly asked her.

'Yes,' Emer said, despite her instincts screaming, *No, no, you love Lars!*

'Your friend who visited,' Henry persisted. 'Isn't he your boyfriend?'

'No,' she replied. 'We had a thing,' she said, 'but it's over now.'

Henry nodded, pouring her another glass of wine. 'Well, that sure makes me glad,' he said, giving her a wide smile.

She was beginning to feel a little fuzzy from all the wine and pie.

'Shouldn't I be getting back?' she said, looking at her phone. 'It's getting late.'

'Don't think I should take the boat now,' Henry said. 'I've drunk too much. Wouldn't be safe. Lynsey's staying over with Susannah, right?'

'Oh yes,' Emer said, feeling a little ambushed. With a jolt, she realised she hadn't even telephoned to say she would be late. She'd been so distracted by the house, by Orla's painting. 'I'll give her a call. Let her know.'

'Sure,' Henry said. 'But maybe don't tell her you're here. You know we have history, right? She could get weird.'

'Okay,' Emer said, feeling a little uneasy.

'Say, why don't you tell her you took the ferry to Rockland for the night, and you'll be back in the morning.'

Emer didn't like lying, but Henry was right. She didn't want to get on the wrong side of Lynsey. Whatever might happen in the future, she needed her job right now. Henry showed her to the phone, and she made the call. Lynsey told her everything was fine. Susannah had gone to bed, and she'd see Emer the next day bright and early. She needed to get back to Salem for Halloween.

Back in the main room, Henry was opening another of bottle of wine.

'All okay?' he asked her.

'Yeah,' she said, collapsing on the couch. 'She's cool.'

'Let's put on some music,' he said, handing her a glass of wine. 'One of the good things about living on your own island is you don't have to worry about the neighbours.'

After complaining that his ex, Mandy, had stolen some of his best vinyl, Henry put on *Astral Weeks* by Van Morrison. It was music that Emer and Orla had used to listen to non-stop as teenagers. Another coincidence.

'Hey,' said Henry, as he settled back down on the couch next to her. 'Fancy some grass?'

It had been years since Emer had smoked any grass, but a part of her craved to let go of everything.

'Why not,' she replied.

They talked for hours. She told him all about her childhood in midlands Ireland, and what happened to her mam. Henry told her about his childhood on the island. His father had been a lobster fisherman, and an alcoholic.

'I swore I'd never fish,' Henry said. 'It's tempting, mind you. Buddies of mine make a ton of cash. But I saw what it did to my dad. If he wasn't fishing, he was in The Sand Bar getting drunk. It's no life.'

Henry explained that all of his siblings had long since left the island, and both his parents were dead. 'I'm the only one left,' he said.

'Will you stay?' she asked him.

'If I find the right girl,' he said, giving her a look so meaningful that she blushed. 'I love running the restaurant in the summer – and don't you think this would be a perfect place for kids? Their own island to roam, safe but free.'

'Oh yes,' Emer enthused, feeling heady from the joint. She could almost see all the little children running through the pine woods. Could hear the laughter. 'Your island would come alive.'

*

She wasn't sure how they came to be kissing on his bed. Her head was spinning with wine, and she was stoned, too. There was a distant voice in the back of her head telling her not to. She was still in love with Lars. He had her heart. She shouldn't be with any other man. But a kind of wildness had possessed her. Besides, she'd led Henry on. He was all over her, and she could sense his need for her. It was good to feel needed.

'You're so beautiful,' he whispered as he kissed her breasts; his lips pressed softly against her skin, all the way down her body.

If she had sex with someone else, it would really be over with Lars. She'd have to let him go.

She put her hands on Henry's shoulders, and he raised his head, snaked back up her body.

'Condom,' she whispered.

'It's okay,' he assured her. 'I won't get you pregnant.'

Again, a distant warning in her head. He'd just been talking about having kids… but he was already stroking her, making her soften, and ache with desire. Her whole being was present in this moment. She wanted him in her.

Chapter 32

Susannah

November 1961

Dearest Katie… Dear Kate… Several times, Susannah sat down to write her sister a letter, but she could get no further than her name. For the first time in her life, words failed her. She decided to wait to hear from Kate, so at least she would have something to respond to. But the mailbox remained empty week after week.

Everything hurt. Her body, from what Matthew had done to her; her heart, from being let down so badly by her mom, and even worse, from Kate not having her back. Her head, from not knowing what to do. It was horrific to think of her sister captive in her marriage with such a brute. But unless Kate herself admitted it and asked for help, what could Susannah do? She missed baby Lynsey, and worried too about her. Would Matthew go as far as harming his own child? Should she go back to the island and try to take Lynsey? At least her niece would be safe then.

Ava counselled her it was more likely she'd end up arrested by the police if she did such a thing.

'I could tell them he's abusive?'

'Do you think they're going to believe you over him?' Ava said. 'Trust me, abusers can be the best actors in the world. And he's a man, too. They will just call you hysterical and dismiss your concerns.'

Susannah hadn't told Ava everything. When she had got back to their apartment in Cambridge, after her escape from the island, Ava had been angry and upset to see Susannah's cut lip and bruised cheek.

'Don't ever, ever go back there,' Ava said, as she held Susannah in her arms.

'But what about Katie?' Susannah said, her voice wobbling with tiredness and emotion.

Ava took a step back and gently stroked the side of Susannah's face.

'I know it's hard to accept, my love, but she's made her choice. We can't force her to leave, because if we do, she'll only go back to him.'

'What's he done to my sister? I don't know her any more!' Susannah said in frustration.

'She knows you're here, Susannah, and that's what's important. She has somewhere to run to, if she ever does decide to leave.'

'She'll never leave Mom,' Susannah said glumly.

Her mother's reaction to what had happened had shocked Susannah deep down. She tried to reason that her mother was afraid of Matthew too, but it hurt her deeply that her own mother had done nothing to protect her daughter.

She hadn't told Ava everything. If she said nothing, maybe the fact of what had happened would fade anyway. But no matter how much she tried to block it – spending hours in the library poring over books, or late nights out with Ava dancing and drinking wine – the memory wouldn't go away. For the first time in her life, Susannah felt fearful.

If she was walking home from the library after dark, she would get tense if a man walked behind her. Often, she'd cross the road back and forth several times, or go on a long roundabout route to avoid it. When she went on a protest with Ava, the whole experience was completely different from before. She no longer felt part of a community, but instead panicked by the size of the crowd and the hostility of the police. The next time Ava asked her to go on a civil rights march, she called off, saying she felt sick.

Worst of all was that the horror of what had happened to her had turned her frigid. Ever since she'd returned from the island, whenever Ava had wanted to make love she'd made excuses – *I'm too tired, I don't feel well* – or even pretend she was asleep. Ava said nothing, turned over and went to sleep, but Susannah knew she was hurting her. She had to forget what Matthew Young had done to her, else she'd drive Ava away.

Christmas came with no word from her family. Susannah and Ava shared the festival together in their apartment. They found the top of a Christmas tree discarded in the street and decorated it with stars and bells they made out of card and string, before putting it in the window. Susannah gave Ava a copy of Joan Baez's new record, *Vol. 2*.

'I know it's not really a surprise; you've been talking about it for months…'

'I love it,' Ava said, giving her a big hug, before putting the record on the turntable. 'Open yours!'

Ava gave her a first edition of Emily Dickinson poetry.

'Oh my god!' Susannah whispered. 'Where did you find this?'

'In a bookshop, dummy!' Ava said, looking pleased with herself.

Susannah felt so overwhelmed. She didn't deserve this woman's love. Ever since that terrible night in Vinalhaven, she'd been pushing her away again and again. Why was Ava still here, when she was so cold to her?

'Darling, what is it? What's wrong?' Ava crouched down beside her.

'I don't deserve you,' she whispered.

'I think that's for me to decide,' Ava said, kissing her tears away, before softly kissing her lips. She paused, took Susannah's hand and led her to the bed. But as soon as they were naked and under the covers, Susannah began to tremble. She tried to still her body, kiss Ava back, but all the passion she had felt when they first kissed had dissipated.

'What is it, Su?' Ava asked her, pulling back.

Susannah shook her head, eyes squeezed shut.

'You haven't wanted to make love for weeks. Don't you like me any more?' Ava said in a small voice.

Susannah opened her eyes. 'Oh no, Ava, that's not it.'

She had to tell her, because if she didn't, Matthew Young would ruin her life as well as her sister's. She turned to Ava, took her hand in hers. Felt the squeeze of encouragement.

'I have to tell you something,' she whispered.

Later, in the darkness of the midwinter afternoon, they went for a walk in the snow.

'I want to kill him,' Ava hissed as the snow fell around them.

Susannah raised her face to the sky, felt the snowflakes landing cold and wet on her cheeks. Already, she felt a little better because Ava knew. She couldn't forget what had happened, but perhaps she could learn to live through it.

They walked hand in hand for once not caring how they might look. With Ava by her side, Susannah felt hopeful for her future for the first time since that dreadful last night on Vinalhaven.

Chapter 33

Emer

30th October 2011

Emer woke to an empty bed and the smell of bacon frying. The scent hit her in the back of her throat. Made her want to gag. She'd always hated the smell of cooking meat, right from when she was a little girl. Orla had claimed Emer was born vegan.

She sat up unsteadily in Henry's large bed, and held her head in her hands. She had a terrible hangover. Her mouth was parched, and she felt dizzy and nauseous. Details of the previous night came back to her. Oh god, how many times had they had sex? Henry's appetite had been insatiable, and in the end, she must have just passed out from sheer exhaustion.

She slid her legs out from under the sheets and stood up, feeling very wobbly. Hunting around, she found her jeans, bra and sweater, but couldn't find her T-shirt or knickers anywhere. She'd have to go commando.

Henry was in the kitchen, frying his bacon. He gave her a big grin and a wave as she staggered in and perched up at the breakfast bar. How come he was so cheery, when she felt like the living dead?

'How you doing?' he asked, pouring a glass of orange juice. 'Hope you don't mind I'm frying bacon. It's my own personal hangover cure.'

'No, it's fine.' She could hardly tell him not to in his own house. 'But I thought you were vegetarian?'

'No, flexitarian. Eat fish, too. You can't live on Vinalhaven without eating lobster. You'll see,' he said, placing a plate with fried tomatoes, mushrooms and a slice of toast in front of her.

She wanted to react to his presumption. There was no way she was ever going to eat lobster, of all things. But she was just too tired to bother.

He slid in next to her at the breakfast bar and kissed the top of her head, before digging into his bacon and tomatoes.

'Hey, last night was so special,' he said to her, his mouth full of meat.

'Yes,' she murmured, not knowing what else to say. She couldn't really remember too much about it, apart from the fact it had felt like two lost souls giving each other solace.

'Like, so amazing,' he continued, and then leant over and gave her a big greasy kiss. The taste of bacon on his lips made her stomach heave.

She quelled her nausea. He really was so sweet, making her breakfast.

'I don't feel so great,' she said, pushing aside her mushrooms.

'Oh, no, baby, I'm sorry to hear that,' Henry said, his face a picture of concern. 'Do you want to go back to bed? You could hang out here for the day?'

'No.' She shook her head, trying to ignore the fact it felt weird he'd called her baby. 'I have to get back. Lynsey's leaving and Susannah needs me.'

'Okay, you go have a rest on the couch. I'll clean up and then we'll get going.'

She wandered into the front room. In daylight, the views were staggering. It was a hazy fall day, the mist rising off the sea, and the sun glowing pink, illuminating the dense pine woods.

Henry's place really was idyllic, and yet she wasn't tempted to hide out here for the day. She was anxious about Susannah. Keen to get back before Lynsey left.

She walked over and studied Orla's painting again. She remembered the preparations for her last exhibition. Orla had been on a high for weeks, having been told she was officially in remission. Ethan had tried to get her to calm down, worried she'd get sick again, but she'd been a frenzy of creativity. Painting non-stop, and organising a show at a gallery in the Back Bay area of Boston. Emer would come home from a night shift at the hospital, red-eyed and bleary, to find Orla still painting, having been up all night.

'Don't overdo it,' Emer had warned her.

'But this is what keeps me alive,' Orla had announced, her face flecked by paint and her studio a cacophony of creative industry.

Sometimes, rather than going to bed, Emer had curled up on the paint-spattered couch, still in her scrubs, and fallen asleep to the sounds of Orla creating. She had found it so soothing.

Emer reached out and touched the surface of the painting now. Her sister could have put her fingertip right in this spot. It sent a shiver down Emer's spine. Orla always signed the back of her pictures. Without thinking to ask Henry whether he minded, Emer lifted the painting off the wall and turned it over. There it was: *Orla Feeney*, her swirling signature in pencil. Ethan's surname was Goldberg, but Orla had kept her own surname when she married.

Above the signature, Emer noticed the gallery receipt still taped to the back of the picture. It was hanging off, so she pressed the tape back down. As she did so, she noticed something else. The date on the receipt was for the previous week. That was strange. Henry had said he'd bought it at Orla's exhibition, last year. But it was there, in black and white. The name of a gallery in Portland, not the exhibition space in Boston, and the date. Exactly one week ago. The day after they'd gone for their first walk.

Emer carefully hung the picture back up again. Should she call him out on it? But he hadn't done anything wrong, had he? In fact, it was touching that he'd looked up her sister's art and had bought a picture.

The ride across the bay was so stunning Emer's nerves at being in a boat again began to gradually dissipate. As she watched sea ducks taking off, her head felt clearer freshened by the sea spray and the clean air.

Henry dropped her at the bottom of Susannah's road.

'Best Lynsey doesn't see us, right?' he said to her as she got out of the pick-up. 'In fact, I wouldn't tell either her or Susannah we're dating, okay?'

'Oh.' She turned around. 'Are we dating?'

'Well, I sure hope so,' he said, looking very pleased with himself. 'Want to go for another hike tomorrow? It's going to be great weather and I can take you to the best viewing point on the whole of Vinalhaven.'

'Okay, I guess, as long as Susannah is all right.'

He didn't pick up on her lack of enthusiasm at all.

'Have a great day, gorgeous,' he called out to her as he drove off.

She stood for a few minutes watching Henry drive off, feeling a little lost and confused. How had she somehow found herself in a relationship with this man? If Orla were alive, she'd say he ticked all the boxes. His own house. A successful sculptor. Owns a restaurant. Passionate lover. Attentive. Maybe too attentive?

It was only as she opened the door into Susannah's house that Emer remembered. Stopped in her tracks. They hadn't used protection. Not once. And how many times had they made love last night? How stupid could she be? She was a nurse, for god's sake. He had said he wouldn't get her pregnant, but how old was that line? She'd have to go to the medical centre and get the morning-after pill as soon as she could. What a mortifying thought. The island was so small – would people find out? She hoped they were discreet.

'So, how was Rockland?' Lynsey asked her, coming down the stairs with her bag packed.

Emer baulked for a second.

'Oh, it was great,' she said, feeling herself redden from the lie.

'Did you go to that cool restaurant, Fog? They've got a great vegan dish, and the cocktails are awesome.'

'Oh, yes,' Emer lied. 'How's Susannah?' she said, hastily changing the subject.

'Well, still criticising me, so she must be okay,' Lynsey said. 'I tried to do some reiki on her and she almost slapped me back.' She sighed. 'I'll be back after Halloween. Rebecca's arriving, so I'll see you in a few days.'

After Lynsey had gone, Emer climbed the stairs to Susannah's room. She was keen to see how she was.

'Well, there she is,' Susannah said as soon as Emer walked through the door of her room. 'I thought you'd gone for good.'

Susannah was sitting up in bed and her eyes were bright. Emer found she was very glad to see Susannah too.

'Well, now, I was thinking about it,' Emer joked. 'But then I missed you!'

'Thought you'd gone off to find your young man,' Susannah said, sniffing.

To Emer's surprise, she realised Susannah was crying.

'Hey, it's fine, I'm here now,' she said, grabbing a tissue out of the box and handing it to her.

'But you should go after him,' Susannah said. 'Don't make the same mistake I did.'

Chapter 34

Susannah

September 1966

The letter arrived the afternoon before they were moving to New York. Ava and Susannah had spent the entire week before packing up their lives in box after box.

'Five years of things all ready to go,' Ava announced as she sealed the last box.

'Who would have thought we'd have so much stuff?' Susannah said. 'When I arrived at Harvard with only one suitcase.'

'Me too!' Ava said, putting her arm around Susannah. 'Are you excited?'

'Of course,' Susannah said.

Things had worked out so well. Ava had work with a civil rights organisation in Brooklyn, while Susannah had secured a teaching position at Columbia. After saving up for months, Ava had bought an old black Ford and they'd driven down to New York the month before, finding a cute apartment in Brooklyn Heights to rent upon their return. It was also on the fifth floor, but worth it for the spectacular views of Brooklyn Bridge and Manhattan Island. They'd made a little holiday out of the trip, and on the way back from New York had spent a few blissful days on Cape Cod, joining friends at one of their parents' vacation homes by the sea.

'Who would have thought Joni was so wealthy?' Ava had said when they'd walked into the mansion.

Being in Cape Cod had reminded Susannah of being home on Vinalhaven. The smell of the sea, watching the fishing boats going out, and even the rhythm of life. Slower, and more connected to nature than the city. It had been a wonderful few days of late breakfasts, swimming in the ocean, bonfires on the beach, and singing songs.

She and Ava were on the cusp of a new beginning and she was looking forward to it. But a part of her was also still grieving for Kate. She hadn't heard from her in over five years and once they moved apartment, her family wouldn't know where she was any more.

'Shouldn't I write them?' Susannah said. 'Let them know where I am?'

'If you really want to,' Ava said to Susannah. 'But maybe it's better to let them go? That's what I've done with my family.'

Ava never went home to the reservation. Rarely talked about it, despite the fact she was so devoted to raising awareness of rights for American Indians. Susannah had once suggested they go visit, but Ava was adamant she never wanted to go back.

'It's not who I am any more. My parents are dead. My brothers and sisters gone I don't know where. Why would I go back?'

Susannah often wondered about the timing of the last letter from Kate, on the very afternoon before the day of their departure. Had it been providential? A sign? If she had known everything would change forever as a consequence, would she have ripped it open so fast to read it?

One sheet. Just a few lines.

Dear Susie,
    Lynsey is five now and I have another little girl, Rebecca – she's two. When I see them together I think of us. I am sorry, dear sister. Can you ever forgive me?

After you left, we were so frightened. We hoped he might
get better after Rebecca was born. But it's worse.
I am leaving him. We have some money saved. We don't care
where we go. Just away from him.

Please come help me. I'm trying to persuade Mom to come
with us. If you come, it will help. Arrive on a ferry first thing
in the morning, any morning. He'll be gone fishing. By the
time he's home, we'll have left.

*

'Don't go,' Ava said.

'But I have to,' Susannah said. 'You told me if she ever reached out, I should be there for her.'

Ava stood among the boxes, frowning.

'That was five years ago! You haven't heard from her in all this time. After what happened, how could you ever consider going back there?'

Susannah went to Ava, took her hands in hers. 'She's my sister, Ava. I have to help her.'

But Ava shook her head. 'Su, he's dangerous. I don't want you on the same island.' She squeezed Susannah's hand. Let it go. 'Why can't you send them a telegram with our address in New York? You don't need to go and get them.'

'He reads all her mail. He'll know.'

Ava was hurt and angry. Susannah didn't blame her. They were supposed to be leaving for New York the next morning. Ava started her new job in two days' time.

'I'll bring them to New York,' Susannah promised. 'I'll be right behind you. We'll take the Greyhound bus from Boston.'

'I don't know,' Ava said, looking worried. 'By the sounds of him, he won't let her go easy.'

'I can't turn my back on my family. Not now she's finally been brave enough to say she'll leave.'

Ava sat on the green chair. It belonged to the apartment, but Susannah would always associate it with Ava. It was the place she always sat to think.

'Okay.' Ava gave in. 'They can stay with us until they find somewhere.'

'Thank you, my love.' Susannah squeezed in next to Ava on the green chair and hugged her tightly.

'Well, I'm not sure what your mom will make of us sharing a bed, though,' she said, giving Susannah a lazy grin.

'Frankly, I don't care what my mom thinks of me any more,' Susannah said, giving Ava a kiss on the lips. 'She must be real frightened of Matthew if Kate says she might come with her.'

Susannah couldn't imagine her mother outside of the island. Would she be able to cope with New York? She had tried to stop caring about her mom after the awful things she'd said to her the night of the rape. *Let her fall off the ferry into the Atlantic*, she told herself. But another part of her couldn't help worrying about her mom, too. Last time she'd seen her, there had been something a little not right about her.

Pushing thoughts of Mother from her head, she looked into Ava's deep brown eyes. 'Everything is going to be okay,' she promised her.

It felt strange to be saying these words to Ava, because usually it was her lover who said it to her. All the times Susannah had broken down in bed, unable to bear Ava's touch. Slowly and gently, Ava had coaxed her back, little by little, and her senses had been reborn. The idea of being apart from Ava, even for a few days, was torture. But she couldn't let Kate down. Not now she'd finally found the courage to leave Matthew.

They made love, curled up in the green chair of their stripped apartment. Afterwards, Susannah often thought about that last hot, late summer afternoon in Cambridge, when she and Ava had been together. Their bodies slick with sweat, melting into each other. Feeling the beat of Ava's heavy heart in the thick, roasting air. All of who they were was contained in their love-making. Their most primal selves, licking each other, wordlessly sensing the urges and wants of their bodies; and their most spiritual selves, looking into each other's eyes. No need for words, for it was said in every tiny gesture – *I love you I love you I love you.*

With the sounds of afternoon stirring the street below as children went out to play after a hot, dusty day in school, lamenting the end of their holidays, and Bostonians emerged from the boiling subway, or sat on the café sidewalks and drank beer, Susannah got washed and dressed.

Ava sat cross-legged on the floor in her damp shirt, staring out of the window.

'I'll see you in a couple of days,' Susannah said, bending down and kissing the top of her head.

Ava caught her arm.

'Are you sure about this?' she asked her. 'I've a bad feeling.'

Susannah had never seen Ava so anxious. Not even at one of their most controversial protests.

'I have to go get my sister,' Susannah said, sounding determined, although inside she was tempted to give in to Ava. Start fresh in New York, and never think about her mom and sister again. But she knew it went against her grain to be able to do that. 'If I was in trouble, Katie would come get me.'

'But would she?' Ava questioned, looking at her with searching eyes.

'Sure she would,' Susannah said, feeling a little thrown by Ava's question.

Ava stood up, padded over to her in her bare feet.

'I'll come with you,' she said. 'Drive us to the ferry. It's five or six hours, right?'

'Honey, you've got to get to New York tomorrow,' Susannah said, putting a hand on her arm. 'Your job.'

'I can defer.'

They both knew that if Ava didn't turn up in two days' time, the job was lost.

'I love that you want to protect me,' Susannah said. 'But honest, it will be okay. I will be there and gone before Matthew even sets eyes on me. He's gone for hours every day, out fishing.'

The wind started to pick up as the bus left Portland. She could feel it buffeting the sides of the vehicle as they trundled down the road. She tried to sleep, but it was impossible. Despite her reassurances to Ava, she was dreading going back to the island. What if Kate had already changed her mind since she sent the letter? What should Susannah do then? Leave immediately on her own, or try to persuade Kate to come with her?

In Rockland, Susannah made it in time for last drinks in The Trade Winds Inn. She ordered a whisky straight, while waiting to see if they had a room for the night. The lights flickered in the near-empty bar as the receptionist came over to her with a room key. Susannah downed her whisky in one and then dragged her tired limbs to bed.

She lay down on the big bed, and closed her eyes. She was exhausted from all the days of packing up their flat and the long bus journey to Rockland, and yet it was impossible to sleep. The wind was rising, as was Susannah's tension. She could hear the inn's sign swaying back and forth, and the trees' branches scratching against her window pane. She recognised the tone in

the wind. A nor'easter was coming down from Canada. Rare at
this time of year, but all the same wild and dangerous. She sat up
in bed. If the wind didn't drop soon, the ferry would be cancelled
tomorrow morning. How would she get over to rescue Kate?

Chapter 35

Emer

30th October 2011

Emer lay down on her bed at last. She felt queasy from the morning-after pill, but also relieved she had got it in time. She was annoyed at Henry. She had sent him a text to tell him she had to go to the medical centre and why, but he hadn't offered to come with her. Not that she wanted him to, but the point was it was also his fault she was getting the morning-after pill, and he should offer to be there. Instead, he'd sent her a barrage of loving texts.

I feel so lucky we met.

Can't wait to see you again tomorrow, baby.

Never felt this way about anyone before ♥♥♥

He was completely over the top. She didn't answer any of them, not wanting to encourage him. How stupid she'd been. The poor guy had completely misunderstood what had happened between them. Tomorrow, she'd tell him she was happy to remain friends, but wasn't ready for anything else. It would be cruel not to put him straight. She scrolled through her phone. Still no messages from Lars. She felt awful now she'd slept with Henry. Even though she and Lars were no longer together, it felt like a betrayal.

'I'm a mess,' she said to her dead sister. 'It's all your fault!'

Anger, pure and unjustified, swept through her whole being. How dare Orla die on her? Leave her all alone? She was fucking everything up without her. If only she could talk to her, Orla would tell her what to do.

She picked up her phone and called Ethan. The closest she could be to her dead sister was Orla's husband. They'd always got on.

'Hey, Emer, how's it going?' Ethan said. 'It's good to hear your voice.'

Ethan sounded better than when she'd said goodbye to him in Boston. They talked for over an hour, memory after memory of Orla. They cried together, but they were able to laugh too.

'Remember her vegan brownies? She wouldn't even tell me the secret to her recipe!'

'Which of you went vegan first?' Ethan asked. 'She always said you copied her!'

'Ah no, it was a pact,' Emer said. 'I never really liked meat, but then Orla suggested we do it together when she was fourteen, and I was fifteen. I was into animal rights, and she just wanted to lose weight!'

Ethan sighed. 'I don't think I'll ever stop missing her, Em.'

'I know,' she said.

'It's not fair.'

'I know.'

They were silent for a minute. Remembering Orla's last days.

'I want to ask you something,' Ethan said, eventually. 'I've some of Orla's ashes. I'm going out to Cape Cod this weekend. Hiring a boat and scattering some in the sea.'

'She'd like that,' Emer said, trying not to think of her spillage in the house in Quincy.

'Do you want to come? It would mean a lot to me.'

'Oh, I don't know, Ethan, I'm looking after this old lady. She's really sick.'

'Just see how it goes,' he said. 'Call me, and I'll collect you from wherever.'

'Thanks,' she whispered, knowing she wouldn't.

'I know I asked you before, but please can I give you some of the ashes too? Would you bring them to Ireland? I know she wanted to have some scattered in the woods where she grew up.'

'Oh.' Emer's voice caught in her throat. 'I don't know when I'll be back home.'

'Think about it. No pressure. I'll keep some safe for you,' Ethan said. 'I think it would mean a lot to your father too.'

After Ethan got off the phone, Emer couldn't help thinking how very strange and surreal it was to be talking to her brother-in-law about her sister's ashes. Different parts of what used to be Orla, being scattered in different parts of the world. In her heart, she knew her sister would want her to take her ashes back to Mammy. But she wasn't ready to go home yet. She'd see things through here, with Susannah, first.

After Lynsey's visit, and Emer's night away, Susannah had appeared so much more vulnerable to her. Now they had just one of Kate's letters left to type up, it was as if she'd let herself get weaker. But still she refused the medication.

'Not until we're finished,' she'd insisted.

Emer's eyes ached from looking at the screen of her laptop. She closed them. Where was Lars now? She pictured his hands. Such beautiful, fine hands, surgeon's hands. Created to save lives. Steady and nimble. Was he in the hospital? Trying to focus on his work, but his head clouded with memories of her, just as her head was clouded with memories of him? Or could he even be in surgery? His mind utterly focused and clear in concentration, because someone's life was literally on the line. Was he able to shut Emer away in a box? Lock her up and one day forget about her? When she thought that way, it drove her crazy. She never wanted Lars to forget her, because he would always be in the back of her mind.

Chapter 36

Susannah

September 1966

Susannah was stuck in Rockland for two nights. On the first morning, when she'd gone down to the ferry terminal in the howling wind, she'd known it was pointless. Sure enough, no ferries were running the whole day. She went straight to send a telegram, which she guessed Ava would get when she arrived at their new Brooklyn apartment the next day.

STORM STOP CANT GET OVER TO ISLAND STOP BE ON OUR WAY SOON STOP LOVE SU

Afterwards, she walked along the main street of Rockland while the rain and wind beat into her. She felt on edge. Only natural, considering she was returning to a place of deep trauma. But she had to get past her own hurt to help her sister. She retreated into a diner, and spent the afternoon drinking cup after cup of black coffee and trying to make notes for her lesson plans for her first semester teaching at Columbia. But her mind wouldn't settle, as dread seeped through every pore of her body. The hours ticked by slowly, while the wind howled outside.

'Say, honey, stay in here until the worst of it's over,' her waitress, Sandy, said. 'It'll start dying down soon.'

At four o'clock, the wind suddenly stopped.

'We're in the eye of the storm now,' Sandy announced.

Susannah felt her heart quicken, a feeling of panic setting in. The uneasy calm was almost worse than the constant battering of the storm. She was desperate to get over to the island. If Kate had finally plucked up the courage to leave Matthew, her situation must be extreme.

As she walked back to the inn for the second night, the wind picked up again. *Please blow away*, she begged nature, *for Katie, please*. Her sister, childhood sprite of Vinalhaven, fairy of the forests. If nature would turn for anyone, it would be for her.

Susannah woke early the next morning. Sunshine flooded into her room in the inn. The storm was over. She looked at her watch. Six fifteen. She'd plenty of time to get the first ferry.

Island folk waved to her with surprised looks on their faces as she rushed through town. It was rude not to stop and catch up. She hadn't been home in five years, and she could see by the curious stares there'd been plenty of gossip about why. But Susannah was beyond caring what the islanders thought of her. Once she left today with her mom and Kate, they were never going to come back.

As soon as she ran into the house, Susannah knew something was very wrong. For a start, the back door was open, and banging, as it hung on its hinges. She called out for Kate, but there was no answer. Where was everyone? It was only eight in the morning. She'd expected to be greeted by her mom and Kate at breakfast, with the girls eating their oatmeal. Then it hit her; of course the storm would have stopped the fishermen from going out this morning. Matthew could still be in the house. She searched all the downstairs rooms, but the door to her sister and Matthew's room was locked, with no key to open it. She banged on it, called out, but there was no answer.

Susannah ran up the stairs to the second floor, calling out again. She was about to search the rooms, but then she heard a child crying. She climbed the final set of stairs into the eaves of the house, and pushed the door open to her and Kate's old bedroom. At first the room looked empty, but then she saw her two nieces under the bed, huddled up together. She gave a little cry to see the two girls. She wouldn't have recognised Lynsey as the baby she'd once minded, but Rebecca was the image of Kate when she was little. Lynsey was holding onto her little sister protectively. She was dry-eyed and pale, but Rebecca was crying, clearly terrified.

Susannah knelt down on the floor.

'It's okay, I'm your Aunty Susannah,' she said to Lynsey, who looked at her with wide eyes. 'Where's your mommy?'

'In the garden,' Lynsey said, her lips trembling.

'Where's Granny?'

'Don't know,' Lynsey said.

'Okay, honey, I'll be right back,' Susannah said. 'Just stay there. Don't come out.'

Lynsey nodded, and Susannah could see in her face it wasn't the first time she'd had to flee with her little sister and hide under the bed. The realisation stabbed her in the heart. She should have come back sooner. Years sooner.

Terror began to take over as she ran down the stairs and out of the back door. She saw her immediately. Her sister in her white nightie, lying face down in the lush green grass.

'Katie!' she cried out, tearing over to her.

She knelt down by her sister, and rolled her over. The weight of Kate's body told her the truth, but it was only when she saw the open, staring eyes that she knew for certain she was too late. Her sister's face was battered with bruises, and Susannah saw a huge red gash on the top of her head. The blood had soaked into the grass surrounding her.

Susannah screamed so loudly that the crows took off. Through the agony of her grief, cold, lethal anger spread through her. She closed Kate's eyes, laying her to rest on the grass. Taking one of the sheets that had blown off the line during the storm, she covered her sister's body. Kate had nearly made it to the sea at the edge of their garden. That was where she'd been running. Leading her demented husband away from her children and into the storm, into the wild waves. She would have drowned to save them.

Susannah stood up and clasped her cold hands together. Took a deep breath. Icy vengeance began to cloud all reason. Where was the monster? And where was her mother?

Back inside the house, she tried the door again to Matthew and Kate's bedroom, but it wouldn't open. If Ava were with her, she'd tell her to take the children and go find help. The police would come and arrest Matthew, and he would spend the rest of his life in jail. That would be the proper kind of justice. But Ava wasn't here, and she couldn't wait for that. He must be in that locked room, and she was going to make him pay. Running upstairs, she went into her mother's bedroom to see if she could find the key. To her shock, her mother was in there. Sitting at her dressing table, quite still, as if a ghost.

'Mom! Mom!' Susannah screamed. 'Katie's dead. Mom, he killed her!'

Her mother looked in the mirror and their eyes locked. She lifted her hand, with the key in it.

'He's downstairs,' she said to her daughter, clearly dazed. 'I locked him in.'

'Mom, go up to the girls; they need you.'

Her mother rose from her chair obediently.

Susannah grabbed the key from her hand, and charged out of the room. She was all fury and instinct. Nothing, not even her love for Ava, would stop her now. She went down to the end of the hall and opened the cupboard. Took out her father's old hunting rifle. Opening the drawer, she found two bullets. She cocked the gun and loaded it. Snapped it shut. She walked down the hall, ready now.

As she unlocked the door to the room where her sister had been abused every day of her marriage, and where she herself had been raped, she had never felt so clear-headed in her life. She was going to the slay the beast for her sister, and for those little girls upstairs.

Chapter 37

Emer

31st October 2011

Henry had been right. It was perfect walking weather. A crisp, bright fall day, not a breath of wind.

'I'm off out for a hike again this afternoon,' Emer told Susannah as she brought her breakfast. Now her patient accepted it in bed every day. No comment made.

Susannah pushed around her toast and jam. Looked up at her.

'You're not going for a big long hike on your own are you, Emer? That's not wise.'

'No, of course not.'

'Who are you going with?'

She thought about telling her the truth, but Henry had been adamant this would be a bad idea. She didn't want to upset Susannah, and besides, she needed to meet him right now, before things went any further. Tell him that in fact they were not dating.

'Shirley from the diner,' she said quickly, because she couldn't think of anyone else on Vinalhaven apart from Peggy Steel, who was in the library all day.

'Shirley?' Susannah looked at her in astonishment. 'She doesn't strike me as much of a hiker. Where you going?'

'Don't know.' Emer shrugged her shoulders. 'She's surprising me by taking me to her favourite place on Vinalhaven.'

'Okay, well, be careful of the ticks! Don't go off the trail.'

*

As soon as she got in his pick- up, Henry gave her a big kiss on the lips. It took her by surprise and his mouth banged against her teeth.

'Ouch!' He grimaced.

'Sorry,' she found herself apologising to him. Then was immediately cross with herself. Why was she saying sorry to Henry for giving her an unwanted kiss?

Before she had a chance to say anything, he was speeding off down the road, chattering away about the place they were going to.

'Okay so, my number one place on Vinalhaven is Big Tip Toe Mountain,' he told her as they drove along the island roads. 'It has the most fabulous panoramic views of the whole of Penobscot Bay. You're going to love it.'

He put a hand on her thigh, gave it a squeeze. She began to wish she'd arranged to meet him in town in the diner.

'Henry, you know I had to take the morning-after pill yesterday?'

'But why did you do that, baby?' he asked her as he parked the pick-up, turning off the ignition and looking at her with concern. 'You didn't tell me.'

'I texted you, and you texted back! Although I suppose you didn't respond about that in particular.' She wanted to say, *You sent me all these lovey-dovey gushy messages*, but stopped herself. That would be mean.

'I didn't get any texts from you,' he said. 'God, I'm so sorry, because you didn't need to do that.'

He took a breath, looked out of the windshield. Took one hand off the steering wheel and held her hand.

'One of the reasons Mandy left me is she wanted kids,' he sighed. 'We tried for years. Had tests. My sperm count is non-existent.'

'Oh, I'm sorry,' Emer said, colouring and feeling immediately awful. 'But at your place, you were talking about wanting to have lots of kids?'

'It's just a dream,' he said. 'But you know, I want to adopt when the time is right.' He squeezed her hand. 'When I meet the right lady.'

She didn't know what to say. Guilt washed over her. She should have trusted him.

'I'm so sorry,' she whispered.

'It's okay,' he said, turning to her. He leant over and kissed her on the cheek. 'Let's not talk about it any more. Let's just have a good time, right?'

They set off on the trail, bypassing Middle Tip Toe Mountain, and scrambling over rock ledges to reach the top of Big Tip Toe. She found herself slipping in her old boots, and Henry took her hand, helped her up to the top. It was worth the climb. He was right, the view was panoramic. She could see the whole of Penobscot Bay, the islands and the ocean from the northwest all the way to the east. Henry walked right over to the edge of the summit, and she followed him tentatively. It was a vertical drop all the way down. She stepped back, feeling a little dizzy.

Henry took off his rucksack and started taking things out. Much to her consternation he'd brought a picnic – sandwiches, cake and chips – and now he spread them out on a gingham cloth, with two bottles of beer. He really had gone to a lot of trouble. Which made the task of telling him there was no hope for them even harder.

'Oh shoot,' he said, looking embarrassed. 'I don't know how I forgot you're vegan; I made egg sandwiches.'

'That's okay,' she said, picking up the beer and taking a swig to fill the emptiness in her stomach.

'Will you not have one anyway?' he asked. 'The eggs are free range.'

'No, I'm fine,' she said, although she was starving. She took one of the packs of chips and ripped it open.

'I won't tell anyone,' he said, winking at her. 'Maybe you should? I mean, you're very thin.'

'I don't want one,' she said tersely, offended by his comment.

'Suit yourself,' he said, biting into his egg sandwich and munching away happily.

She drank the whole bottle of beer quickly, which she knew was stupid on an empty stomach, but she needed some Dutch courage. Henry finished his sandwich, and put his arm around her shoulder. She could smell his eggy breath as he leant in and tried to kiss her. She pulled away, wriggled free from his embrace and stood up.

'Hey, sorry,' he said, looking up at her. 'What's up?'

'I'm not in the mood for kissing,' she said.

'Is it the sandwiches, honey? We'll go. I'll get you some fries at the diner in town.'

She shook her head.

'It's not that,' she said, taking a breath. 'I'm sorry, but this whole thing is going too fast.'

He stood up and walked over to her. Took her hand. 'I know, it's scary, but what we have is so powerful – why wait?'

'But what is it *we* have?'

He looked genuinely surprised. Picked up her hand and kissed it, looking into her eyes.

'I'm in love with you, Emer,' he said, to her horror. 'It's the real thing.'

'Henry,' she said, pulling her hand away. 'I'm so sorry, but I don't feel the same way.'

He stared at her, the smile slowly fading from his face.

'But we made love all night,' he said. 'What was that?'

Emer tried to speak as kindly as she could, although all she wanted to do was get away from him.

'I know, I was drunk and stoned, and so sad about my sister...'

'You used me?' he asked her, coldness creeping into his voice. 'You still in love with your ex?'

'No,' she lied, shaking her head. 'It's nothing to do with him. You're just—'

'What am I?' he interrupted, an edge to his voice she'd never detected before.

'Too much,' she said, emphatically. It was time to be clear. 'Too soon. I feel suffocated.'

Henry's face coloured. He looked angry.

'She got at you, didn't she, that old lezzy bitch?'

'What are you talking about?' Emer asked, confused by the dramatic change in tone of his voice.

'You know what I mean. Susannah Olsen. Lying, conniving old cow.'

Emer felt as if she'd been smacked in the face, she was so shocked. 'This has nothing to do with Susannah.'

'Of course it does! She broke me and Lynsey up, and now she's getting in the way of us.'

'No, Henry, Susannah doesn't even know I'm out with you.'

The charming, chilled-out man of the woods had been replaced by a jilted lover, angry and mean. 'Everyone on the island knows what she really did,' he said. 'They all kept quiet because you never tell on another islander, but we all know.'

For the first time all afternoon, Emer didn't feel safe. She must have been crazy to put herself in this position.

'I want to go back now,' Emer said, in a quiet voice. But Henry ignored her. He kicked her rejected sandwich off the side of the hill and she watched as it fell through the branches of the trees.

'I'm going, then,' she said, trying to stay calm and making for the trail. As she began to clamber down, her heart was pounding in her chest.

'Ask her about what really happened to her sister's husband!' Henry called out to Emer.

She stopped walking, turned around, feeling her breath tight in her chest. She knew she should move on, ignore his taunt, but her curiosity got the better of her.

'How do you know about all of that?'

'Matthew was my uncle. My father was his brother, Silas Young,' he said, taking a step towards her. 'That's why she put an end to Lynsey and I. Sent her off to stay with old friends of hers in Florida, just to stop us being together.'

Emer had frozen in her tracks. A part of her was screaming – was it Orla? – *Don't listen to him! Go now!*

'Susannah always claimed Uncle Matthew ran into the sea after Kate died. Killed himself,' Henry continued, ranting. 'But my dad told me he didn't mean to hurt Kate. He loved her. It was an accident. That's what my daddy said.'

Henry had almost reached her now. Emer began to back away. There was a look in his eyes completely unfamiliar to her.

'My Uncle Matthew loved his girls more than anything in the world. He wouldn't have drowned himself. Not Uncle Matt, he wasn't a coward.'

A murder of crows took off from the tops of the trees, cawing loudly. Emer edged away again.

'It was Susannah who killed Uncle Matt. In revenge for what happened to Kate. She's the murderer, not him.'

Chapter 38

Susannah

September 1966

The body was so heavy she had to get her mother to help her. She put every ounce of strength into dragging it across the garden as quickly as she could. Her brother-in-law hadn't been a big man, but he was all sinew, apart from the beer gut. She tried not to look at his face, nor to think of him as a human being as she and her mother flipped him over and into their small row boat. The horror of the last hour seemed surreal, but she was only too conscious of the fact that Silas might turn up any minute wondering why his brother wasn't at The Sand Bar. For once, her mother was speechless, working almost as a machine as she helped Susannah weigh the body down with granite rocks. Once Susannah was ready to launch the boat, she gave her mother quick instructions.

'Go back to the girls,' she said. 'Give them some lunch.'

'But Kate?' Her mother pointed to the still form beneath the white sheet. Her face was pale with shock, and she was shaking non-stop. Susannah wanted to scream again with loss, but held it in. It helped to remind herself of what this monster had done to her sister. He deserved to be dropped to the bottom of the ocean and eaten up by fishes.

'When I get back, we'll get the cops,' she said. 'But wait till I'm back. '

She pulled the outboard and it sputtered to life. Praying none of their neighbours were looking out of their windows, she sped out of their small cove to sea, bumping up and down on the choppy water in her haste.

The official story went like this: Susannah had arrived on the morning ferry to discover her mother and nieces cowering upstairs in terror, her sister murdered in the garden and her brother-in-law gone. The boat had still been there, so all she could assume was that after he'd killed his wife, his shame had driven him into the ocean and his own self-inflicted end.

For days after they'd taken Kate's body away to the mainland for an autopsy, Susannah had sat staring out of the kitchen window at the sea, half-expecting to see her brother-in-law emerge from the ocean like a sea-monster and come to wreak his revenge on her family. Silas visited often, and was all over her. Constantly questioning her about where she thought Matthew might have gone. Implying Kate's death had been an accident. Susannah knew that Matthew's family didn't believe her. Especially Silas. Every time she went into town to market, she felt the eyes of the whole island on her. They were a spectacle. She couldn't wait until the cops had concluded their investigation and they were free to leave.

When she'd sent Ava a telegram with the news that her sister and brother-in-law were dead, Ava had immediately offered to come get them all in the Ford. But Susannah had stopped her. She didn't want Ava to be dragged into anything on the island. She'd sent a hasty telegram back. They would come soon. If not her mother, then she and her nieces. She was going to take the girls as far away as she could from the island. Rebecca was so little that hopefully she'd remember nothing of the night of the storm. But she was worried about Lynsey. She kept asking for her mom. And crying when Susannah tried to explain she'd gone to the angels. Some days, it was hard even to get up. Susannah would curl up in bed with Lynsey and Rebecca. The three of them under the sheets.

As for her mother, it was as if the events during the storm had dislodged something in her mind. She kept asking Susannah where Kate was. Or even calling her Kate, sometimes. And every day at three, she'd run into the kitchen and start boiling a pot of water.

'Better get the potatoes on, Kate,' she'd call out to Susannah. 'He'll be back soon.'

'Mom, it's Susannah,' she'd reassure her, taking the pot out of her hand. 'He's not coming back. Not ever.'

Her mom would start to tremble as she remembered the night of the storm.

'Oh, Susie,' she sobbed, 'he killed our Katie.'

The two of them would embrace. In the losing of her mother's mind, Susannah had never felt closer to her.

Finally, six weeks after the murder, the case was closed and they were allowed to bury Kate. There had been no sign of Matthew Young since the night of the storm. A national manhunt had been set up, but seeing as he had not been seen on the ferries that day, nor had he taken his boat, it was assumed he'd committed suicide by walking into the ocean.

Ava drove up all the way from New York for the funeral. Susannah fell into her arms in relief. She'd been holding it together for her mom and the girls for so long. To see Ava broke her.

'It's gonna be okay,' Ava kept saying, stroking her hair.

But nothing was ever going to be okay again. Susannah had to carry a deep, dark secret to her grave. It would eat away at her own life, and it would shadow the lives of all around her. No matter how much she wanted to, she could never tell Ava what had really happened to Kate's husband.

A storm blew up the day of the funeral, but it didn't stop the islanders coming out to show their respects. Everyone had loved Kate. Matthew's family stood a little apart, Silas and Rachel, pregnant again, with three small children hanging off her. Rachel was sobbing but she didn't go over to Susannah and speak to her. Just kept staring at the coffin, devastation etched on her worn-out face. Susannah didn't want the Youngs there, but she couldn't be bothered with Silas' antagonism if she told him to go. As it was, Silas was giving her dirty looks, especially when Ava put her hand in hers. But she didn't care. She was leaving Vinalhaven soon, and forever. She and Ava would raise her sister's girls in New York and ensure they would never become the victim their mother had been.

As Kate's coffin was lowered into the ground, the rain lashed into them and their neighbours cowered in the downpour. The deluge mirrored Susannah's sorrow, extreme and intense, biting her with icy cold down to the bone.

That night, Susannah and Ava's love-making was the most intense surrender Susannah had ever experienced. Without words, Ava took her loss into her own heart, and held her. Susannah sobbed in her arms, wishing she could tell Ava the truth. But she knew she never could.

The next morning, after breakfast with her nieces, Susannah announced to the girls they were going on an exciting journey with Aunty Susie and Aunty Ava to the great New York City.

Rebecca didn't understand what was going on, but Lynsey frowned.

'We can't leave Mom,' she said, a fierce expression on her face.

'We'll come back and visit her once a year,' Susannah lied. She had no intention of ever returning to Vinalhaven.

'But what about Granny?'

'She's coming with us,' Susannah reassured her niece.

Her mom turned from the sink, her arms covered to the elbows in suds. 'We're not going anywhere, Susie,' she said, her mouth set in a grim, determined line.

'I told you, Mom,' Susannah said patiently. 'It's for the best for the girls. You don't want this hanging over them for the rest of their lives.'

'We belong here.'

Her mom looked quite lucid. But last night, after the funeral, she had agreed wholeheartedly they should pack up home and go to New York. It would be a squeeze in the little apartment in Brooklyn, Ava had said, but cosy, and they'd find something bigger soon. Ava's job was going well. It would only be a matter of time before she was promoted, and Susannah had her lectureship in Columbia starting when she got back.

'I'm staying here. With Katie,' her mom said, adamant.

'But you said it was a good idea last night,' Susannah told her as Ava locked eyes with her in alarm. They needed Susannah's mom to come with them to mind the girls while they were both at work. Besides, no matter how mad Susannah was with her mom, she really didn't want to leave her alone to deal with the Youngs.

'We're island women,' her mom said. 'You, me, Katie, Lynsey and Rebecca. But she don't belong here.' She pointed at Ava. 'Get her to go!'

'Mom, stop it, you're not making sense,' Susannah said, getting up from the table. But her mom pushed past her.

'I ain't going nowhere. You hear me?'

Lynsey started to cry.

'It's okay, honey,' Ava consoled her. 'Let's go out. You can sit behind the steering wheel of my car.'

Ava picked up Rebecca and took the two girls outside. Susannah went after her mom. She found her in Kate and Matthew's old bedroom. She and Ava had stripped the bed of all its sheets, and packed everything they could away. But the room was still full of Kate. Her jewellery box, open on the chest of drawers. A small jar of dead flowers she'd clearly put in the window.

'Mom, please, you've got to come with us. It's the best thing for the girls.' Susannah approached her mother. 'Don't you see, we need to take Lynsey and Rebecca away from here? It's not good for them.'

The older woman turned with her back to the window, crossed her hands and looked at Susannah coldly.

'We're staying,' she said firmly. 'Otherwise I'll tell the cops what really happened to my son-in-law.'

'Why would you do that, Mom?' Susannah gasped, horrified.

'I will!' she threatened, looking wild-eyed. 'I'll tell them the truth. How we dragged his body out like he was an animal. And you threw him in the sea like trash.'

'He was trash, Mom!' Susannah found her voice rising.

'It was a sin,' her mom said. 'We've got to spend the rest of our lives asking forgiveness for it. That's why you've got to stay with me, Susannah.'

The walls of her sister's old room closed in. Panic swelled up inside her. Her mom was giving her an impossible choice. In fact, it was no choice. She was trapping her on this island, for the rest of her mother's life. And no matter how much she loved Ava, Susannah knew she couldn't let her stay too. She would have to let her go. This was the price she'd have to pay to protect her family.

Chapter 39

Emer

31st October 2011

She stumbled along the trail. All she wanted to do was get away from Henry. Why had he been so duplicitous? Not told her who he really was?

She followed the track as fast as she could, not sure what she would do once she reached the parking lot. It didn't look the same as the trail they'd taken up the mountain. As she rounded a corner, she saw the sea, and that part of the trail was submerged by seawater. She'd clearly gone the wrong way. She turned around and headed back the way she'd come, trying to remain calm. Shadow came bounding towards her, and next thing she knew, Henry had rounded the corner.

'Thank god,' he said, all concern. 'I saw you'd gone the wrong way. At high tide that trail is dangerous.'

'I just want to go home,' she said, close to tears.

'I'm sorry, Emer,' he said, all his anger gone now. 'I didn't mean to scare you. That's the last thing I wanted to do.'

'None of this has anything to do with me,' Emer pointed out. 'It's a tragic story from the past.'

'But don't you see?' Henry said, passion flashing in his eyes again. 'Susannah's been walking around free as a bird all these years. What happened to Matthew destroyed my parents. My dad never got over it. Hit the bottle real hard.' His voice cracked.

'And what that did to my mom was even worse. The stress of his drinking pushed her into an early grave.'

'I'm really sorry about your parents, but I don't want to talk about it any more,' Emer said firmly. 'Just bring me back, okay?'

Henry gave her a long, measured look.

'I clearly got you wrong,' he said coldly. 'Thought you were kind, at least.'

He walked fast through the woods, and she almost had to run to keep up, tripping over tree roots, getting hot and sweaty. At last, they arrived in the parking lot. To her astonishment, she recognised Susannah's pick-up, parked next to Henry's. The driver's side door opened, and Susannah climbed out, clinging onto it.

'Susannah!' Emer called out in shock. 'My god, what are you doing here?'

'I came to get you,' Susannah croaked, looking as if she might collapse. How on earth had she managed to drive all the way across the island? 'I was worried.'

Henry put his hand on Emer's arm. 'You're staying with me,' he ordered.

Emer felt fury rage up inside her. How dare this man tell her what to do? 'Let go of me,' she said, pulling her arm away.

'Emer, please do as I say,' Henry said to her, trying to pull her back. 'I'm begging you, don't go with her. Come back with me. She's a liar, and she's dangerous.'

'Are you crazy? She's sick, and she needs me,' Emer said, shrugging him off.

'Let her go, you bully!' Susannah yelled at Henry, her voice hoarse with effort.

'You just can't stop yourself, can you?' Henry snarled at Susannah, and took a step towards her. He looked like a giant, glowering over the tiny Susannah.

Emer pushed him aside and stood in front of Susannah to protect her. 'Leave her alone,' she told him.

'She'll brainwash you, just as she brainwashed Lynsey against me,' Henry declared. 'She's plain evil. You old witch!' He spat on the ground at Susannah's feet, before turning on his heel and getting into his pick-up, Shadow jumping up beside him. He roared off out of the parking lot at breakneck speed.

As soon as he'd gone, Emer felt her heart slow down again.

'Come on, I'll drive', she said, helping Susannah into the passenger side of the vehicle. The older woman was breathless, almost panting as she clambered back into the pick-up.

'Susannah, what were you thinking of driving all the way out here?' Emer asked her, as she reversed the vehicle and began driving back down the road.

'I got to thinking,' Susannah said. 'Wondering why you were so secretive. I mean, Shirley really isn't the hiking type. So I went down to the diner.'

Emer glanced across at Susannah. Her hair fell around her face in soft silver folds, and her eyes were the clearest blue. Emer knew in her heart she trusted her implicitly, despite what Henry had said.

'Course, Shirley was there. But she told me you been seeing Henry Young. I was real worried you'd gone off with him then.'

'Why?'

'Henry's not a good guy,' Susannah sighed. 'I know his dad, Silas, messed him up a lot. But when he dated our Lynsey, I could see how things were going to go. Just like with Katie.' Susannah clasped her hands in her lap. 'Besides, they were cousins. I had to put a stop to it.'

'Is that why you and Lynsey fell out?'

'Yeah, she said I broke her heart. But he would have done worse.'

Emer remembered Henry's strange behaviour. Trying to force her to eat the egg sandwich, his assumption they were dating, even his behaviour in bed the night before. Had he been lying about his sperm count? Could he have tried to get her pregnant to trap her? It was abuse. Subtle, all the same. But without her realising it, he had been controlling her since their very first walk.

'I'm sorry, Susannah, I'm an idiot.'

'That's okay,' Susannah said, putting a cold hand on her arm. 'I'm just glad it didn't get out of hand between you two.'

Back at Susannah's house, Emer helped her into bed. It was clear that the old woman was now in a lot of pain, trembling all over as Emer put her in her nightie.

'Emer, will you give me something?' she whispered, her voice tight with pain. 'It's real bad.'

'Sure,' Emer said.

It had been the first time Susannah had ever asked for morphine. Emer tried to make her as comfortable as possible. It touched her deeply that Susannah had left the sanctuary of her home to rescue her. She knew in her heart this old lady would never have killed anyone, even the man who had abused her sister. And she wasn't going to insult her by ever asking about it.

Chapter 40

Susannah

September 1966

Gripping the gun under her shoulder, with her free hand trembling, Susannah unlocked Kate and Matthew's bedroom door. Kicked it open. She swung into the room, gun raised, but her brother-in-law wasn't standing up ready for her. He was lying face down in the middle of the bedroom.

Susannah dropped the gun in shock. Blood was seeping into the rug on the floor, a big lake of red. Matthew was completely still and utterly dead. She saw a dent in the back of his head where it had caved in. On the floor next to him was her mother's heavy iron pot, the one she used for boiling all his potatoes.

Everything spun in the room and Susannah tried to steady herself. She had been expecting a showdown with her brother-in-law, but not this.

'I killed him,' her mom said in a small voice.

She was standing right behind her, like a ghost.

'Couldn't bear it no more. Him beating up our Katie.'

'Oh, Mom!' Susannah wailed, turning to her mother.

'I killed him for you, Katie,' her mom said proudly, her eyes bright with strength. 'I done it for you, darling.'

Susannah grabbed her mother, and pulled her to her chest.

'You don't need to be afraid no more,' her mom kept rambling as Susannah sobbed into her old cotton dress. 'See, Susie will come back now. Don't need to be mad at me no more,' she said to her daughter. 'Us girls together again at last.'

Chapter 41

Emer

1st November 2011

In the morning, Susannah was very weak. This was how it was with pancreatic cancer. Everything stable for weeks, and then a sudden, fast descent. Emer helped her in and out of the bathroom. She looked so tiny and frail in the bed, as if she were a child again. Her skin was turning yellow and Emer could see her life force fading, just as it had for Orla. Why, when she'd seen the look of death approaching, had she run out of her sister's hospital bedroom? Why, when she'd known the end was coming? Run, run out of the hospital. On to the T-line in her scrubs. All the way to Lars' apartment and into his arms.

She wasn't going to run now.

After she'd dosed Susannah with more painkillers, she made two phone calls. First, she asked for one of the assistant physicians from the medical centre to call in. Then she called Lynsey. Told her she needed to come straight away.

'But it's All Soul's Day,' Lynsey protested. 'My biggest time of year. Besides, Rebecca's arriving on Friday. Can't we come then?'

'I'm sorry,' Emer said. 'But I really think you should come today.'

Emer climbed the stairs to her room at the top of the house. She was exhausted from all the tension with Henry, and looking after Susannah. She lay down on the other bed for once, on top of the second quilt, closing her eyes. There was something inside the quilt, digging into her back.

She sat up and investigated the quilt. Sure enough, there was a secret slit in this one too. She pushed her hand inside and searched blindly, feeling with her fingers. At last, she got a hold of a piece of paper folded so small, it was its thick edges which must have stuck into her back. She pulled it out, and unfolded it. Another letter. But this time, it wasn't a letter Kate had received from Susannah. This letter had been written by Kate to Susannah. The fact it was hidden in this quilt proved she'd never sent it.

Curling up under the covers, Emer read the letter. In Kate and Susannah's story Emer recognised the love between the two sisters, like the love she'd shared with Orla. Emer sat up, perched on the end of the bed and stared out of the window. Now, before it was too late, she must read this letter to Susannah, no matter how much it might upset her. She went back downstairs and pushed open the door into Susannah's room, the letter still in her hand. Susannah was awake, reading in her bed. The beside lamp glowed beside her, filling the room with warm hazy light.

'What is it, dear?' Susannah asked her, seeing the look on her face.

'I've found another letter,' Emer said.

It was time Susannah heard what Kate had to say to her at last.

Chapter 42

Kate

December 14th, 1965
Vinalhaven, Maine

Dearest Susie,

I have sat down to write this letter so many times over the last four years and never managed to finish it. But today I am determined I will. Get Mom to take it to the post office for me, as I can't show my face for a while.

As I write, I'm nursing two broken ribs, a black eye and a cut lip. You know why. I don't have to tell you how I got them, after what happened last time you visited. Oh Susie, I am so ashamed. How weak I am. Why can't I leave him? Even after what he did to you? Why do I still love my husband? Because I do. Mixed in with all the fear, all the hurt and anger, there is true love. He is a tortured soul, and I know he loves me so much. Every time he hurts me, he's on his knees begging for forgiveness. And I forgive him, because I live in the hope that the boy I once met, all those years ago in high school, will return to me.

If only he'd stop drinking. It's like a poison, Susie. Transforms him into a man I hardly know. And when he's bad, I want to leave. But we have no money, and nowhere to go. I can't land on you.

What he did to you is unforgiveable. At the time, I couldn't let myself believe it. And Mom kept saying you had led him on. I knew she was wrong. Because of Ava, because of who you are. Oh Susie, I've ruined everything. I miss you so much. Every day I think of you, and the only reason I never wrote to you before is I want you to be happy and far away from our island of broken hearts, mine and Mom's.

I've had another baby. A girl I've named Rebecca. She's so easy, Susie. As if she knows to be quiet. You wouldn't know Lynsey. She's quite the little girl, and such a good one. Always by my side. My daughters are my whole world, they bring me joy. But I worry for my girls. I have to hope as they get older, Matthew will get better. Surely his instinct as a father will prevail and he will look after his girls? Care for their mom? How could he not?

Some days he is the kindest, sweetest man and really it makes up for the days he's not.

I can see you shaking your head. I know you think me a big fool. But Susie, I never had what you had. You're so clever, and independent, and strong. I would never have been able to go off to Harvard and do what you did. Be truly yourself. I am so proud of you.

There is a reason I am writing you this letter. And you must promise me when you read it, you will do as I say. One day, I might write to you again and beg you to come help me. Please don't come. Promise me, you will turn away from my plea. You are quite entitled to. I did not help you, and I deserve to face my trials alone. Never come back to Vinalhaven, Susie, because I fear if you do, our island will destroy you. With all my love, Katie.

Chapter 43

Emer

1st November 2011

Lynsey arrived on the last ferry of the day, all purple velvet and black lace. Emer sent her straight up to Susannah. They'd spent the whole morning together, as Emer had read all the old letters to Susannah yet again, reading the last one from Kate time and time over at the end. Susannah had held her hand tightly the whole time.

'Do you know where Ava is now?' Emer had asked Susannah gently.

She shook her head, her eyes brimming with despair.

'Shall I try to find her?' Emer asked, but all Susannah said was: 'It's too late.'

When Lynsey came back down from Susannah's bedroom, she was crying. Emer made her tea, and sat down with her at the kitchen table.

'Shall we have something stronger?' Lynsey suggested, blowing her nose. 'Got any wine?'

Emer opened up a bottle of red and poured two glasses: one for her and one for Lynsey.

'She really is going,' Lynsey said, her voice still thick with tears. 'Can you believe it? She actually said sorry to me.' She looked at Emer in disbelief. 'I mean, my aunt has never apologised to me. She is always right. But she actually said, *sorry, Lynsey*. I asked, for what?'

'I think she feels bad about what happened to your mom,' Emer said, careful not to bring Henry into it.

'It wasn't her fault,' Lynsey sighed. 'I've been angry at her for years, but not because of what happened to my mom and dad.'

Emer watched Lynsey as she pulled off her purple wrap. She truly was a beautiful woman, with her dark red hair and deep blue eyes.

'I spend my life reading people's tarot, working as a sort of counsellor, and sometimes I feel such a fake. Not because the cards don't work, because they always do, but because I'm such a mess myself.'

'Believe me, I've worked in the medical profession long enough to know the most unhealthy people can be doctors and nurses.'

'I've been angry all these years because they never talked about what happened. Granny and Aunt Susie,' Lynsey said, taking a big gulp of wine. 'It was this great big secret. But you see, I've these memories. And they make no sense to me.'

Lynsey looked out of the window.

'I remember seeing my dad hit my mom once,' she said in a small voice. 'I was very frightened and I hid under the kitchen table.' She sighed, her eyes swimming with tears. 'I thought he was the bogeyman. I didn't realise he was my father.' She spread her hands on the table, her nails painted black with tiny silver crescent moons on them. 'I remember Susannah's special friend, Ava, too,' she said, smiling, wiping the tears away. 'She let me sit on her lap at the steering wheel of her car. I loved that! Made me feel so grown up.'

'What happened to her?'

'She left. Not long after my mother's funeral, I believe,' Lynsey said. 'I always felt that was Rebecca's and my fault. Aunt Susannah sacrificed her life in New York to look after us. My sister doesn't look at it like that, but I do.'

'Do you know where Ava is now?'

Lynsey shook her head.

'I know she was some big-shot lawyer, because sometimes Aunt Susie would see her name in the paper and point it out to us. Do you remember Aunt Ava? she'd say. Look what important things she's doing. What was her second name?' Lynsey mused. 'Ava Greenman. That's it!'

The next day, Rebecca arrived. The presence of the favourite niece immediately picked up Susannah's mood. The house suddenly felt full of positivity.

'Thanks so much for taking such good care of her,' Rebecca said, giving Emer a warm hug. She was tall and slender with blonde hair, and indeed looked very like her mother Kate from the picture Emer had seen on Susannah's desk.

'You're welcome to stay,' Lynsey said. 'It's clear our aunt is very fond of you.'

'But if you want to go, we can take it from here,' Rebecca said as she put her arm around her sister. The two of them leant into each other.

'Oh,' Emer said, taken aback. She hadn't considered they might ask her to leave.

'Please don't think we're asking you to go,' Rebecca continued, obviously reading Emer's thoughts.

'Yes. You're very, very welcome,' added Lynsey.

Emer retreated into Susannah's study while the two sisters caught up over wine. She guessed her purpose had been served, but she had no idea where she should go now. She looked through Susannah's bookshelves at all the beautiful old books, and one slim volume caught her eye. It was Emily Dickinson. She pulled it out and the cover fell open. Written on the flyleaf was a dedication to Susannah from Ava. *With all my love forever.*

Was it true that love could last forever? Emer believed that for Orla and Ethan, it could have.

She put the book down carefully, and took a breath. It was clear to her where she needed to go now.

Chapter 44

Susannah

November 5th, 2011

Her girls were with her now. As they moved around the room, gently adjusting her and helping her in and out of the bathroom, they were their younger selves again. Her two daughters, not by birth, but by default. Her sister's daughters. Lynsey and Rebecca – the redhead and the blonde.

Susannah had lost track of time. Only knew when it was day or not by whether it was dark or light outside. Either Lynsey or Rebecca were giving her drugs, helping keep the pain at bay. She was tired now. A couple of times, she'd wondered where the young Irish nurse had gone.

'Emer's left for a couple of days,' Lynsey told her. 'But she said she'll be back.'

Susannah wasn't afraid, because she felt love surrounding her. Of the living, and of the dead. In the room with her was her mother, her sister, Kate, and even her lost daddy. She only had one regret.

Every time she closed her eyes, she saw Ava's face. As clear as day. The black hair, cut straight with bangs, thick dark eyebrows, and dark eyes which swallowed her up. Why had she let her poor mother blackmail her all those years, when she had clearly been suffering from dementia? Would anyone have believed her? Susannah knew in her heart it had been an excuse. She had been afraid to leave the island. Afraid to trust Ava with her secret. She had lived the rest of her life in grief, not just for her sister, but also for Ava.

Someone had opened her window. It was a warm day, even though she knew it was Fall. She smelt the crispness of the trees outside, and a blackbird sat on her window sill, filling the room with the most beautiful song. She took one breath, then another. She was still alive.

Lynsey came into the room, followed by Rebecca.

'You're awake,' Lynsey said gently. 'How are you feeling?'

'Okay,' Susannah croaked. It felt as if a knife was twisting in her stomach, but she didn't want them to dope her up just yet.

'Someone's here to see you,' Lynsey continued, and Susannah could see there was a careful look in her eyes.

'Is Emer back?' she asked.

'Yes,' Rebecca told her.

Susannah was glad. She'd become very fond of the young Irish nurse. Almost viewed her as family.

'She's brought someone with her,' Lynsey said, speaking very slowly, as if Susannah was deaf. 'Went all the way to New York to get her.'

Susannah looked between her two nieces, not fully comprehending what Lynsey had just told her.

'Ava's come, Aunty, do you want to see her?' Rebecca chirped, unable to keep it in any longer.

Susannah's heart gave a leap and she gasped in shock. How did the girls know? Was this a dream?

She lifted her frail hands to her face.

'But I look bad,' she whispered. 'Is it really her?' She looked up at Lynsey.

'You're beautiful, Aunty,' Lynsey said, patting her arm. 'I'll go get her.'

She was in a dream, she was sure of it. In the last blissful illusion, before death caught up with her. Ava had come back to her at long last.

Chapter 45

Emer

5th December 2011

They walked the woods of her and Orla's childhood. Crunching through the thin films of ice on the puddles, the mud hardened with frost. On her back, she felt the weight of what she was carrying in her backpack. She knew exactly where she needed to go.

Through the trees, rustling in the chill winter's breeze. Their sound reminded her of the sea, and yet again, she thought about her strange time on Vinalhaven, and its end. Her most abiding memory was of Ava and Susannah reunited, albeit for just a few days. It had been surprisingly easy to find Ava, once she'd arrived at Ethan's place in New York. He had even heard of her and knew the firm where she still worked, despite the fact she was in her seventies.

When Emer had turned up at her office, Ava had been shocked, but easily convinced to come with her once Emer had explained the urgency of the situation. Her initial delight at hearing her lost love had finally sent a messenger for her had turned to distress to hear of her sickness.

On the long drive to Vinalhaven, Ava had told Emer how much she'd regretted all the years apart from Susannah.

'I never did fall in love again,' she said. 'There were other women, sure. But none like Su.'

'Why did you never try to get her to come back to New York?'

'Oh boy, I tried, but her crazy mom made her stay. I couldn't make her leave her mother. She was so loyal to her and her little nieces.'

'But couldn't you have stayed in Vinalhaven with Susannah?' Emer continued to question her.

'I said I would, but Su wouldn't let me. Insisted I leave. I thought she didn't want me any more.' Ava sighed. 'I was young and stupid. A love like ours doesn't come twice in one life.'

As Ava talked, Emer couldn't help thinking about Lars. The whole episode with Henry had made her realise that what she and Lars had found was so real, so rare, she shouldn't turn her back on it.

'I buried myself in my work,' Ava said. 'Poured all my passion into human rights.'

Once on the ferry, Ava had grown quiet. Gone to stand on the deck by herself and watch for the island. Emer could see the young woman within her more and more as they approached Vinalhaven. Her dark eyes, strong brows and chin.

As the ferry pulled in to the harbour, Ava took Emer's hand.

'You said she doesn't know I'm coming. Do you think she'll really want to see me now, when she's so sick?'

'Of course she will,' Emer reassured her.

'I'm frightened,' Ava said, her hand shaking.

'It's going to be hard to see her so ill,' Emer warned. 'And I know I'm only the nurse, but please, you must go talk to her. Give her peace.'

'Child, you are so much more than a nurse,' Ava said, putting Emer's hand to her face. 'Indeed, I believe you must be an angel!'

Emer was stunned by Ava's declaration. She found herself unable to speak, as tears choked her throat. Her sister had always been the angel, not her.

*

Emer had left Vinalhaven before Susannah had passed. The house had felt very full at that stage, and she knew it was time for her to go. She remembered her last conversation with Susannah, and what she'd promised. Never give up on true love.

This was why she was here in her home woods in Ireland, right now. They walked in unison, her and Lars. He took her mittened hand in his, wordlessly. She knew he was with her every step of the way, on the hardest walk she had ever taken through her childhood woods.

The trees cleared and they came to the edge of the lake. She had been afraid it would be frozen, but the water lapped gently against the shoreline. She stared into its depths and longing rose within her as a dark shadow. For a moment, she let it consume her. The longing for Orla would never go away, but she had to learn to live with it. Try to let her go. She took the backpack off and unzipped it.

'Are you ready?' Lars asked her.

Emer nodded, unscrewing the lid of the container Ethan had given her in New York.

She closed her eyes, waiting for the right moment. As she did so, she heard an incredible sound, a rhythmic beating above her head. She opened her eyes again and looked up to see two white swans flying above her. Intuitively, she threw the ashes out across the lake, watching them scatter upon its surface and sink.

They stood in silence for a while. The sky darkened and it began to snow. White, feathery ice, fluttering all around them. Emer smiled. Of course, Orla would bring some magic to the occasion.

She turned to Lars. His nose was blue with cold. He was there by her side. Her love for him was limitless. She knew that now. It almost took her breath away.

'Come on,' she said, holding out her hand. 'Let's go home.'

A Letter from Noelle

I want to say a huge thank you for choosing to read *The Island Girls*. If you did enjoy it, and want to keep up to date with all my latest releases, just sign up at the following link. Your email address will never be shared and you can unsubscribe at any time.

www.bookouture.com/noelle-harrison

The Island Girls is inspired by the love between sisters, and the bond between women while exploring both joy and darkness, in love and in loss and longing. *The Island Girls* refers not just to the sisters who grew up on the remote and very beautiful island of Vinalhaven in Maine, but also to the bond between women in male-dominated environments in the past such as at Harvard. These women were islands in a sea of male voices. They inspire me in all that I write as does the wild and lush autumnal landscape of Maine with its glorious foliage, piles of pumpkins and deep blue ocean.

I hope you loved *The Island Girls*, and if you did, I would be very grateful if you could write a review. I'd love to hear what you think, and it makes such a difference helping new readers to discover one of my books for the first time.

I love hearing from my readers – you can get in touch on my Facebook page, through Twitter, Goodreads or my website.

Thanks,
Noelle Harrison

 NoelleCBHarrison

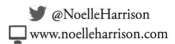 @NoelleHarrison
www.noelleharrison.com

Acknowledgements

First and foremost, huge thanks to my editor Lydia Vassar-Smith for sharing her creativity and passion with me, and to my agents, the wonderful Marianne Gunn O'Connor and Vicki Satlow for their unerring support of my writing. Special thanks to the fabulous team at Bookouture for their dedication and skill. Thank you to my dear friend Becky Sweeney for travelling with me to the island of Vinalhaven and for her feedback as first reader. Special mention to my second reader and good friend Alyssa Osiecki, for her help in building an authentic picture of life in Maine. Gratitude to all the lovely people I met on Vinalhaven, in particular the Vinalhaven Historical Society. I wrote this novel while completing my Master's in Creative Writing at Edinburgh Napier University. Huge thanks to my tutors, David Bishop, Daniel Shand, and in particular my mentor Laura Lam for their guidance and inspiration as well as my fellow cohort.

Without the support of all my friends and family all over the world, it would be impossible to continue in my work as writer. I am blessed to be surrounded by so many inspirational humans and really it would fill a whole book to mention everyone, but I am so grateful to you all, especially my close family, in particular Barry, Helena and Corey. Thanks too to all my gorgeous colleagues at Tribe Yoga in Edinburgh. What a joy it is to work with you all!

Most importantly, thank you to all my readers for picking up my books and engaging in the worlds of my characters. Every single word you read is appreciated. Namaste.